The second book of ORDER series

DISORDER
OF
THE WORLD

ROHIT DHARUPTA

A sequel to *Order of the World*

For my mom

Rohit Dharupta

CONTENTS

SPRING 1

CHAPTER ONE 3
CHAPTER TWO 11
CHAPTER THREE 19
CHAPTER FOUR 26
CHAPTER FIVE 34

SUMMER 43

CHAPTER ONE 45
CHAPTER TWO 53
CHAPTER THREE 59
CHAPTER FOUR 67
CHAPTER FIVE 76
CHAPTER SIX 85
CHAPTER SEVEN 94
CHAPTER EIGHT 101

AUTUMN 113

CHAPTER ONE 115
CHAPTER TWO 120
CHAPTER THREE 126
CHAPTER FOUR 135
CHAPTER FIVE 143
CHAPTER SIX 152
CHAPTER SEVEN 159
CHAPTER EIGHT 168
CHAPTER NINE 175
CHAPTER TEN 183
CHAPTER ELEVEN 191

WINTER **201**

    CHAPTER ONE *203*
    CHAPTER TWO *211*
    CHAPTER THREE *219*
    CHAPTER FOUR *227*
    CHAPTER FIVE *234*
    CHAPTER SIX *242*
    CHAPTER SEVEN *249*

SPRING

"Love"

Chapter One

Her breathing made a whistling sound, as if she was gasping a hundred gallons of air and puffing it all out into the wild the very next second.

Her heart pounded like angry sticks mercilessly thumping a drum beat, as if pumping a hundred barrels of blood through her arteries.

Her arms swung like a complete novice swimming against the ocean's tide, desperate to stay afloat.

Her legs hastened as if the next step would cause her to glide into the air, never to alight back on the ground.

And she ran, in despair, into the bushes. The mud soiled her shins. Pebbles flicked off her ankles. Twigs pierced her calves.

The tall grass unsuccessfully attempted to block her way, only to get trampled. But a rock stood its ground and caused her to trip. She fell to the earth, groaning in excruciating pain.

Her petrified wail jolted me to the core.

It was then I woke up and realized I'd had the same dream again. I still didn't know who she was. Why did she dart haphazardly into what looked like a dense forest? Why did her anguished shriek rattle me wide awake each time? Could she be me?

The mechanical timepiece resting on the side table—a gift from my Mom—struck two a.m. My dried-up mouth suggested I could use some hydration. I slipped into my flip-flops, wobbling slightly, and tiptoed down to the kitchen, careful not to wake anyone.

I advanced toward the stove that pressed against the new backsplash tiles. I had installed them on the wall after persistently nagging Viru. He simply didn't understand the difference between a wall and a wall with tiles. He only began to understand the benefit of the backsplash when the wall developed cracks due to the seepage and frequent water splashing.

Forget the kitchen; we would not have tiles even in the bathroom if he were left alone to design the interior of our house. My husband's focus was on his dull job as a project director, which kept him away from home for days on end.

I turned on the light over the stove to ensure minimum illumination.

"Oh, Ma!" I blurted, suppressing a scream as I noticed a dark silhouette on the wall. It belonged to a brown figure sitting at the kitchen table.

My tongue always presented the word *Ma* in reflex to startling situations. The spontaneity was such as if Mom was present to save me in any scary situation. The irony, though, was that she was also the one who frightened me on this occasion.

"Mom! You scared the hell out of me! What are you doing here?" I asked in one breath.

"Munni, is that you? When did you come in?" she returned meekly.

"Just now. What are you doing sitting here all alone? Are you okay?"

"I am okay, my child. I'm … fine," she said after a pause, as if not truly present in the moment.

I filled two glasses from the water filter, offered her one, placed the other on the table, and sat next to her.

As I waited for the water to trickle down her throat (esophagus, to be more specific), I could not help but notice the years of caring and sacrifice in the vivid veins on her wrinkled neck.

"What is it, Ma? Can't you sleep? Is something bothering you?"

"I told you, Munni, it's nothing. I woke up and couldn't go back to sleep, so I came down here," she returned. Her words didn't seem to match her expression.

"Are you happy, Mom?" I pressed her hand. "You don't like it here?"

"Are you kidding me? You're here, my grandkids are here... Where else would I want to be?"

"Really? There isn't something wrong?"

"Yes, really. You're just overthinking, Munni."

"Overthinking? Mom, if I'm a student in that department, you're surely the principal."

We both giggled softly, still being careful not to wake anyone.

After helping Mom to her bedroom, which adjoined the living room, I tiptoed back up to my bedroom.

"Mom!"

"Revu, why are you up?" I opened the slightly ajar door to Reva's room.

"What happened? Is Grandma okay?" my daughter asked.

"She's fine, honey. It's a new place for her. Takes some time to get used to, that's all. You go back to sleep."

"Okay, g'night, Mom!"

I had a waker and a sleeper in my two kids. Reva would wake up at the drop of a hat. Even a little activity at night couldn't escape her notice.

I couldn't say the same for Ryan. The mysterious world of sleep presented itself as a much more appealing place for him than our mundane world of Loka. As for Caesar, he didn't leave his master alone even in his sleep.

In bed, I wondered if Mom was finding it hard to adapt to the lifestyle here in a country she had not lived in before. I could tell she was hiding something by her efforts trying to convince me otherwise.

Was it right to pull Mom out of her comfort back in India and move here to help me with my comfort, especially at her age? Was I being selfish?

Then, I pacified my guilt with a generalizing thought that

all kids are selfish, and all moms are selfless. I would do the same for Reva or Ryan had they needed me.

My train of thought then switched to my unusual and frequent dream of some lady running for her life in the woods.

What did the dream mean, and why did I keep having it? Who was the lady, and why did I only see her back and not her face?

It was four in the morning. Sleep, the least friendly companion of my eyes, evaded, as it often did.

To go back to sleep, I needed to steer my thoughts away from Mom or my strange dream into something boring like Viru's unfunny work jokes that he usually cracked at the dinner table, which only amused Reva.

Two weeks back, he told us about a conversation between his two colleagues, Tom and Jerry, on a conference call. The joke didn't end here as Tom and Jerry were not nicknames given to them inspired by the animated cartoon, but their real names: Tom Williams and Jerry Anderson.

So, in the conference call, Tom asked, "When are you going to do the needful?"

To which Jerry replied, "Sure, I will do the needful, but do you want me to prioritize it over the needless? I can manage both the needful and needless simultaneously. Remember, doing the needless is unproductive but necessary."

Nobody except those two on the call understood what they meant. Viru later found out that they used code words. Any task assigned to them by their boss was needless, and everything else they did was needful.

The mischievous father-daughter duo then made it a running joke for almost a week, chuckling all the time. Anything I asked to do would be turned into a joke by them.

For instance, if I asked, "Revu, could you please draw the curtains?" Viru would promptly say, "Revs, could you please do the needless for your Mom?"

And daddy's girl Reva would return, "Mom, needless is

now done."

Viru would top it by saying, "Remember, doing the needless is unproductive but necessary."

Annoyed by their giggling, when I asked Viru to cut it out, he said, "What, aren't you the boss of the house? Tom and Jerry consider everything their boss asks as needless."

*

A ticklish pressure on my palm woke me up. With my half-closed eyes, I saw Caesar on the bed next to me, tapping my hand gently with his paw.

After the tired eyes, I moved another part of my stationary body, my dazed head, in the direction of the clock to confirm what my brain had already registered, thanks to Caesar's idiosyncrasy.

It was quarter to six, and Caesar displayed his eagerness to get out of the house by sprawling on top of me and wagging his tail.

I had always been reluctant to acknowledge Viru's contribution to the household chores, for he was far from being a role model husband, or a father. Still, there was one quality I could not ignore in him: punctuality.

Despite hating walking Caesar and frequently grumbling about his clumsiness, Viru would hit the road with him at five-thirty in the morning without fail. The same applied to his work, where he would never skip his business travels, like on this occasion, thereby passing the onus of the only significant duty he performed in the house onto me.

By ten past six, the reluctant woman and her exultant dog were cutting through the chilly breeze of bright spring morning to conquer the Mount Mary Hills.

While heading up the slope, I smiled slightly at the thought of deliberately recalling Viru's jokes last night to help me doze off. I was amused to realize that Viru's jokes were senseless, but not useless. They actually worked, not to make me laugh, but to sleep. I even came up with the proportionality relationship in my mind, like Viru often did, to prove his bizarre logic mathematically. His unfunny jokes were directly proportional to the probability of me going to sleep.

The stupider the joke, the quicker I would fall asleep.

A familiar face greeted us with a warm smile and wave as she jogged past us along the gravel road that bordered the cemetery. Though Samantha and I would barely talk other than exchanging pleasantries, we shared a bond of tacit understanding of the supernatural existence only known to us.

Before, it amused me to catch sight of her running every morning. But for the last two years, standing at my bedroom window shortly after waking up waiting to see a glimpse of her was a comforting practice for me, and she never disappointed.

And it wasn't only me; Caesar also longed to see someone to ignite his mornings, and did not have to wait long.

"Hello, Mandira!"

"Good morning, Mrs. Walker."

"It's you today? Where's the funny man?"

"Seattle. Business trip," I returned. "Hey, Tulip! Look at you, cutie pie!" Bending forward, I gently ran my fingers over Tulip's forehead.

"Seattle? Wow, that far."

"Yeah, Viren is a workaholic. Never misses his work trips. He'll be back on Saturday," I said, still cuddling Tulip.

"Saturday! He will be missed. That man cracks me up every morning. Where does he get all those jokes from?"

"No idea, but one can put his jokes to good use," I said, recalling how they helped me sleep last night.

"Bet you can," she giggled. "The other day, he said, 'Mrs. Walker, Is Tulip still in kindergarten? I tell you, with that IQ, the school should promote her to the middle grade.'" Mrs. Walker chuckled, and I joined in superficially.

I wondered how Viru made people laugh with those borderline offensively bad jokes. What next? Would he ask her if Tulip could read? Or write? Or if she has gross and fine motor skills? Viru had a knack for improvising his jokes to the point where they became unbearable.

Was it a mediocre sense of humor or sixteen years of living with the man that had made me immune to his jokes? Either way, thanks to Mrs. Walker, I could use another joke for my sleepless nights.

I beamed at the thought as I stroked Tulip again.

Tulip was a milky white, thick-furred Siberian husky. Her eyes were like transparent glass marbles with blue sapphires at the center. The most beautiful dog in Abbynton, Tulip, had wolf-like grace and childlike charm. According to Viru, if there were a benchmark of beauty among dogs, she would qualify as Angelina Jolie.

The best part was that she was aware of it. When the owner is mindful of their worth, they become irresistible in the eyes of the beholder. All the enchanting dogs of the proud morning walkers lingered for proximity, but she would not let anyone sniff her, let alone permit any physical contact. Caesar had tried all the antics in the dog handbook to impress her, but this supermodel of dogs would not budge.

After another unsuccessful attempt by Ceasar to gain Tulip's attention, we made a lap of the lake before heading home. On our way, we saw three groundhogs enjoying breakfast by the lake, who rushed back into the shrubs when they sensed our presence.

At home, Caesar darted back to his first love, the sleeping beauty, Ryan. There was no chance of success there either, as instead of waking Ryan up, Caesar ended up snoring in sync next to him on the bed.

Reva served me lemon and honey water on the kitchen island. Taking a sip, I waved at Mom through the sliding glass door. She was up by now and taking a stroll in the backyard.

9

"Mom, what's with Grandma?" Reva asked softly as we watched her in the garden.

"What do you mean?"

"She doesn't seem okay."

"She's fine, Revu. I told you, she's spent all her life in India. It's hard to get used to a new place at her age."

"I don't think that's it."

"What is it, then?"

"A few nights ago, she came upstairs."

"Upstairs?"

"Yeah, it must've been around two a.m."

"What, into your bedroom?" I frowned with confusion.

"No, she was in the hallway, I think, and then she went back down. I thought it was you, but then I heard her slow steps down the stairs; you know how she walks."

I nodded. "Then what happened?"

"I came downstairs and found her bedroom door open. She was standing by the window looking outside as if something was there."

"Looking outside? Like at the street?" I asked, a bit unsettled.

"Yes, at Mrs. Bergenza's house across the street, or maybe at the trees? I'm not sure what she was looking at. I asked her, 'Grandma, what's wrong?' And when she turned around, she had this expression of fear on her face. It scared the crap out of me, Mom."

"Then what happened?"

"Then she calmed down as if nothing had happened and said she was fine, that she just couldn't sleep. Something about it being an 'old people problem,' and then she smiled. I asked her what she was doing at the window and she said it was an old habit, that she stands by the window when she can't sleep. Then she said, 'You go back to sleep, my dear girl. I'm perfectly fine.'"

Chapter Two

The glass shutter of the counter was closed. From the sitting area, a lean man, perhaps in his late twenties, glanced at me momentarily before looking back to the file on his lap. I took a seat two chairs from him. He continued to study his file without raising his eyes again.

A few minutes passed in uneasy silence before I heard the approaching sound of shoes lightly knocking on the freshly mopped floor with every step. The owner of the shoes paused beside me.

"Nobody in yet?" she asked, pointing her head toward the counter.

I shook my head in response.

"I'm Charlene," she said.

"Mandira."

"So, what's your story?" asked the curly-haired, moderately curvaceous Charlene as she sat next to me.

Taken aback by this stranger being so upfront, I asked, "My story? What do you mean?"

"You look like a non-traditional. So, what is it?"

Before I could say something, the counter shutter slid open, and a soft female voice interrupted my reply, "Hello there!"

Looks can be deceptive, but so can sounds. I'm not sure about the others in the room, but the voice's owner deceived me as when I turned toward the counter, a middle-aged man was sitting there, sporting a wide grin.

"Welcome! My name is Terrance Henson," he said, approaching the waiting area. "You can call me Terry because ... well, everybody does. I'm the admin coordinator." He grinned, stretching his protruding tummy, adding additional responsibility to the two buttons at the bottom of his shirt against a wardrobe malfunction. "You need to fill in these forms, and these are the keys to your offices," said Terry, addressing the three of us. "You must be Mandira," he stated, handing the form and the keys to me.

I nodded and smiled in response.

"And you?"

"Charlene."

"And I'm Ali," the young man, who was hitherto calm, said, springing out of his chair.

"Okay, Charlene and Ali, take yours." He handed them their forms and keys. "Follow the arrows; all the offices are on the left. I will join you in your offices shortly."

How did he guess my name? Is it because I'm older than Charlene and Ali? I wondered as I walked up to the office. Usually people said I looked younger for my age.

Sitting on a moderately comfortable chair, I waited in the small office. There was nothing much to do other than to gaze at the bulletin board pinned haphazardly with colorful papers or stare at the desktop computer's black screen.

After five long minutes, Terry came in.

"How's it going, Mandira? Comfortable here?"

"Yes, thank you, Terry."

"This is your office," he said, spreading his arms as if showing me a hockey stadium. "You can walk here or here," he continued, taking an animated stroll from one corner to another that took no more than a few steps. "And the chair you're sitting on is yours."

"Thank you, Terry. That's great."

"Let me introduce you to this smart guy. Hello, Mister Computer," he said, hitting the power button. "See this icon, *Informa*? You will find all the work files here. I call it Missus Informa. So basically, Missus Informa sits on Mister Computer's lap.

"It's read-only access. That means you can access them only to read but cannot modify them. And this icon over here, you see? That's Internet Explorer. You can surf the internet by clicking on it. The internet is like a web of information. There's tons of content out there."

I couldn't tell if this was how Terry usually talked or if he exhibited this comedic talent only for my benefit. If indeed this was an attempt at being funny, his sense of humor felt somewhat like Viru's, the difference being that Viru's jokes did not make me feel ancient.

One would only explain the meaning of a self-explanatory term like "read-only access" or the purpose of the Internet Explorer icon to someone who they presumed to have traveled to the present day through a time machine. I was glad that he did not begin by explaining the function of the computer—or the purpose of the table it sat on, for that matter.

Why wouldn't I know about the internet? After all, we both grew up in the eighties, with the internet scaling new heights at the same rate I did. Even Mom could talk about the internet, despite spending most of her life without technology.

And the chair I was sitting on in the office allotted to me was mine? How unexpected.

And Missus Informa sitting on Mister Computer's lap? *Really?*

After sharing more unnecessary and obvious details, like how to slide the drawers under the desk or locate the light switch and power socket on the wall, Terry finally shared his first nugget of meaningful information.

Per Terry's instructions, at nine a.m. sharp I arrived at the conference room one floor above my office and sat next to Charlene. Ali was sitting on the other side of the large oval-shaped table.

A few minutes later, a lady and a gentleman wearing white aprons, perhaps in their forties, entered, and the gentleman began to address us.

"Good morning, all! How are you doing today?" He

gave a closed-mouth smile. "Victoria Hospital welcomes you to the pre-medical shadowing program. I am Dr. Adam Jalil, and I'm the program director. My colleague here, Dr. Maria Lopez, heads our teaching wing for observation programs."

She nodded in greeting with a similar tight-lipped smile.

Dr. Jalil continued, "Dr. Lopez will be your supervisor during the shadowing period. Let's start with a brief round of introductions, shall we?" said Jalil. His eyes danced from side to side until resting on me.

But before I could speak, Ali chimed in, briefing them about his biology major from Abbynton College, followed by research work and a series of volunteer jobs as a crisis and emotional support responder.

Charlene grabbed the next opportunity to impress Jalil and Lopez by describing her paper presentation skills, healthcare publications and her rehabilitation counselor job.

Finally, I spoke when no more eager candidates were waiting in the queue to cut in, and I finished promptly, as there was not much to talk about other than passing my eligibility tests.

Dr. Lopez showed curiosity about my work, and I described my previous job in public health, which prompted another question from Jalil:

"When was this?"

"About eight years ago."

"And why did you stop working?"

"Um, I wanted to spend more time with my family, since my kids were young," I returned hesitantly.

We talked for a little longer, and the doctors left after giving their instructions for the day.

Chatting briefly with Charlene, I asked what she meant before when she asked if I was non-traditional.

My ignorance seemed to amuse her. "Anyone who doesn't directly transition into the medical field after finishing their undergrad is a non-traditional medical applicant. Like the ones who take jobs or switch careers. Or those with gaps of employment of two or more years, like you," she explained.

"I see. Well, forget medical; my missing years make me non-traditional for any field," I returned with a self-deprecating joke.

"I work as a rehab counselor; I'm a non-traditional, too. And so is Mr. Emotional Support Responder. See him pretending to read his file?" she whispered. "I'm sure he'll need some emotional support here. Mr. Responder has a lot to ponder."

We both chuckled softly and Ali's brows raised slightly, making me think he perhaps overheard us.

Charlene couldn't believe I had a teenage girl and a pre-teen boy.

"Fifteen and eleven? Wow! How old are you?"

"Not very. I married in my early twenties and had my girl just a year later."

"Good for your son. Having an older sister is like having, like, another mother. Like, she can watch him while you're here," said Charlene, and I smiled at her comment and the overuse of the word "like."

Charlene was right. To focus on observing the doctors, I needed someone to observe Ryan, another benefit of having my Mom come to live with us for a few months. Though I felt guilty for bothering Mom, I couldn't think of a better person to look after my child than the one who had raised me.

Though Reva was responsible and capable of supervision in my absence, and I couldn't agree more with Charlene on her older sister/another mother comment, I did not want Reva to waste her best years worrying for Ryan. I wanted her to live her life.

It amazes me how a woman can be a selfless mother and a selfish daughter at the same time, I thought.

I reminisced about the past on my metro on the way home. Twelve years ago, when Viru and I, along with toddler Reva, moved to Abbynton, I was fired up to make a mark in the medical field. I had enrolled in pre-medical programs to boost my chances, as my degrees from back home did not carry much weight in Canada. I also took a job in public health administration that went on for a few years.

Then Ryan came along and filled our lives with joy. Not only was I hopeful about my career, but I was also blissful about my life in general.

However, the joyride soon became bumpy, marred by Ryan's silence. He did not chortle like Reva had when she was his age, or chatter like our neighbor Britney, who was a year younger.

By the time Ryan turned three, his lost, watery eyes had extinguished the fire in me to become a doctor. My developmental goals took a backseat to his developmental milestones. I quit my job and the dream I had pursued, for the only dream left now was to see him speak and grow like a normal child.

This morning, I could not help but notice a mild flinch pass on Jalil's face when he enquired about why I quit my career. How could he understand that my most important job back then was being a mother? Perhaps he would have, had I told him the full truth, but I was too proud to blame my career stagnation on my son's difficulties.

My train of thought derailed abruptly by the momentary gaze of a man sitting next to the door of the sparsely occupied metro train.

He was neatly dressed, except for his shirt, which was unbuttoned at the top. He was perhaps in his fifties, with thin hair and a crimson face, and looked to be either inebriated or in pain.

His bloodshot eyes, so red it was as if multiple tiny blood vessels had burst and trapped beneath the eyes' surface, instantly made me uneasy when they met mine. I noticed his leg was shaking incessantly, and he seemed to breathe slightly faster than normal.

Suddenly, he rose from his seat and grabbed the

stanchion handle at the center of the compartment. He stood there for about fifteen to twenty seconds, then anxiously sank back into his seat.

Though the man had my undivided attention, strangely, nobody else seemed to notice him. I wondered if my fellow passengers intentionally ignored him or if only I could see him.

The latter thought made me uneasy. This was not an isolated or far-fetched idea, considering my extraordinary experiences in the past.

I would try to rule out anything odd in every stranger by one key aspect—ensuring that others could see them. If they could not, I would attribute such presence to having something to do with me for a purpose beyond human comprehension.

Experience begets wisdom, but supernatural experience breeds skepticism.

Bang!

Suddenly, the man with red eyes collapsed on the metro floor, and all the healthy eyes turned to him.

His legs shook like a piece of dry cloth on a clothesline, fluttering in the gusting wind, seconds away from slipping out of the clothespin's grip. His eyes, now partially closed, dangled beneath his eyelids like the pendulum clock in my grandma's old house.

Two young boys rushed to hold him, and a gentleman called 911. An elderly lady handed the boys her bottle, anticipating that the man on the floor could use some water.

Ironically, my initial reaction was relief, realizing that everybody could see him, but the thick white foam bubbling out of the man's mouth soon made me sick and concerned.

The metro halted at the next stop, Saint Thomas Metro Station. The first responders turned out to be fast responders, already waiting at the station to give medical attention to the man, who now looked unconscious. I remained at the station for some time, observing them carry him off on the stretcher.

Walking back to my house, I wondered if I, the aspiring doctor, could have helped the man with bloodshot eyes. But to be a doctor with adequate skill and confidence to treat a patient was a distant dream at this point.

Chapter Three

"How was your day, Munni?"

"Fine, Mom."

"You look tired. Did you eat something?"

"I had lunch, Ma."

"Must've been five hours ago now. Let me make you something with tea."

Mom returned to the kitchen without waiting for my answer.

Mom's adorable inquiry made me smile, reminding me of my years during school and college, always being greeted by the same question upon returning: Did you eat something? I wondered how my meals were still as important to her as they were back then.

A mother's appetite gets satiated when her child eats, not when she does.

"Why so quiet today? Where are the kids?" I asked.

"Boy's in the yard throwing that disc you bought him…"

"A frisbee!"

"Yes, frisbee. And the girl's in her room. Your children are so quiet, Munni. They hardly make any noise. I remember you and your brothers at this age would cause a ruckus. The entire neighborhood would complain about you three."

I stepped out into the backyard, anticipating the monotonous cycle of Ryan throwing the disc and Caesar bouncing around, bringing it back to him, but I was pleasantly surprised.

"Hello, Mrs. Sharma! We've been playing since five and haven't dropped once. Isn't that cool?" said an excited Britney Hayden, standing near the birch tree.

"Yeah, but Ryan dropped it," interjected Theodore King, affectionately known as Ted, stationed next to the cabana. "Two times."

"He didn't! He just missed it, but Caesar caught it."

"That's called dropping."

"No, you silly. Dropping means the frisbee touching the ground. Caesar grabbed it before it could land. Doesn't it, Mrs. Sharma?"

I acknowledged Ryan's quiet "hello" by waving at him. The non-stop chattering of Britney and Ted almost muffled his soft voice, which floated from his spot close to the shrubs.

Excited, Caesar welcomed me by running up to me, wagging his tail profusely. But before my fingers could reach his forehead, Caesar took a giant leap back toward the shrubs, grabbing the disc again that Ryan had missed, perhaps due to distraction caused by me. Caesar's agility did not surprise me, as I had witnessed his potential before.

"See, he dropped it again."

"No. Caesar caught it."

"But Caesar isn't playing."

"Yes, he is."

"Oh really? What point is he playing on?"

"He's playing on all the points. Ryan's, yours, and mine."

"That's not allowed. How can he play on all points?"

Before the two talking machines, Britney and Ted, could ramble on with their pointless argument about Caesar's point, I cut in:

"Hey, Ted, where's Tim? I haven't seen him for two days."

"Must be in his room with his iPhone," returned Ted without taking his eyes off the disc. "Where else? He's always listening to music. And he doesn't let me borrow his iPhone. Mom said she'll buy me an iPhone next year, and I won't share it with Tim, even if he asks. Or I can get an iPad. Mom says you can only have one—iPhone or iPad. I haven't decided yet…"

Ted continued to ramble until the divine aroma of whatever snack Mom had made in the kitchen teased my nose and tantalized my belly, coaxing me back inside.

Before eating, I headed up to fetch Reva. I found her in bed, reclining against the headboard with AirPods stuck in her ears, and her eyes closed. I had to shake her to wake her up, as my voice was perhaps a tenth of the song's volume reaching her ears.

"Hey, Mom! When did you get home?" said Reva loudly. Her voice returned to normal as she took out her AirPods, "How was your day?"

After exchanging pleasantries with Reva, we all assembled at the kitchen table to relish Mom's evening snacks. Britney joined us, but Ted decided to head home.

We enjoyed tea with bread pakora—a sandwich stuffed with spiced potato and onions, dipped in gram flour batter, and fried. Mom received compliments for her cooking, especially from Britney, who named it a "super awesome triangle sandwich."

I owe my culinary skills to my Mom. She can cook any typical dish flavored with a valuable ingredient called love.

We talked for a while, with Britney initiating and leading the conversation most of the time and Mom gazing at her face in awe, perhaps wishing her grandson was as chatty as her.

After eating, Britney's Mom, Elena—my close friend—returned from work to fetch her, and they both headed home next door.

Later, we had a light supper upon Mom's insistence despite us having hardly any appetite left, thanks to her savory evening snacks.

Before going to bed, I stopped by Reva's room.

"So, how long have you two not been talking?" I asked her.

"To who, Mom?" returned Reva, putting down her ever-present AirPods that she was about to stick into her ears.

"You and Tim. Who else?"

"How do you know we aren't talking?"

"Well, isn't it obvious? Ted told me he stays in his room listening to songs, and here you are, doing the same in your room."

She chuckled. "Mom, you're a genius. A sly genius."

I sat next to her as she folded her legs to make room for me. "I am no genius, nor sly. I'm just Mom. Tell me, what's the matter?"

"It's nothing much, Mom. Just a stupid fight. We haven't fought in a while. So, it's healthy." She smiled again, but not the usual smile that would light up her face.

"Something personal? Or you don't want to share?"

"Nothing like that, Mom. It's the same old story. Tim wants me to join Abbynton. I told him to wait another year, let Ryan finish his elementary, and we both could join him. He goes, 'You must choose between Ryan and me,' and I said, 'That's easy, I choose Ryan.' And now he's sulking. He's such a drama king."

Tim studied at Abbynton International Academy, a distinguished school for middle and high school grades, the dream of every young Abbyntoner. Despite his insistence, Reva would not leave Saint Augustine until Ryan became eligible to join Abbynton along with her.

"I'm with Tim on this one, Revu. You've got top grades. Your dad and I also want you to join Abbynton."

"Don't tell me you're taking his side, Mom," she whined.

"I'm taking your side, honey. This is about your future. You deserve the best. You deserve to be happy."

"What about Ryan, Mom? I can't choose happiness at his expense."

"Who said you are? Ryan is a grown-up boy. He's made progress in the last two or three years. Did you know he was playing frisbee with Britney and Ted this evening? How many times have you seen him participating in games? Isn't that a huge milestone?"

"It is, Mom. But you don't understand. School is hard for Ryan. There are so many bullies at St. Augustine. They make fun of kids like him and even get rough with them. They stay away from Ryan because they know his sister will kick their asses."

"Language, Revu."

"Sorry, Mom. Kick their butts," she corrected.

"How does 'butts' make it better?"

Reva was a tough nut to crack once she made up her mind. Viru often used the analogy of a sewing machine for her. Most of the time, a sewing machine runs smoothly, stitching a variety of clothes meticulously. But sometimes, the needle gets stuck and doesn't budge, even after tearing the cloth. Reva was easygoing, like a sewing machine, except for those rare times when she would form a firm opinion like a needle stuck in the fabric.

Back in my bed, I could see why Reva felt protective toward Ryan. She didn't know something about him that only I knew. With a choked throat and wet eyes, I could only thank the Almighty for blessing me with a caring daughter.

Something woke me up.

It didn't take much to figure out what it was when a creaking sound from the hallway reached my ears.

In the darkness, the luminous radium hands of the vintage timepiece sitting on the side table declared quarter past one.

Within no time, I jumped out of bed, storming barefoot into the hallway, fighting a head rush from standing up so quickly.

In the dim light of the passageway, I saw someone standing at the half-opened door to Ryan's room, peeking inside.

"Hey! Who's there?" I asked in a quivering voice.

Someone turned around, and the feeble moonlight soon overpowered the shade, exposing the pale, terrified face.

"Mom? Is that you?"

She made no reply. I noticed her hands trembling.

"Mom! What are you doing here?" I whispered.

Her face and lips twitched. "Munni…"

"Munni, what? What happened, Mom?"

"M-Munni…" Mom was fighting for words.

"Okay, okay. Take it easy, Mom. Let me take you downstairs. Here, hold my hand. Watch the steps. Slowly."

After settling her on her bed and gulping two glasses of water, Mom calmed down.

Sitting next to her in bed, I asked, "Tell me, Mom— what's the matter?"

"It's nothing, Munni. I'm fine."

It was times like this that Mom became annoying, and I had to get harsh with her. She didn't understand that not talking about the problem can be more torturous than the problem itself.

"Mom, are you kidding me? You were peeking into Ryan's room at one-fifteen in the morning. One fifteen! You scared the crap out of me with your petrified face. I'm pretty sure Reva heard us. And you say it's nothing, Munni? Cut this crap and tell me now."

"Munni!" she scolded. Then, after a pause, "If I tell you, you'll think I'm going crazy."

"Try me, Mom. If there's someone who can take in any amount of crazy, it's me. Go on."

"I saw Ryan," returned Mom.

"Yeah, I know. I saw you at his door."

"In the street."

"What?"

"And Caesar."

"What are you saying, Ma?"

"Munni, I saw them in the street."

"The street outside? Saint Thomas Street? When? Where?"

"A few minutes back. Through this window. They were standing right in the middle of the street next to the streetlight."

Confused, I walked up to the window and looked outside. The street was empty.

Standing next to me, Mom pointed. "Down there, Munni. Under that pole."

"Do you see them right now?" I whispered.

"Not anymore. When I saw them, I could not believe my eyes. So I went upstairs and found Ryan and Caesar sleeping in his room."

As I gazed at her gloomy face, Mom continued, "Two days back I saw Caesar out there, but tonight I saw Ryan too. I don't know how they could be in two places at once."

I remained silent, continuing to stare at the street for some time.

"I knew you'd think I'm losing my mind," Mom said. "Some days, I wonder if I am."

Chapter Four

"What took you so long?" I asked my husband on Monday morning as he returned from walking Caesar.

"The smooth, butter-like path and our docile dog. What else?" No prize for guessing he meant the opposite. "I tell you, Mandy, this whole road construction thing is a hoax. A big joke."

"A joke! A funny one?" I asked sarcastically.

"What?" he asked, momentarily pausing as he took off his shoes.

"Nothing. Go on."

He continued, "They're digging everywhere as if looking for the waterbed."

"Water table," I interjected.

"Yeah, yeah. Water table, Miss Dictionary. All I could find was digging and detouring. I wonder if they are playing some dig here–dig there game."

Viru had returned from Seattle on Saturday evening and so had his jokes. The upside to it was that I would gain an hour of sleep not having to walk Caesar, and the downside was having to wake up to Viru's usual morning grumble.

"I tell you, Mandy, construction is just a hobby for these workers. The construction sites are playgrounds, and those traffic cones are their toys. If someone asked me what Abbynton is famous for, I'd say traffic cones. Can't imagine roads without them."

Caesar approached me with adorable eyes and wagged his tail like a fan, triggering Viru further.

"And this shameless hormonal dog! He keeps smelling Tulip's butt."

"Smelling Tulip's butt?" I repeated with a chuckle,

moving my fingers on his forehead.

"Yes. He embarrasses me in front of Mrs. Walker, and I have to crack silly jokes to diffuse the tension," called Viru from the hall.

"Silly jokes! Imagine, even by your standards."

"What?" Viru returned to the door, leaning against the door jamb. "I know what you're doing, Mandy. You don't find my jokes funny. You should see Mrs. Walker. If there was a mattress instead of soil, she would be rolling on the ground laughing every morning."

"Now that's a funny joke, Viru." I giggled. "She laughs because you make jokes about Caesar. Poor chap. He's not that bad."

"Not that bad? Tulip is a divine dog, Mandy. Like an angel. She's way out of his league. She's royalty, and he's reality. There's no match. He should be charged a fine for even sniffing her, let alone licking."

An hour later, Viru left for the office after complaining at the breakfast table, this time about the weather and daylight saving time, and dishing out trivial remarks every time, prefixed by his helping words, "I tell you…".

As usual, Reva and Ryan were almost late for school, thanks to Ryan's lethargy in getting up. Tagging along an unenthusiastic Ryan, Reva rushed to board the school bus that almost left them behind. Out of habit, Caesar chased the bus for about half a kilometer.

According to Viru, Ryan could not be rushed out of the house even if it were in flames. Nevertheless, it was tremendous progress that for the last two years, I only had to wake him up, and he would reluctantly get ready all by himself.

I was last to leave the house but first to arrive at the Victoria Hospital clinic. Shortly after, Charlene and Ali came in and headed to their offices after stopping by for a brief greeting.

Charlene complimented my bag that I had forced Viru to gift me for my last birthday, and I returned by praising her shiny black belly shoes.

Blushed by my mention of his new haircut, Ali perhaps felt pressured to reciprocate when he instinctively replied, "You too."

Getting started with work, I accessed the online database of patients' medical records to study the files of those who would be consulted by our supervisor, Dr. Maria Lopez, throughout the day. In Terry's language, I poked Missus Informa, sitting on Mister Computer's lap.

Thirty-nine-year-old Mr. Sahaye was diagnosed with BPPV (benign paroxysmal positional vertigo) on his last visit. He had dizzy spells and had been feeling off balance, as if the world around him was spinning. Mr. Sahaye's treatment involved an exercise called the Epley maneuver.

Vertigo is caused by tiny particles in the ear being dislodged from their normal location. I found it incredible how particles in the ear could literally shake a grown man's world. It oddly reminded me of a childhood story from my grandma about how ants crawling up its sensitive trunk caused a humongous elephant to dance.

Fifty-year-old Miss Cooper had an abnormal spine curvature, tilting her upper body sideways. The medical term for this condition was scoliosis, and Dr. Lopez had referred Miss Cooper to a physiotherapist for core strengthening exercises.

Ten-year-old Tyler was treated for pneumonia after a persistent fever and coughing up mucus. Dr. Lopez prescribed him the antibiotic azithromycin.

Reading Tyler's history reminded me of those sleepless nights worrying about Reva burning with fever. Reva, when small, would frequently fall sick. Viru would not leave her bedside until the sweat took away her body's heat.

Sometimes, I felt guilty about giving so much of my attention to Ryan, even Reva's share. But then I felt better, thinking Viru compensated by caring for her more.

Compensate and complement were the pair of scales that balanced my family.

A voice behind me snapped my bubble of thoughts.

"Hey, Mandira! I see Missus Informa is keeping you occupied."

"Good morning, Terry! Indeed, she is. Missus Informa is one hell of a storyteller," I returned with a smile.

Terry grinned, then said, "Yeah, but she's all about painful stories."

"Yes, sad and painful stories from the heart. But don't forget the happy endings—Missus Informa has mastered them."

"Here, another painful story for you. Find the happy ending," said Terry in a colder tone, placing a file on my table.

My playing along had not amused Terry.

What's the deal with these self-professed funnymen? The moment you match their pun, they lose the fun. You add a bit and cease their wit.

I wondered if having a comedian at home worked to my disadvantage with the comedian at work. The real question was why I had to put up with these comics wherever I went.

I sighed and picked up the file.

My shadowing role was akin to delivering an opening act before the featured act stole the show. While the opening act would help as a filler, the audience came for the star headliner.

My task was to receive the patient in the OPD; ask scripted questions I had memorized by now; jot down the answers in my notebook; accompany the headliner Dr. Lopez , who would make the diagnosis and update Informa; jot down more notes; present a summary; and ask Dr. Lopez about any doubts at the end of the day.

I made Mr. Keith Howard comfortable in the consultation room and enquired about the purpose of his visit with a friendly smile. The young man pulled one side of his pants up to his knee and rolled the temporary bandage open. My plastic smile withered away at seeing his severely bruised and battered lower leg.

He told me he was riding his bike in the woods that morning when a raccoon came out of nowhere and attacked him fiercely. He fell off his bike and struggled to shove the raccoon off his leg, for it wouldn't let go. He grabbed a rock, striking the raccoon's head, loosening its grip and giving him time to clamber back onto his bike. Despite the blow to its head, the violent raccoon chased Howard for almost a mile.

I fetched Dr. Lopez, who carefully examined the blood-stained wounds that exposed the inner parts of his calf. It seemed that the raccoon had bitten off a chunk of his calf.

"Mr. Howard, these wounds need to be stitched up. The nurse here will wash the wounds, and I am referring you to the ER for stitching and a vaccine shot," said Dr. Lopez, writing the prescription slip. I caught a glimpse of the letters PEP written at the end.

Charlene, Ali, and I assembled in the conference room in the afternoon to discuss our morning cases with Dr. Lopez. Ali volunteered to go first, followed by Charlene, and Dr. Lopez suggested improvements in their presentation.

Learning from their mistakes, I incorporated her suggestions into my summary of cases, which seemed to go well per Dr. Lopez's affirmative nod.

Charlene pointed out my lack of mention of Keith Howard's medical history, and I told her he didn't have a record, being a walk-in patient visiting the clinic for the first time. My answer did not satisfy her, as she turned to Dr. Lopez for support, who chose not to say anything.

Charlene's speaking out of turn made me a little uncomfortable.

Dr. Lopez solved my query about PEP that she had scribbled on Howard's prescription slip. Post-exposure prophylaxis is a combination of rabies immune globulin (RIG) and rabies vaccine administered for raccoon bites. It causes the body to create antibodies that prevent the rabies virus from developing.

After finishing with us, Dr. Lopez carried on with her work. Charlene and Ali called it a day, and I stayed back, browsing the internet, curious about raccoon bites. Raccoons do not attack humans unless they are ill, cornered, or feel threatened. I wondered why the raccoon charged at Howard while riding his bike and minding his business. Perhaps the speeding cycle made it curious.

"Are you okay, Mandira?" Terry asked, looking at the webpage opened on my computer.

"I'm doing good, Terry."

"That guy with the raccoon bite was an ER case. I knew it the moment I saw him limping into the clinic. It's a given thing," Terry proclaimed.

In my mind, I returned, *Really, Doctor Terry?*

"I wonder why he came here," he continued.

"Mr. Howard looked like a tough man. One who doesn't visit the doctor often," I responded.

"Anywho. Mandira, I've got some feedback for you. Keep in mind that I have your best interests at heart when I say this." I nodded, and he continued, "I feel you should open up a bit more. Come out of your shell. I'd like you to look and sound more confident in your interactions with people."

"You don't think I am?"

"You are, kind of. But you're either a little shy or hold yourself back. It seems like you are in two worlds, one in your head and the other in front of you, and you hang out more in the former. And believe me, doctors here are quick to notice."

"Terry, did Dr. Lopez say something? Because she seems happy with my performance, as far as I can tell."

"No, no. I'm talking like a concerned friend who knows how things work here. There was a girl like you in the last shadowing program. She was old. Not that I'm saying you're old! But she barely had any work experience and mostly kept to herself. And you know what? She didn't pass the program. Now, I don't want this to happen to you. Again, this is just my feedback as a friend."

I had one word of feedback for Terry that I didn't share with him—judgmental.

Two years back, when I first shared my desire to apply for medical school with Viru, he initially regarded it as an impractical whim. He knew that Ryan was gradually gaining independence, which meant less attention and nurturing on my part. Viru suggested I take up a job or a side hustle instead to keep my mind occupied. But when I ordered the prep books for the MCAT exam, he realized it was not just an impulsive decision born out of boredom.

"It won't be easy, but then easy is not your thing. So, let's do this," said Viru.

I loved the side of Viru that stepped up when it mattered. All his other sides were simply annoying.

Viru's belief strengthened when the blood and sweat of a year and a half yielded results. I cleared the MCAT.

But when I applied and didn't even qualify for an interview on my maiden attempt, I realized clearing the eligibility test was just a drop in the ocean. I needed to embellish my application with academic and non-academic laurels to get the selection committee's attention next time. My quest for gaining an edge brought me to the shadowing program at Victoria Hospital.

In bed later that night, I told Viru how humiliated I felt by Terry's "advice."

"I don't think you lack confidence in any way. He thinks you're distracted. Here's the thing: Negative feedback is hard for anyone, but it makes room for self-analysis. If you leave his sarcasm and rudeness aside, there could be something worth paying attention to," said Viru.

I hated it when Viru turned from a husband into a philosopher. All I wanted him to say was, *"Honey, that guy is mean, and his feedback is meaningless."*

Was that asking too much?

"Now, where are you off to?" asked Viru, seeing me get out of bed.

"I'm going to do some self-analysis. Obviously, I can't do that sleeping next to you."

"Oh, c'mon, Mandy. I'm just being honest with you."

"Yeah, I know; you're giving me honest feedback. I get feedback at work. Then, I get feedback at home for the feedback at work. Can't you simply say, "I got your back" instead of, "I got you feedback"?"

I walked out of the bedroom, leaving Viru to do some self-analysis.

I disliked three things about Viru: 1) He gave his opinion on everything, 2) it rarely matched mine, and 3) it affected me every time.

But before I knew it, his viewpoint cooled my temper like an antipyretic drug cooled the temperature. To suggest the idea that I could be distracted was not wholly unfounded. Mom's supernatural experiences at night troubled me. She perceived those sightings as a sign of losing her mental state. I felt guilty about having Mom fly seven thousand miles to Abbynton and thrust her inadvertently into ambiguity.

It occurred to me that I was doing self-analysis in the living room, sitting on the couch, sipping water.

I walked to Mom's room and quietly pushed the slightly ajar door, hoping to find her sleeping peacefully.

There she was, like a crumpled piece of paper, wilted under the weight of uncertainty, looking out of the window.

Chapter Five

There were three worlds. One, the world we lived in that humans knew existed. It was called Loka, and all its living things were referred to as minners.

Second, Shloka—the world of sleep. The living things, or minners, regularly journeyed from Loka to Shloka in what they believed to be sleep and stayed temporarily in Shloka before returning to Loka. I was unsure which was temporary though, the stay in Loka or Shloka.

Third, Parloka—the world of the dead. Parloka was a place where minners resided after death. It was also home to the central authority called Kendram, operated by certain forces that worked to maintain order and peace. These forces controlling all three worlds were called keepers. Chief Joseph, the headkeeper, was at the apex of Kendram, the titanic organization.

Shloka, in a way, formed a link between Loka and Parloka, being the only place where minners, living and dead, could coexist.

During that long night, I opened up to Mom about what I knew, the secret I had not even shared with Viru or Reva, let alone anyone else. Mom listened to me with her eyes wide open and seldom blinking.

I emphasized to Mom that Shloka and Parloka, though beyond human comprehension, were legit like our world, Loka, and not a mere figment of my imagination.

And then came the part where you expect to excite but manage to fright—when I told Mom that Chief Joseph wished Ryan to succeed him as the next chief of Kendram.

Kendram's local entity that managed our world, Loka, was called Rudram. Caesar, just another mischievous dog in the eyes of the neighborhood, was the leader of Rudram. Behind the disguise of an imbecile dog was a faithful commander who would go to any length to protect his master, Ryan.

In my epic tale to Mom, I skipped mentioning the bad fish in the pond, the unscrupulous keepers of Kendram called daggers. I left out the horrifying account of how Hogdon, the wicked son of Chief Joseph, had almost succeeded in wiping out Loka in his greed for the throne. And the part where he deceived me into believing my supernatural experience was mere hallucinations and conspired to destroy my family with the help of his accomplice, the hideous black bear Duma.

"Mom, I don't know why you see Ryan and Caesar out in the street at night. I also can't explain how they can be sleeping upstairs at the same time. But I am absolutely sure about one thing: these are not hallucinations, and you're not losing your mind.

"There exist things beyond the conception of us mere mortals—or minners, as Jack, the faithful keeper of Kendram, would call us. And Ryan is a significant part of those things. Your grandson, who everyone thinks is a special child, is indeed one. A child born for greatness. For a purpose. A purpose that our world, Loka, cannot comprehend, let alone serve."

After listening for hours, blinking back tears that occasionally trickled down her cheeks, Mom spoke at last:

"Munni, do you still see that old man, Jack?"

"No. I haven't seen him in two years."

"How does he look?"

"Handsome. Don't worry, I'll fix you up with Jack when I see him next."

"Shut up. You bugger," chuckled Mom.

"Why? You're still hot. Jack will come running for you. I bet you can corrupt that honest keeper with your charm. Make him a permanent resident of Loka."

We both laughed. We lay in bed holding hands,

reminding me of nights during my childhood when Mom would comfort me during scary thunderstorms by wrapping her arms around me.

We slept like two babies.

*

Her tired feet begged her legs for mercy, desperate to skip as much ground as possible. The setting sun peeking from behind the branches of trees kept pace. Dust erupted from her footsteps, filling the moist air, which, in turn, filled her exhausted lungs. The lungs that gushed air out of her dried mouth.

She ran. Ran into the wilderness. Ran out of breath. But she didn't stop until a rock forced her to. Her scream as she tumbled down reverberated in my ears.

I woke up from the same dream about a woman I didn't know. My eyes opened right as she fell and was about to turn around.

I found Viru leaning against the door jamb.

"You okay, Mandy?"

I nodded and yawned. "When did you get home?"

"Just now," he returned.

"Dad! Come down! I've got your honey lemon water!" Reva yelled from the kitchen.

"Coming, Revs!" called Viru. "See? She never forgets. Such a wonderful girl. Only she cares for my health."

"Yes. Only she does. I'm just feeding you grease. What are you doing loitering in the hall? Come in or go downstairs."

"I can't find one of my earbuds. Wireless is not for me; I should stick to the wired ones. Either you use both or lose both. Now, what will I do with one earbud? I tell you, technology is just one big scam. Wasting people's time and money."

"It's in the cupboard. I found it in the track pants you

wore yesterday. The man keeps one earbud in each pair of track pants."

"Great! Why didn't you tell me before? I was feeling guilty for no reason. And don't be mad today, Mandy. It's a big day. We've got things to do."

Viru was excited that Saturday morning. It was Holi, the festival of colors.

In my childhood, I had been mesmerized by the legend of Holi. At Grandma's, I always insisted on hearing Prahlada's tale during bedtime, and her endearing and animated storytelling would never disappoint:

The demon king, Hiranyakashyap, possessed a boon of five powers. He could neither be killed by a man nor an animal, neither during the day nor at night, neither indoors nor outdoors, neither on land nor in the air nor water, and from no man-made weapon. Intoxicated by power and immortality, Hiranyakashyap regarded himself as invincible.

Prahlada, the son of the demon king, was an ardent devotee to God Vishnu, much to his father's anguish. He commanded Prahlada to acknowledge him as the supreme deity and warned against worshiping Vishnu. When Prahlada refused, Hiranyakashyap decided to kill him.

After several failed attempts of filicide, thanks to God Vishnu's blessings, Hiranyakashyap called upon his sister Holika for help. Holika had a boon in that fire could not harm her. The demoness sat in the burning pyre with Prahlada on her lap. The evil designs backfired. Holika scorched to death, and Prahlada came out unscathed.

Eventually, God Vishnu appeared as an incarnate Narasimha, part human and part lion (neither man nor animal). He attacked Hiranyakashyap at twilight (when it was neither day nor night) on the threshold of a courtyard (neither indoors nor outdoors) and placed the demon king on his thighs (neither earth nor in the air or water). Narsimha, fired with divine rage, disemboweled the demon using his claws (not a human weapon) and thus saved Prahlada.

The term Holi, coined after Holika, signifies the victory

of good over evil.

Initially, after moving to Abbynton, the idea of celebrating Holi did not excite Viru. According to him, we would look silly to the people in the foreign land alien to the festival, smearing our faces and getting wet.

"When in Rome, do as the Romans do," he'd added.

Viru shed his inhibition a few years later, expressing the need to celebrate our traditions and not forget our culture. He proclaimed his desire to draw his children closer to their faith and roots and that he didn't care what people thought.

To my jibe of reminding him, *When in Rome, do as the Romans do*, he replied, "But honey, we are in Abbynton, not Rome. I definitely don't care what Romans do or think."

I knew this overnight change of heart was neither for the love of customs nor out of remorse for neglecting the culture. Viru was jealous of his friends from back home, posting pictures and videos of their Holi fun on social media.

That's what peer pressure does to you. One wants to score even on the virtual goalpost.

Britney Hayden, who must've been four at the time, was the first curious soul who instantly joined our maiden Holi play in the backyard. A colorful activity with a license from the elders to soil their clothes—little Britney could not have wished for more. The green-eyed, bubbly Britney spent the following year asking when we could do it again.

Inspired by their daughter's excitement, Elena and Jim (who was still alive back then) joined us the following year.

Eventually, encouraged by the attention on social media and in the neighborhood, Viru turned the small family event into an organized bash.

For the ladies in the house, the morning of Holi began with the grand cooking task. This year, I was relegated to deputy chef, and Reva's rank had slipped to kitchen porter. With my Mom's culinary prowess, I stood no chance of leading my kitchen.

The head chef, like a professional, planned ahead of

time. She had made her mouth-watering sweets the day before and had us do the cutting and chopping work last night for the morning's preparation. I wondered why my folks never started a restaurant business to do justice to Mom's talent.

Viru occupied himself with making the Holi-special beverage, his only contribution to the culinary department, to which he would go to any lengths to get the recipe right from his friends back in India.

Reva participated in the chores wholeheartedly. She wouldn't share, but looking at her sad eyes, I could tell that her weeklong matter with Timothy King stood unresolved. My house did not appeal because of its décor, but due to Reva's giggles. I hoped to see the beauty of my home restored soon.

Ryan, clad in a slightly worn-out t-shirt and old jeans that I planned to throw away later rather than toss in the laundry, kicked off the play with Caesar, who wore nothing more than a wide grin.

Caesar's excellent matrix-like reflexes helped him maneuver through the streams launched at him by Ryan's loaded plastic gun after sucking water from the bucket Viru had left in the backyard.

Britney joined them shortly, initially gasping at the jet of cold water that splattered her moist skin, making her ditsy floral dress wet, then squealing joyfully. It didn't take long for my backyard to become a waterpark.

Elena became filled with childlike joy as she chased Britney around the yard, pink powder clenched in her fist. The wrinkles on her forehead, cut deep by single parenting woes, had temporarily faded in the bliss of her daughter's uncontrollable laughter.

Britney successfully dodged her Mom by taking momentary refuge behind Ryan's back and then mine, followed by frolicking around every corner of the backyard.

Stopping by to catch her breath, Elena gently smeared the pink powder on my face, which was already unrecognizable due to the mishmash of colors thanks to Viru's careless smudging.

I reciprocated by dabbing yellow color on Elena's red cheeks, and we both uttered the words simultaneously: *Happy Holi.*

Viru had not even spared my head. My hair was bathed in a green powder and somewhat clumped due to water splashing from Ryan's gun and Ted's water balloon landing on my back. A hair wash nightmare awaited me later.

Only Ryan was excused from the color as the sensation of particles on his face made him uncomfortable. He loved getting soaked in the water, though.

However, the texture of the powder seemed okay to Ryan when rubbed by Britney's hand, a privilege that she boasted about joyfully to everyone.

The red, pink, blue, yellow, and green heaps of powders were consumed shortly by excited faces, casual tops, loose-fitted overalls, and (in my case) hair and ears, as well as Caesar's entire body.

Mrs. Bergenza, famous for her four cats, dipped her fingers into the powder and made yellow marks on everyone's faces that looked like cat paws.

Tim and Ted's parents, Tom and Debra King, danced gracefully to the slow music Viru had arranged. Sylvain danced around his wife Molly comically, and everybody laughed.

Simple joys of laughter and merrymaking break the boundaries of faith and transcend the limits of culture.

To my pleasant surprise, Timothy King showed up. Reva's eyes met his and it was as if the surrounding noises of laughter and music ceased to reach their ears.

Tim moved his red fingers softly down Reva's moist left cheek like water flowing on a marble slate. Moments later, Reva reciprocated by running her colorful fingers on his cheeks. They did not speak a word, but I could hear their eyes talking and laughing.

Reva and Tim sat on the deck under the blue sky. Her

giggles returned, and so did the beauty of my house. I choked back my tears and thanked God.

It turned out I had one more person to thank for this. Noticing Tim glancing at Viru with a smile and his returning the same took me by surprise. It didn't take long to guess what went behind the scenes.

Viru blushed at my gaze, then heaved a sigh. "Times have changed, Mandy. This boy makes my daughter happier than I do. Imagine! He doesn't even have a sense of humor like me. It kills me to see her sad. God, I hate sharing Reva's love with this doofus."

Viru had never objected to their proximity for Reva's sake, but he was not fond of Tim. Tim rarely visited our house as he did not feel welcomed by Viru, who would turn monosyllabic near him. Realizing Viru had not only initiated a conversation with Tim but also invited him over for Holi spoke volumes of how much Reva meant to him. I choked back more tears.

Kids and enthusiastic parents aside, the Holi celebration piqued the interest of the reclusive adults, like Mr. Bergenza, thanks to the beverage that Viru had spent hours perfecting—*bhang thandai*. Despite the meticulous preparation of us ladies, Viru's cold drink made of milk, blended with almonds, pistachios, walnuts, and, above all, infused with cannabis, would prove to be the showstopper item for yet another year. According to Viru, food and *Bhang Thandai* complemented one another in that the former satisfied the belly, and the latter set the mood.

Viru sat down with his friends on the lawn he had cut neatly with the mower the previous evening. Two glasses down, they laughed hysterically at Viru's jokes, which lowered further in standard by the intoxication, and wept nonsensically over Sylvain's funny account of the trekking expedition.

Another unexpected entry was Mrs. Walker, who arrived with Tulip, assuredly making Caesar's heart bloom.

My faith in Holi's magic had soared after Tim and Reva

made up, which evoked a spark of hope for Caesar. But Tulip, the Miss World of dogs, was one touch-me-not plant no dog in the city of Abbynton had managed to impress.

The spark I'd hoped to discover did not kindle. I realized the burden of matchmaking could not be thrust on the Holi bash alone, as it only afforded the ambiance. The initiative needed to come from the individuals.

However, the unusual occurrence of the day was Caesar's indifference toward Tulip. Viru would regard Caesar's morning walks as nothing more than the pursuit of Tulip, and here, aside from an initial moment of interest, Caesar paid no regard to her amid the merriment. It just didn't add up.

On the contrary, Caesar shook his brown coat, no longer visible in the mélange of colors, violently and repeatedly in displeasure, which somewhat concerned me.

Viru made Mrs. Walker laugh, and Caesar made Tulip curious.

Two tables from the living room were joined in the yard to serve the buffet lunch. The tantalizing aroma wafted into the air, teasing nostrils and tickling bellies. Mom's cuisine became an instant hit: hot *rajma* (creamy curry of red beans), blazing *palak paneer* (cottage cheese dipped in buttery spinach gravy), sizzling *aloo gobi* (a dish made of potatoes, cauliflowers, spices, and herbs), steamed rice, and warm butter *naans*, to name a few. The praise garnered by the cooking and sweets, especially *gujia*, satisfied Mom's appetite.

Everybody laughed and ate, and those under the influence of *bhang thandai* even more so.

"Loss"

Rohit Dharupta

Chapter One

The revelation of the unknown worlds, Shloka and Parloka, and their functioning had lifted Mom's spirit to some extent. I couldn't tell if she believed me, but she had not shown indifference either. Regardless of my playing it down to Mom, attributing it to the grand scheme of things, her puzzling encounters at night had bewildered me.

I analyzed the situation. Caesar, being the leader of Rudram, the sister concern of the ultimate organization Kendram, handled the affairs of Loka, our world. What affairs? I could not tell. But it sounded like a huge responsibility.

As far as I, an ordinary minner, could tell, Caesar's day started with a morning walk with Viru, followed by loitering about in the house through the day, waiting for Ryan to return from school in the afternoon, and spending the remaining day cuddling and prancing around with his buddy.

Considering the unproductive days, nighttime seemed about the right time for Rudram's headkeeper to get things done. Since Ryan was Caesar's master and the prospective candidate for the top job of Kendram, he was likely to know and participate in Caesar's work.

But why would Ryan need to be with Caesar at night when they lived together? How could both be present on the street and in bed simultaneously? And above all, how could Mom see them?

After Mom told me, I spent a few nights gazing through my window, hoping to catch sight of Ryan and Caesar dawdling on the street, but in vain. I could only see a quiet road with a car or two cruising by occasionally, and the lonely sidewalk flashed by the milky white light of the seemingly tired lamppost. It seemed that the old buddies— road, sidewalk, and lamppost—always together through thick and thin, did not wish for another's company in the middle of the night.

Mom told me she saw Ryan and Caesar under the lamppost with four large dogs and a girl. A large gathering occupied every inch of the street, the sidewalk, the alley, the gravel road bordering the cemetery, and the cemetery itself. Men, women, lions, tigers, elephants, giraffes, zebras, horses, rhinos, chimpanzees, bears, camels, and deer, to name a few.

Mom felt as if she was witnessing a congregation assembled for silent contemplation presided by Caesar, Ryan, and others under the lamppost. The view from her window looked like an elaborate painting of an animal kingdom on a black canvas. It lasted only a minute before the street returned to its former lonely self. The uncanny feeling, however, lasted longer.

I guessed Mom saw the Watch Force with Ryan and Caesar. The four dogs were perhaps the dog army, the D-Force, as the keeper Jack would call them, deployed for our protection.

I remember the time they encircled Ryan and me when the scary bear Duma had attacked us after Jack and I caught Hogdon red-handed, disguised as a psychiatrist, Bob. They were larger than average-sized dogs: two brown, one black, and their leader, Tormon, had a white coat with black spots.

The girl could be Samantha. She jogged up Mount Mary every morning.

I wanted to make headway, but Caesar could not speak, and Ryan would not talk. Ryan was more absorbed in the other world I knew so little about than the one we shared. As a mother, I was at a loss in both worlds. I yearned for information in the former and attention in the latter. Ryan would not give me either.

I would not mistake Mom's visuals for hallucinations, as

I had been misled once into that trap by Hogdon. I wondered if Mom had magical powers, like divine vision.

Was it not enough with Ryan and Caesar? Now Mom, too? Why do all superheroes have to be from my family? Why not one of my neighbors, like Elena or Britney? Or maybe Mrs. Bergenza, with the four cats? People already call her Catwoman.

I hoped I would not discover a superpower in Viru.

Well, he already has one: killing people with his jokes.

That thought broke my yawn into a chuckle as I changed my position on the bed.

The next thing I knew, the superhero of killer jokes, back from walking Caesar, was standing at the bedroom door, studying me.

Viru gave me a queer look. "Look at you, smiling by yourself in bed."

"An idiom just flashed in my mind. Think of the devil, and he shall appear," I said with a chuckle.

"I see … you find the lousy idioms you pick for me funnier than I am! By the way the correct usage is *speak* of the devil. Not think."

"Works either way. Where's Caesar?"

"That menace?"

"What now?"

"What now? This dog is an embarrassment, Mandy. *That* now. He wouldn't let me pet Tulip. I reached for a gentle pat on her neck, and he barked like a mad dog."

"Caesar barked at Tulip? That's strange. Was he jealous of you petting Tulip?"

"I've petted her before. Why would he be jealous now? And not some regular gruffing. Crazy barking. Like "stay away or I'll kill you" barking. Scared the crap out of Mrs. Walker."

"But Caesar likes Tulip. It doesn't make sense."

"I tell you, this dog doesn't make sense, Mandy. He was sniffing her behind a week ago and now he's howling at her like a lunatic," Viru said, strolling into the bedroom.

"Why would he do that? There must be some reason."

"Haven't you heard of barking up the wrong tree? This stupid dog took it literally."

"I don't get why Caesar would attack Tulip, of all dogs. And I also don't get the use of the idiom in this context."

"Tulip is the wrong tree, and Caesar was barking at her. What part do you not understand? Mandy, I'm talking about his ludicrousness, and all you're thinking about is the idiom usage?" Viru grumbled, standing at the foot of the bed.

Viru did not possess an inclination toward any art. However, he pursued one inadvertently. The art of exaggeration. He could easily turn a funny account into a horror story. His art would reach its peak when it came to Caesar.

Once, when Caesar briefly chased a beaver at the lake, Viru proclaimed that he grabbed its tail by his mouth and swirled it around like a spinning top. If there were an award for the art of exaggeration, Viru would surely win. It seemed Caesar also fanned Viru's annoyance toward him on purpose and enjoyed the reaction.

Usually, I would ignore Viru's morning whining, attributing it to another noteworthy performance of exaggeration. But I had noticed Caesar's discomfort in Tulip's presence a few weeks ago during the Holi celebrations. Given Caesar's previous liking for Tulip, I had found his behavior unusual at the time, but thought no more of it since.

Viru's claim of Caesar attacking Tulip sounded like a stretch, a concoction of his inventive mind, but I would concur that Caesar was up to something. I wondered if it was a ploy to capture Tulip's attention.

Is he trying some reverse psychology technique on her, switching from caring to carefree, or playing hard to get to mess with her mind?

If indeed he was, he had perhaps succeeded in mystifying her.

I would not think that for an ordinary dog, and though aware of Caesar's intelligence, it still seemed a far-fetched idea.

*

Charlene rattled me in the hospital by informing me that our first evaluation would be discussed that afternoon. Ali had also apparently known about it since last week.

Terry was unapologetic about not telling me.

"Didn't I tell you, Mandira? I thought I told everyone. Sometimes I get super busy with work and forget I have a life. But don't you worry, the evaluation is no big deal. They talk, you listen."

"Yes, but if I knew, I would have come mentally prepared to listen. And perhaps appreciate it better."

"Trust me, Mandira, I haven't seen anyone appreciate the evaluation. They evaluate you every day. In the first three weeks, I bet they had decided who would pass the program and who wouldn't. So relax."

I made no reply.

"Remember, Mandira, I'm telling you as a friend: Performance speaks for itself. Others can't cut in line when it's your moment to shine."

I could not fathom why Terry Henson would forget to inform only me of a key milestone of the shadowing program and act as if nothing had happened. On the one hand, he advised that I build my confidence; on the other, he clearly did not mind risking shattering my confidence by withholding information.

And what's with the sharing of misplaced wisdom? I thought. "*Others can't cut in line when it's your moment to shine.*" *That's like misleading a traveler looking for directions and, when caught red-handed, telling them they were meant to find their own path.*

Per Viru, who understood work politics better than I did, I should ignore his barbs and focus on the positives. But with Terry, I struggled to find positives.

My daily recaps of the events at the hospital to Viru for the last six weeks had made him appreciate the staff much like the characters of *Grey's Anatomy*, with perhaps more drama infused by me. It turned out I was no less of a storyteller myself.

Viru believed that Terry sought attention equivalent to the doctors, and I needed to balance moderately obliging him and staying clear of the negativity. In his words, "Pay attention to the person, not to his perspective."

Every night in bed, Viru gave a patient hearing to my complaining. Not that he really had a choice. When Dr. Lopez enquired about me eating an apple one afternoon, I told her I sometimes liked to keep it light by eating fruit for lunch. She said she always kept it light by eating food for lunch.

Viru noted that she rhymed her sentence with mine as she thought I wanted to keep her away.

I knitted my brows, and he clarified, "Haven't you heard an apple a day keeps the doctor away?" Viru laughed.

I knitted my brows again, this time in vexation.

After shadowing him for three days, Dr. Kumar complimented me for sounding calm and confident in front of patients.

"Sometimes I am, and sometimes I am not," was my humble reply.

To this he snapped, "Well, you must be good at masking emotions then."

Viru was not impressed when I told him. Assuming an air of wisdom, he remarked, "Compliments are to be taken with a smile and a thank you. One must not respond with an explanation."

One would wonder if Viru was the same person who remarked that Caesar was barking up the wrong tree this morning.

Viru was like a coconut; what you saw on the outside was in total contrast with the inside. The dichotomy of Viru's disposition could inspire another Jane Austen title—*Senseless and Sensibility*.

Adapting to the doctors' distinctive patient management approach was my most significant learning curve and perhaps the most challenging one in the shadowing program. Patient management could be broken down into problem management and time management. While Dr. Ralph regarded active listening to the patients as vital for the diagnosis, Dr. Kimberly believed in controlling the conversation to prevent the topic from derailing. Dr. Kumar reckoned that patience with patients went a long way, but Dr. Herschelle, who worked in the ER, was aware they didn't have all day.

I had to keep the modus operandi of each doctor in mind when engaging with their patients. Active listening after a point would be an inconclusive sermon for Dr. Kimberly, and extra patience would not be a virtue for Dr. Herschelle.

Ali and Charlene went in for their feedback spiritedly but returned dispirited.

After knocking on the door, I entered the conference room, greeted by suppressed smiles. Dr. Adam Jalil, the program director, was seated at the head of the oval table, and Dr. Maria Lopez occupied the third chair to his right. At her gesture, I took the seat opposite her.

"Mandira, we would like to hear your views about the program. How do you think it's going for you?"

"I think it's going well, Dr. Lopez. I learn something new every day. I keep asking how to improve my interactions with patients and the case presentation to the doctors, and the doctors are kind enough to share tips and tricks. And I do my best to apply them."

"Well, we have the feedback from our team of doctors. Everybody believes your patient interaction is good. You're polite with them and keep your calm. But with patients, one must build rapport. Only then can you get the most out of them. Perhaps your shy nature can sometimes come across as less empathetic to the patients.

"As for your presentation skills, they're impressive. You structure your summary very well. However, sometimes you seem to hold yourself back on your expression. We have seen this hesitation in people who don't have much work exposure, like you. The team agrees that you are resilient, Mandira, and due to your adaptive nature, we are sending you to the Department of Internal Medicine on a three-week rotation."

Viru had once explained a feedback sandwich to me, and I noticed that Dr. Lopez had just served me a sizzling one:

"Like the sandwich slices," he'd said, "you begin and end with praise and express the critical part in between—the stuffing. It would help if the bread did not fool you, as the essence of feedback is in the stuffing. Bread slices only provide a cushion to the impact of the blow from the stuffing. The more the stuffing, the harder the blow.

"Feedback can only be positive when it does not have a follow-up sentence prefixed with *but*, *however*, or *by the way*. If indeed such a conjunction is used, the real feedback follows after the prefix."

So, based on this, the gist of my feedback was that I was shy, less empathetic, holding back, and had less work exposure.

According to Viru, critical feedback is an unwanted gift people are happy to give but don't wish to receive. Accepting it with humility is the only way to be the bigger person in the room.

Given a choice, I'd rather be a happier person, but I came out of the conference room as a bigger person.

Terry sounded bothered by the news.

"I can't believe they're sending you to Internal Medicine. I recommended Ali, but you should be fine, too. I'll help you like I do here."

I could not tell if my transfer to the Department of Internal Medicine over Ali or Charlene was a reward or a punishment.

Chapter Two

A squirrel darted up a tree, stopped where the trunk branched into two, and stayed still, perhaps reminiscing about the day almost passed or wondering about the night befalling shortly. Or maybe she confided in the other squirrel, crouched on the branch looking out for her.

Between the partially visible protruding roots of the tree grabbing the earth firmly, small holes cut deep, perhaps to the origin of the rootlets. A thousand laborious ants marched on the brown soil, like the fresh stroke of a paintbrush running on the coarse fabric, before disappearing into those chambers. Many carried pieces of green leaves thrice their sizes to breed the farmland of fungus, their dependable food reserve, under the ground.

A monkey family relaxed on another tree. Adults bonded over picking particles off each other's fur and slipping them into their mouths in a grooming ritual. Young monkeys jumped from one branch to another, with the mama monkey occasionally pulling their legs to keep them close.

A hare chased another on the thick, ungrazed grass. Balancing on two feet, they briefly engaged in a scuffle, before the female gave in to the teasing, and both hopped back together behind the bushes.

Far away, like a melted hot iron, the sun slipped into the moss-wrapped rocks, paving the way to twilight.

Suddenly, thousands of birds hidden in the leaves, twigs, and buds shot off into the sky, stripping the soul out of the splendid trees.

The birds flapping and fluttering aimlessly and squealing at the top of their voice, almost in chorus, filled the space and broke the calm of the bewildered sky.

The incessantly screeching monkeys climbed on the higher and leaner branches, shaking them haphazardly.

The noise of chaos suddenly trampled the fragrance of peace and the melody of harmony.

A fawn emerged from the bushes and sprinted hither and tither. His face was blank, eyes clueless, and his flight severely marred by one limping leg. Where he was running to or what he was running from was not clear.

The mystery unfolded in the next moment. A pack of twenty-five or thirty howling hyenas surrounded the fawn.

Those frenzied eyes and ugly salivating mouths knew no mercy. The jarring whines and whoops of the hyenas grew louder in the excitement of bordering their prey. Like a deer caught in the headlights, his trembling limbs had seemingly given up, staring nervously into the eyes of the hideous and inevitable death closing in.

One of the stronger and more overexcited hyenas pounced on the fawn. But before the hyena could grab the fawn by his canines, a deer appeared out of nowhere and pushed the fawn away with lightning speed. The hyena backed up a little to process the unexpected event.

The deer stayed there, unmoving, all eyes on her now, while the fawn fell outside the perimeter of bloodthirsty beasts thanks to her forceful jerk.

It was easy to guess but hard to express the relationship the deer and fawn shared.

The mama deer knew she could easily dodge those beasts with her strong athletic limbs, but her injured baby deer could not. So, she made an impossible choice only a mother could make: sacrifice herself for the sake of her offspring.

There was no scale yet designed to measure the length a mother can go to protect her offspring. How could another life be more precious than her own that she didn't think twice before offering to be mangled in exchange for it?

The grass field where the two hares had boxed playfully a few minutes back was now witnessing a massacre.

The entire jungle of Billaria teared up along with the baby deer, helplessly witnessing mama deer torn into pieces. His spindly legs sunk into the ground in guilt for being the reason for Mama's merciless slaughter.

His oversized ears strained to hear Mama's last sounds of goodbye, muffled under the shrilling laughter of delirious hyenas. The mother that before fed him milk to live now fed her flesh and bones to see him off alive.

The little fawn must carry on. He must not throw away the ultimate gift his mother had given him for the second time—the gift of life.

As the baby deer darted away, mama deer, dying in a pool of blood, heaved a sigh of relief. Her gradually closing eyes opened abruptly one last time when the little one stumbled, as if asking with concern, "Are you hurt, son?"

The fawn galloped on with the wind. He dashed across the grass field, sped past the bushes, hastened down the shallow canal, and hurried along the mossy rocks. Oblivious to his surroundings, it seemed, at his pace he would soon cross the jungle of Billaria and reach the outskirts of the town of Driffin.

But how far could those weak and hurting limbs take him?

Exhausted by running and trauma, he did not realize a pack of hyenas, perhaps outcompeted by their aggressive accomplices for mama deer's flesh and bones, was still chasing him.

The pack leader of ten lept up to attack. His jaws brushed the fawn's injured limb, tumbling him down, crashing against a large rock cushioned with moss.

The fawn didn't get back up. His hope of living withered in the face of death as the jubilant hunter stepped forward to nab his prey.

Perhaps it was one of those days when the entire universe conspired to protect the little deer. The leader hyena grabbed the fawn by his neck. But instead of feeling pressure on his jaws, the hyena felt pressure on his own neck. Before he could understand, the hyena was jerked violently against a nearby rock—this one much sharper than the last.

The pack backed up. A large, white-furred wolf stood tall, guarding the fawn lying listless on the ground.

There was something in the fierce eyes and wild snarl of the giant wolf that ten angry and whining hyenas—embarrassed leader included—could not muster the courage to come anywhere close to.

The hyenas' whines and whimpers continued for a few minutes, hesitantly taking three steps backward for every one forward until another pack of thirty joined them, restoring confidence.

They collectively charged.

However, undeterred by their number, the mighty wolf flung them forcefully on the ground, keeping them away from the fawn.

The fierce brawl continued for a long time. The wolf began to slow down, exhausted by the noisy, persistent hyenas. Whenever he grabbed one, the others snuck bites from his tail, legs, and underbelly. Still, none managed to come close to the fawn under his watch.

When it looked like the wolf was overpowered, another pack showed up. A pack of wolves this time.

One pack against another.

Though the hyenas still outnumbered the wolves, even fifty of them would be no match against those ten looming and snarling wolves.

The savage wolves showed no mercy, tossing the hyenas in every direction. They slaughtered many of them on the spot. Those who survived hastened back, howling to where they came from, picking up their battered bodies on broken legs.

The original wolf walked closer to the fawn, who lay motionless on the ground as the other wolves guarding the area looked on.

Examining closely by sniffing, licking, and repeatedly

pressing above the underbelly with one paw, he applied what looked like a CPR technique. The other wolves looked assured by his actions, as if their leader had studied animal medicine in the jungle of Billaria.

About three minutes and twenty chest compressions later, the fawn finally moved. His head first, followed by the rest of his body. He slowly came to his senses and, with help from the wolf, stood back up on his lean, unsteady limbs. He seemed calm, surrounded by these new beasts. He darted hither and thither, this time fearlessly.

The leader wolf, visibly satisfied, noticed a black shadow by a distant tree. Upon paying attention, he realized it was a dog with black fur. Their eyes communicated respectfully, and the dog disappeared behind the tree.

*

I strolled on the green carpet of my neatly mowed backyard lawn. The air smelled like a bowl of grass leaves and sandalwood chips. Walking barefoot on the moist, trimmed grass on the warm summer morning was bliss. Natural acupressure.

Mom is the discoverer of such natural pleasures. Since arriving, she had always walked barefoot on the grass, removing her sandals on the deck. Initially, I made fun of her strange quirk, but now I was shy to admit that I loved doing it, too. So I tiptoed to the yard early in the morning while Mom slept to avoid getting caught by her triumphant, "I told you so" gaze.

Britney caught my glimpse from her house and slid open her glass door, holding a cup of coffee.

"Morning, Mrs. Sharma! You're walking without sandals, like Ryan's granny."

"Hi, Britney! How are you, honey? You're up early. When did you get back from your trip?" I returned, changing the topic, thinking now everybody would know about my new habit.

"Yesterday afternoon. It was awesome, Mrs. Sharma. The best vacation ever! Miami was so cool! They have such tall buildings downtown. Mom says they're called skyscrapers. And the beach! It's so beautiful and huge! We walked and walked, and Mom got tired and dehydrated, and we headed back to the hotel. We ate so much at dinner that our tummies were aching. Miami is hot…"

Busy recounting the minute details of her trip, Britney did not notice her Mom, Elena, appearing briefly behind her and waving at me through the glass door.

"…Then we went to Niagara Falls. The waterfall was so cool. Mom says it's enormous. We did a boat tour. You know, Mrs. Sharma, it took us so close to the falls that the water spray soaked us. Mom says it's called mist. They gave us plastic rain jackets. Mom says it's called poncho…"

Elena appeared again behind her, snapping the fingers of her hand together and apart in a *blah blah blah* gesture. I chuckled. Elena's hand went down before Britney turned back.

"It's poncho, isn't it, Mom?" asked Britney, and Elena nodded animatedly.

"It was so cool!"

I could not help but notice Britney's frequent use of the word "cool" and the mention of terms from Mom's vocabulary, either peculiar or less familiar to her.

"…we were tired and it was getting too late to drive back to Abbynton, so Mom said, 'Let's stay in Driffin for the night.' You won't believe it, Mrs. Sharma—there's a jungle nearby! And the animals make so much noise we could hear them in the motel. Howling sounds. Like *woo, woo.* Mom said they were wolves. And birds screamed all night in the sky, and Mom could barely sleep. Isn't it true, Mom? But I slept like a baby…"

And the ten-year-old chatterbox went on.

Chapter Three

"Hello, Mandira! Remember me?" said the familiar face, tipping his hat and exposing his bald head.

I looked up in shock, and he continued, "I bet you do. You're the only minner who has seen me. Well, other than Monsieur Ryan, of course. You and I met a few times in our last mission," he said, briefly rubbing his long, conspicuous nose.

"Let me remind you anyway. I'm Jack, the keeper. I oversee the three zones that lead to Shloka—Antar, Jantar, and Mantar. Minners journey daily from Loka—your world—to Shloka and back through these three zones. You minners perceive these repeating journey cycles as sleep and Shloka as dreams. See! How nicely I summed up the biggest secret minners don't know," said Jack, proudly running fingers across his chest, straightening the crease of his black cloak.

Of course, I remember you, Jack, I thought, but couldn't say aloud. *You're the one who dragged my son and me into your grand, otherworldly schemes two years ago. And I haven't slept peacefully ever since, constantly worrying about Ryan's safety. How can I forget you? You have no idea how it kills you to see your child suffering, even more so when you don't know how to help them. Be a mom for a day, Jack, and you'll know. Keep a child in your belly, Mr. Keeper, and you'll know what keeping means.*

"Hmm, I am sensing sarcasm in your eyes, Mandira, which means you have not forgotten me," said Jack, surrounded by a thick mist, making nothing else but him visible.

I don't forget, Jack. I also know that I'm sleeping right now, roaming somewhere in one of your zones, and you're talking to me from the border of Jantar and Mantar, where there's only mist. You can speak directly to me, but I can only listen, I thought, hoping the words in my head would reach him.

"Well, it's my pleasure to see you again, Mandira. You will be happy to hear that Monsieur Ryan is now a popular figure in Parloka. His work has earned him respect and praise from some of the senior committee members of the apex organization, Kendram."

His work? The only work I know he does is his schoolwork, which he rarely completes. And that work does not earn him respect, but complaints from the teachers. As for praise, I haven't heard that word and Ryan's name in the same sentence in years.

I often wished I were actively involved in other worlds, Shloka and Parloka, that acknowledged and appreciated Ryan. But on second thought, those worlds were mysterious and dangerous. So Ryan being unappreciated but safe in Loka was a better proposition for me than otherwise.

"Monsieur Ryan is eleven, according to your minner calendar. In one year, he will be ready to participate in the greatest carnival arranged by Kendram—Korsi, or 'The Meet' as it is sometimes called. I can't wait to see him there. Believe me, Mandira. There's nothing bigger and better than The Meet. Even a chance to be a tiny part of such a grand show is an honor. Everybody in Parloka is excited for Monsieur Ryan. The chief wishes to see him as his predecessor. No, I mean, successor," Jack fumbled and then paused momentarily. "I don't know … whichever 'cessor' it is. Minner language is complicated, and I don't get to use it much. I'm out of practice, you know. But I think you get me."

I chuckled at seeing him still struggling with the language after two years, correcting Jack in my head.

"Remember, Mandira, we all are rooting for Monsieur Ryan. Time to go; a lot of work. I am getting old. I also need one of those predecessors. Or successors. There we go again. Why do you people have to make two words sound similar? You are smart enough to know which 'cessor' I meant. I will know it soon, too, as I am taking lessons from the great Professor Lingua Franca of Parloka. Sir Franca speaks all the languages that are known to exist. Watch out for my new avatar. Bye, Mandira!"

The fog engulfed Jack. And moments later, the darkness in my bedroom engulfed the fog. I had woken up.

My eyes fixed on the ceiling after adjusting to the dark.

That was odd. Why would Jack show up suddenly after two years and remind me of The Meet? I knew, as per the guidelines of Kendram that the chief and the keepers followed religiously, I must be on board with the idea of Ryan participating in The Meet and contesting for the next chief. I had the right to decide for my minor child. They feared I might deny them my blessing, considering it a high-risk responsibility for Ryan, still very young, surrounded by dreaded enemies like Hogdon.

And what had happened to Hogdon? Could there be a misadventure looming like the last time? Why else would Jack appear unannounced and talk to me in such a reassuring tone? I didn't think he was simply paying a courtesy call. A professional keeper like him would not visit me without reason.

Jack could have visited me rather than addressing me from the border of Jantar, clouded by the mist of mystery. If he met me in person, he knew I would ask questions he perhaps wanted to avoid.

There were plenty of questions begging for answers. To begin with, more insight into The Meet would have been great. What was supposed to happen in that so-called grand event, and what was Ryan expected to do?

And Jack mentioned that The Meet would occur in Parloka. As far as I understood, Parloka was akin to an afterlife destination where one could be only after death. How were we supposed to enter Parloka while alive? And even if we could, and I gave the green light, there was no way Ryan would be going without me.

I had more pressing questions for Jack that bothered me

frequently. Were Ryan and my family safe? Where was that wicked Hogdon and his accomplice, the ugly bear, Duma? Were they in captivity somewhere, or roaming free, contriving their evil designs? I would also enquire about the strange sightings of Mom through the window in the middle of the night.

Least important, but I would also ask him about Professor Lingua Franca.

I mean, really? Is that the name of a real person?

Jack's sudden appearance acted like an unhealed wound suddenly exposed by rolling the bandage open. The wound of disquiet was always there, but covered by the mundane trifles of day-to-day life.

The radium hands of the mechanical clock at my side table struck two. I had little hope of going back to sleep, or speaking literally, journeying to Shloka via Antar, Jantar, and Mantar. That journey sounded even more complex at this hour.

I wondered if Mom was sleeping. Quietly slipping out of the quilt Viru grabbed tightly from the other end like it was the last shred of clothing on his body, I tip-toed down the hall.

As usual, I gently pushed open the slightly ajar bedroom door and found Mom at the window.

Seeing her wrinkled face glowing despite the darkness, the guilt of dragging her into my problems engulfed me. But in the next moment, I thought to myself, *She's my Mom! Who else would share my troubles if not her?*

I entered the room, letting the momentary guilt exit my head. I joined Mom at the window. The street was empty and exposed by the luminous lamppost, as expected.

"You okay, Mom?" I asked softly.

Mom was so engrossed studying the lamp that she had not noticed me enter the room. My voice in the dark broke her bubble, and she shuddered in fear.

"It's okay! It's me, Munni."

"Munni! Oh dear God! You scared me," said Mom,

breathing heavily with a hand on her chest.

"Sorry, Mom! I didn't mean to scare you. You okay? Need some water?"

"I am okay, dear," returned Mom, collecting herself.

"Come, sit here, Mom."

"Wait a second," she said, looking out of the window again. "Very well, now they're gone."

"They're gone? Who is gone, Ma?"

"Who else, Munni?"

"Ryan and Caesar? Did you see them again?"

"Yes."

"But when?"

"Just now. A second before you scared me."

"I don't believe it. I was standing next to you; I didn't see anything. Where did you see them, Ma? What were they doing?"

"Same place. Right under that lamp." Mom pointed to the street. "Ryan, Caesar, and that other dog."

Who? Tormon? The one with white fur and black spots?"

"Yes, do you know him? Have you seen him before?"

"Mmm … not really. Jack told me about him. Remember I told you about Jack, the keeper from another world? But never mind. What else did you see?"

I fumbled as I had not told Mom about the horrifying face-off with Hogdon and Duma when I first saw Tormon, lest I should scare her. Mom only knew the bright side of my supernatural experience, not the dark one.

"I also saw a wolf. A big wolf…"

"A wolf? Oh, wait! Was it another dog?" I cut in, thinking Mom was confusing a wolf with a dog, another member of Tormon's D-Force.

"I don't think so. It was a wolf, larger than this dog. What did you call him again?"

"Tormon."

"Yes, Tormon. Definitely a wolf, about the same height as Ryan. A giant wolf."

I recalled all four dogs of D-Force were bigger than an average dog, but about the same size as each other.

"And there was a little deer. A baby deer."

"A baby deer? Like a fawn?"

"Yes. Must be a few months old. So beautiful. He had some trouble with his foot. He was limping."

"A giant wolf and a small lame deer. What else did you see, Ma?"

"That's about it. Yeah, that's all. All right under that streetlamp."

"What were they doing?" My curiosity had no bounds.

"Nothing. They did nothing. That's the strange part—they don't do anything."

"That's the only strange part?" I chuckled sarcastically, thinking, *What part of this isn't strange?*

But an event, however unique, when repeated frequently makes you focus on the particulars associated with it more than the existence of the event itself. For instance, we hardly contemplate the remarkable phenomenon of regularly getting hungry to address the body's need to function like a well-oiled machine. Instead, we focus on what and when to eat.

"They kept staring at each other, except for the fawn hobbling around them. And then you came, and they disappeared," said Mom.

I spent some time with Mom analyzing the finer details of her visual experience and concluded that we should go back to sleep.

After tucking Mom into bed the way she always did when I was little, I quietly walked upstairs.

I peeked into Ryan's room through the half-opened door. Sleeping on his stomach with hands wide open, Ryan seemed to hug the bed tightly as if nothing could separate him from the comfort of the soft, cozy bedding. Curled beside him, Caesar snored like an airplane with his mouth open.

The portion of the comforter still on the foot of the bed

covered Ryan's feet, and the remaining sprawled on the floor. The room looked nothing short of a shrine to blissful sleep. There was no sign of him leaving the bed, let alone leaving the house.

Besides sleeping here in Loka, the only other place Ryan and Caesar could hang out simultaneously was somewhere in Antar, Jantar, Mantar, or Shloka.

Being in bed and on the street contradicted the concept of the mesmerizing journey to Shloka that everyone did unknowingly in sleep, and I had experienced it in the state of consciousness with Jack two years back.

I knew further analysis at this hour would not give me the answers. So, I returned to my room, knowing my movement would not have escaped Reva in the other room, no matter how hushed.

Slipping into bed, I gently pulled one end of the comforter that Viru had wrapped around his body like an old gift in new wrapping paper.

"What are you doing walking around at night?"

"You awake? I thought you were still in Shloka."

My eyes widened upon realizing my slip of the tongue.

"Where? What did you say?"

"Nothing. I thought you were sleeping."

"Do you see me sleeping? You mumbled something else. What were you doing?"

"Nothing. Went to the loo."

"For how long? I woke up a while ago and you weren't here."

"I was checking on Mom. She has difficulty sleeping sometimes. Okay, Sherlock Holmes?"

"You and your Mom! I've married into a family of insomniacs. Why don't you people start a business of night watchmen?"

"Viru, you're not funny at any hour of the day or night. Go back to sleep. It's four a.m. You have to walk Caesar in an hour."

"Very well, Madam Sentry Guard. Spoil my sleep and

then assign me the morning duty. You people should seriously consider this business."

"Haha, very funny," I returned mockingly. "Caesar will be up in a jiffy."

"I tell you, Mandy, if your mad dog barks at Mrs. Walker and Tulip today, I will throw him in the lake."

Viru's comment made me once again consider Caesar's odd behavior toward Tulip. Once bewitched by her charm, Caesar had become increasingly hostile toward the adorable dog lately.

I knew analyzing Caesar's odd behavior would not give me the answers in the wee hours of this very confusing night, so I forced myself to focus on sleep.

As I closed my eyes, hoping my worries withered away, I had an uncanny feeling that not everything was as it seemed.

Chapter Four

"You're here early, girl. Where do you live?" Nurse Dolma asked.

"I live close by: Saint Thomas Street, near the metro station."

"I see. Got a boyfriend? Or you single?"

"I'm married. I've got two kids."

"Oh, how old?"

"Fifteen and eleven. A girl and a boy."

"Oh, shut up, girl. Really?"

"Yes."

"You look too young to be the mom of a fifteen-year-old! Was it a child marriage or something?" The nurse looked amazed.

"No, not child marriage." I chuckled. "I guess I look a few years younger than my age."

"A lot younger! You've gotta give me your secret, girl. I look a few years older than my age."

Young Sophie, the receptionist, giggled at the counter.

"Now, what are you laughing for, Sophie? You think I'm lying? Do your work, girl."

Sophie, accustomed to Nurse Dolma's banter, continued to giggle.

"By the by, Mandira, don't go to room one-oh-seven."

"Why, Mrs. Dolma?"

"The new patient in there is nuts. Abusing everybody left and right. You know what he said to the resident doctor last night? He said, 'What are you? A dummy doctor? How do you people pass your medical tests?' Poor boy, such a gentle doctor. He was so upset that he left early this morning."

"That's not good. Why would he say that?"

"Not only that. He refused to take his medicine, and when the nurse said, 'How will you get better if you don't take your meds?' He goes, 'Why don't you take the meds instead? You'll definitely get better and stop asking stupid questions.' He's on a roll, girl, insulting everybody," said Nurse Dolma as she focused on the machine that was brewing a fresh batch of coffee.

"Any idea why he's so worked up?"

"God knows. I ain't going in to talk to him. Can't control myself if someone mocks me. You too, girl. Stay away from him."

"But I need to fill out the history form before Dr. Green comes in," I said anxiously.

"Well, you better go see him with Dr. Green only. Don't tell me I didn't warn you," said Mrs. Dolma, walking toward the staff lounge with her coffee.

Sitting at the desk near the conference room, I became thoughtful. It had been a week since I had joined the Department of Internal Medicine. Dr. Jalil, the director of the shadowing program, and Dr. Lopez, the teaching head, both from the Department of Family Medicine, had sent me here for a three-week rotation. My colleagues Charlene and Ali continued in Family Medicine.

I shadowed Dr. Steven Green, the attending physician and a teaching professor of the interns. On the first day, Steven Green briefed me about my work with an expression that indicated I was just another hindrance in his busy work schedule. He directed me to fill out the questionnaire by talking to the admitted patients every morning, followed by observing him on the rounds the rest of the day. I had no idea how much it helped Dr. Green, but filling out the form was the only productive part of my day to which I could contribute.

I looked up the notes from the resident doctor on Informa (or Missus Informa, according to Terry).

Paul Martin, a fifty-year-old male known for chronic hypertension and uncontrolled diabetes, presented with acute heart failure due to noncompliance with his medications—a difficult patient.

A few minutes later, I walked into room one-oh-seven.

"Good morning, Mr. Martin. I'm Mandira. How are you doing today?"

"Here comes another one. Now, what are you? Another dummy doctor?"

"I'm a student. I'm shadowing the attending physician, Dr. Steven Green," I returned, already apprehensive that I had made a mistake.

"Shadowing? What's shadowing?'

"Well, shadowing means I follow the doctor closely during his day-to-day work."

"Follow the doctor? Like a stalker? So you do nothing?"

"I make myself available for any assistance, like filling out this questionnaire. I'm applying for a medical school test next year."

"Oh, so you haven't joined med school yet! Not even an intern, like that guy last night. What is this place? Run by you dummies! When will I see the real doctor?"

"Dr. Green will commence the morning round shortly. He will see you with his team in an hour."

"And you're a student? You look too old for college. What'd you do, fail your classes?"

I felt like storming out of the room, but it was too late; I had come in here alone, and now I had to stay. I wondered why I'd thought he would treat me differently.

I made no reply to his jibe. I knew anything I said would continue the loop of insults. Paul waited, perhaps ready with another remark in his head.

"Do you have a mute button? Why have you gone quiet?" Paul asked.

I shook my head.

"What, are you offended now? Do you know how traumatic it is to live with this condition? High blood pressure and diabetes and whatnot? You people say, 'Do this, do that; take this, take that; eat this, don't eat that.' Like I'm some toy. Do you even understand me?"

"Yes, I totally understand, Mr. Martin," I replied, expecting him to mock me again.

"And that boy last night! That dummy doctor goes, 'Oh, Mr. Martin, you have uncontrolled diabetes. What have you been doing?' What have I been doing? I started living! A normal life, like a normal person. Do you understand me, Ms. Not-a-doctor?"

"I do, Mr. Martin."

"And that nurse! She goes, 'Mr. Martin, take your meds. How will you get better if you don't take your meds?' Well, what do you know, Ms. Another-not-a-doctor? I lose my erection when I take those meds. That's why. There you are. Now you know. Cat's out of the bag. But the mouse is still in the pants." He chuckled.

Checking himself, Paul continued, "Now I want to enjoy life. Go cycling. Make love to my lady. Eat the meals of my choice and have my favorite drink. Tell me, is it too much to ask . . . what'd you say your name was?"

"Mandira," I returned, amazed by him asking my name.

"Yes, Mandira. Is it too much to ask? Get me out of here, please? I don't feel good lying here in the hospital."

"Of course, Mr. Martin. Dr. Green will visit you shortly and explain everything. We don't want to keep you for long. That's why I want to fill out the questionnaire."

"Alright. Let's get this over with. Ask me."

As I took the form out of the file, I felt like a triumphant warrior swinging her sword after conquering a fort.

Jubilant, I struggled to keep a straight face as I asked, "Okay, Mr. Martin. When did you first experience the shortness of breath?"

Dr. Green called me over before commencing his morning round. He had checked the questionnaire attached to Paul Martin's file and read my note—reassuring me that he noticed my work.

"Mandira, you wrote that Paul Martin has concerns about erectile dysfunction due to medication. Did he tell you this?"

"Yes, doctor."

"Isn't he a difficult patient? Everybody's been telling me that he refuses to speak to anyone. How did you manage to get this info?"

"He is. But somehow, he shared that with me," I returned with humility.

Green smiled at me for the first time. I joined him in the round along with two resident doctors. Like a skillful goldsmith mindful of the finer details of his craft, Green handled Paul Martin like a pro.

"Mr. Martin, I know your concern about medication causing erectile dysfunction. BP medicine can occasionally cause ED. I'll change your medicine, and that should help. Also, keep in mind that if ED occurs, sometimes it's anxiety that triggers it, rather than the medication. We need to weigh the benefits against the side effects. Take your medicine on time, follow your diet, and continue exercising and you'll be fine."

Surprisingly, Paul paid attention to Dr. Green, nodding along and barely interrupting. Upon his only inquiry about being discharged, Green granted his wish the following day and gave the necessary instructions to the resident doctors.

When we were ready to leave the room, Paul said, "Doctor, I like this lady. It would be good if you had more doctors like her."

A slight contraction appeared on Green's forehead, but he collected himself the next moment. "Of course, Mr. Martin. Mrs. Sharma is a smart lady. Anything you observed she did differently?"

"She listened."

"Thank you for the feedback, Mr. Martin. We will keep that in mind," said Dr. Green, momentarily glancing at me as I blushed awkwardly.

I was not trying to be humble when Green had asked me about Paul. I didn't know why he shared the details with me, and there was no deliberate decision to listen on my part. Perhaps he took pity and spared me, was all I could think. While Paul kept talking, the questionnaire occupied my mind, and I plugged it into the conversation at the first opportunity.

Later, sitting at the metro station, I wondered when I had last received a compliment. Viru's compliments did not count because, well, for starters, it was Viru. Secondly, he went overboard with cheesy lines like *The Best Cook in North America*, *Mother of the Nation*, or *Mother India*. And when he chortled as he said it, it sounded like a joke rather than genuine praise.

I did get compliments for cooking when we would throw house parties occasionally. But then, which guest wouldn't appreciate the hospitality of their host? I couldn't tell if the praise was out of the delight of their taste buds or merely out of courtesy.

The only person who would make me feel special with his compliments was Sebastian, the old homeless man who always stood by the escalator of Saint Thomas Metro Station. The way his face lit up upon seeing me with a box of fresh food would be enough for me to take pride in my culinary skills.

Sebastian was fond of sweets I made on special occasions, such as hot *gulab jamun* soaked in sugar syrup, which he called "tasty sugar balls." Perhaps every word from his mouth sounded sweet because of his sweet tooth. The deprived homeless man's positive outlook on life would inspire me and keep me afloat in the sea of my sorrows.

At Saint Thomas Metro Station, as I was heading for the escalator, I glanced toward the candy shop at the corner. The middle-aged owner smiled at me awkwardly.

The day I figured out that Sebastian was Joseph, the chief of Kendram, whom nobody else in the Saint Thomas

Metro Station could see, was the last time I saw him. It was Diwali, two years ago, when I last spoke to him at the escalator, and he savored my sugary *gulab jamun* before disappearing. The candy shop owner disclosed that he had never seen any homeless man and thought I just talked to myself.

He probably still thought I was an eccentric woman.

Back home, I found Mom sitting on the couch, absentminded—her usual demeanor nowadays—and Ryan playing frisbee in the backyard with Britney, Ted, and Caesar.

After securing Daddy's blessing, Reva was out at a movie with Tim and friends. Though he would not admit it, lately Viru had relaxed about Reva's friendship with Tim that once bothered him.

Another reason for his generosity to Reva on this occasion was the guilt of his absence from dinner. Viru would be late as he and his colleagues were celebrating with a customer for closing a large deal.

I couldn't tell if it was a mere coincidence or if my smart girl deliberately chose this day to go to the movies, expecting the maximum probability of Daddy's approval. My permission was not much of a task for Reva, as all I cared about was her happiness.

After a quick chitchat, Mom got busy with dinner preparation. Since Mom had arrived, she had taken over the kitchen, relegating me to a mere helper doing chopping work.

The kids finished playing outside and joined me in the living room. Britney and Ted argued non-stop about the scariest rides at Abbynton Amusement Park, ensuring my participation by repeatedly asking, "Isn't it, Mrs. Sharma?"

They headed home after Elena returned from work.

After my forgettable contribution in the kitchen with Mom, I found Ryan in his room playing with Caesar.

"What're you two doing up here? How was your day, honey?" I asked, sitting next to Ryan on the bed.

"Good day, Mom."

And how was school? Is Miss Miranda back from leave?"

"Yes, Mom."

After that casual inquiry, I came to the reason I had come into his room.

"By the way, I saw Jack," I said.

There was a pause, and then Ryan looked me in the eyes.

"In my dream. Do you remember him?" I prompted.

Ryan nodded and looked away.

"He talked about you, said you're doing a great job. Everybody's happy." I paused for reaction and continued when I didn't get one, "Listen, honey. Mom knows about everything you see that others can't. You know that, right?"

"Yes, Mom."

"So you can tell me anything. I promise I will believe you and keep it to myself. Do you understand that?" I asked.

Ryan nodded without looking up.

"Would you tell me what you do that makes Jack and everybody happy?"

"Don't know what he's talking about, Mom," Ryan returned sheepishly.

I didn't know why it was so hard to discuss the otherworldly things despite both of us knowing they existed. Ryan's reluctance to share would make it more awkward whenever I brought it up. Talking to Reva about puberty was easier.

Ryan's comfort with speaking had improved over time, but expressing himself had not. His breaking eye contact on this subject felt as if the guilt of being different eclipsed the realization of genius. I wondered if Ryan was too ashamed of his superpowers to even share about them with me.

"Do you sleep well, dear?"

"Yes, Mom."

"And … do you wake up at night? You or Caesar, sometimes?" I asked hesitatingly.

"No, Mom. I don't wake up."

Caesar sprawled out on his tummy beside Ryan as if caught with his mouth in the cookie jar.

"Okay, that's good. I'm happy you sleep well. Um, have you… Do you sometimes see animals? Like dogs, wolves, deer? I mean, randomly?"

Ryan made no reply. Asking questions that would seem ridiculous to a regular person was not the only hard thing; interpreting Ryan's silence was another hurdle.

"Promise me one thing. Look at me, Ryan." I waited until his hesitant gaze met mine. "If ever you're in trouble, you'll tell me, won't you?

Ryan nodded.

"Promise me, honey."

"Promise you what?" Reva appeared at the door. "What are you two talking about?"

"Revu!" I turned around. "Hi! When did you get back?" I asked, fumbling as if caught shoplifting.

"Just now, Mom, when you two were making promises. What was that about?"

"Nothing. Just mom talk. You're early. Did you have a good time? Where's Tim?" I asked, segueing the conversation.

"Where'd you think? At his house."

"Did you like the movie? How long were you standing at the door?" I asked inconsistent questions, interested more in the latter.

I hoped Reva had not heard any more than she admitted, as the last thing I wanted was another family member sucked into the mystery wrapped in an enigma.

The situation was akin to a secret closet in the house that Ryan and Caesar practically lived in. Viru and Reva had no idea, and Mom and I could barely figure out anything through the peephole.

The phrase "complete ignorance is bliss; partial knowledge is an abyss" came to mind.

Chapter Five

Viru's friend Sylvain visited on Sunday afternoon. I served tea and samosa, and Sylvain served the story of his latest escapade.

The previous weekend, Sylvain had flown solo in a single-engine private aircraft, an Aeronca Champion, borrowed from his dad. He could not keep the joy of flying to himself and decided to share his adventure with us.

When I enquired why his wife Molly did not join him, Sylvain explained, "Mandira, she just doesn't get how good a pilot I am. She says, 'I can't trust you on the ground, let alone in the air.' When I tell her I have completed thirty hours of flight time, she goes, 'You have completed forty-five years walking and still walk clumsily. What good will thirty hours of flight time do?'"

I smiled, and Reva laughed aloud.

"Flying over Abbynton and Driffin is all right, the usual buildings and cars, etcetera," Sylvain continued. "The real kick you get is by the jungle of Billaria. I flew at a low altitude, about five hundred feet above the trees. It looks fantastic from the top. A bushy green carpet below and a clear blue sky above. And the animals! Their weekend seemed to be more fun than ours. I watched a herd of deer running as if competing in a four-hundred-meter track race."

"Really? Do you see them qualifying for the Olympics this year?" Viru returned jokingly.

"Depends upon the coach, you know. They had a very talented one: Coach Tiger. When he arrived in the field, one deer sprinted so hard he broke the world record," Sylvain improvised, and we chuckled.

"Only one? With such a killer coach, all of them should break records. Or else the coach will break their necks."

We all laughed.

"I also saw beavers on grassland across the canal, heading somewhere. Hundreds of them, together," said Sylvain, dipping samosa in the ketchup.

"Hundreds! Were they attending a wedding? A beaver wedding feast?" Viru joked again, encouraged by the last response.

"Could be. Or maybe a gala. A Beaver gala."

"Absolutely. The beavers gotta have fun. Or maybe going to the movies."

"Could be a movie, yes. A bunch of beaver movies are released every Friday in the jungle multiplexes."

"Like, *The Beavers in Black*. Or *What Beavers Want*," Viru garbled, munching a cookie.

"Or *The Beaver with the Dragon Tattoo*."

"Yes, that would be a psychological thriller beaver movie."

"Or *Iron Beaver*. And *Iron Beaver II*," Reva chimed in, anxious to contribute.

"Yes, very well, Reva. Beaver superhero movies. *Iron Beaver*, *Spider Beaver*."

And they continued spoiling movie titles for some time.

"I believed that animals were lazy like us. I didn't know they did so many recreational activities." Sylvain winked. "The entire jungle was one big carnival full of hustle and bustle. And I spotted so many hyenas wandering about like they were deranged."

"Hyenas? In North America? Aren't they found in Africa and Asia only?"

"I thought so too, my friend. Turns out, if you look from the top, they can also be in Billaria."

"I see. Hovering over Billaria on a private aircraft is the proper way to find hyenas!" giggled Viru.

"Absolutely. I don't know if it was heatstroke; they were going crazy—shrilling laughter. Some even howled at the sky."

"Perhaps they saw you. Did you say hi?" asked Viru, still enthused to tickle our funny bone.

"I did. Like this," Sylvain returned with a waving gesture. "I actually said, 'Hye,' and they went, 'Na.'"

"Hye na! Hye na!" both repeated simultaneously, becoming more animated each time.

Sylvain then reminisced about the flying trips with his dad during his younger years. One time, he flew a friend who couldn't hold it midway; Sylvain had to land on a grass strip to accommodate the friend's nature call. This diversion cost him a lot of fuel, and they barely managed to arrive at the destination, with the tank on empty. Following this incident, Dad forbade him, and rightly so, to fly his aircraft until the latest trip, years later. That's why Sylvain was excited to share his experience.

"No wonder Molly didn't join you. You, my friend, have an impeccable record of risking lives. Hope you didn't land in Billaria to take a closer look at those hyenas," joked Viru.

"I didn't. Safer to say *hye* from a distance." Sylvain laughed aloud. "Apparently, Viren, hyenas have a sense of humor. They laugh all the time. People say they laugh more when they are frustrated. Like ironic laughter."

"Perhaps they laugh at themselves. Self-deprecating humor. The highest form of humor."

The two funny men continued their friendly banter amid Reva's giggling and Ryan's usual blank expression. I couldn't tell if Ryan was paying attention. Caesar, another house member unimpressed by Pilot Sylvain's flying adventure stories, found licking Ryan's hand a better pastime.

*

The following morning in the hospital, I was engrossed in the files of admitted patients when a familiar deceptively feminine voice called my name.

I looked up. "Hi, Terry. What a pleasant surprise! How

are you?"

"Charming as always, Mandira! How are you?"

"Well, I'm charming too," I returned with a smile.

"Look at you. You look happy! Are the internal med folks treating you well?"

"Yes, they are. Keeping me busy. The staff is friendly."

"Oh, learning the tricks of the trade! You must laugh with the staff to get your foot in the door." Terry grinned, though I sensed he spoke with a tinge of sarcasm.

"How are Charlene and Ali doing?"

"Hanging in there. Your friends are good hangers." Terry grinned again.

"So, what brings you here, Terry?" I posed a direct question, as his one-liner remarks made it challenging to maintain small talk.

"Paperwork, Mandira. This hospital runs on paperwork. I'm the glue that binds the departments together. Also, I came to give you this," he said, handing me an envelope. "Give it to Dr. Steven Green. He needs to fill out your feedback. I would give it to him myself, but I'm swamped."

"Okay, will do. When do you want it back?"

"Don't worry about getting back. Just hand it to him and I'll collect it next week from the office."

"I see." I nodded.

"Look, Mandira, I don't mean to scare you, but between you and me," Terry spoke softly, sounding like a child whispering, "don't fret too much over your feedback. Internal med doctors don't care much for the shadowers. Sometimes, they don't even fill out this form. I'm not saying that'll happen to you; just a heads-up not to have high hopes. Serious assessment happens in Family Medicine. I'm telling you as a friend."

I just smiled at the friendly advice, missing the friendly vibe.

"Gotta go. See you next week," Terry said.

"Bye, Terry. Say hello to Dr. Lopez and Dr. Jalil."

Terry walked out, exchanging an awkward glance with

Nurse Dolma on the way.

Mrs. Dolma noticed me deep in thought. "You okay, girl? What was Mr. Big Mouth here for?"

"Oh, you mean Terry? Feedback form." I held up the envelope.

"I hope he's not bugging you with his know-it-all stories. He thinks he's the founder of the hospital. One time, he said, 'I am the eyes and ears of Victoria Hospital.' We call him Victoria's Secret."

Sophie at the counter burst out laughing.

"Slow down, girl. It's a hospital," Dolma scolded Sophie, then turned to me. "Sophie is a big fan of Victoria's Secret. Not the one that just left."

Now, both laughed aloud, and I felt lighter. I loved the welcoming environment in the Department of Internal Medicine. Nurse Dolma was protective, and her banter with Sophie was fun. Resident doctors were helpful, my interaction with patients was fulfilling, and it seemed Dr. Green was gradually noticing my work more and more.

There were no piercing eyes scrutinizing my every action, no Charlene and Ali eager to outscore me, and above all, no Terry running me down at every opportunity.

The whole point of the shadowing was to obtain excellent references to help me apply for medical school. Terry's allusion to Dr. Green's indifference to feedback bothered me, but not more than the thought of returning to the old department in a week.

Terry's unexpected visit left me with no time to go through the patient files, and I headed to room one-oh-five to see the new patient admitted last night, Keith Howard. The name sounded familiar, and so did his face, except for sullen features and red eyes.

"Hello, Mr. Howard. I'm Mandira. How are you today?"

"Could be better," he returned, raising himself against the backrest pillow with a little effort.

"You'll be fine, Mr. Howard. I'm shadowing Dr. Steven Green and am here to ask you a few questions. Is that okay?"

"Mandira, haven't we met before?"

"I think we have. I was trying to remember where."

"Here, in this hospital. A month back. A raccoon bit me, remember?"

"Of course! I do now."

I was good at remembering people, but the Keith Howard I had seen before was a handsome, athletically built man, unlike an emaciated fellow with a pale face and sunken eyes lying in the bed.

"I'm not a fan of hospitals. Rarely visit one. Guess that's why I remember you."

"Well, in that case, you should've forgotten me as soon as you left."

"Right. One way to look at it," Keith chuckled. I noticed a slight heaviness in his breathing.

"So, what happened, Keith?" I asked hesitatingly.

I was supposed to stick to the questionnaire, but I couldn't suppress my curiosity. I wondered what lightning had struck this young man, making him look like he had aged by twenty years in just a month.

"I've no idea, Mandira. Something weird is going on. I'm anxious all the time. And irritable." His face twitched. "I'm always scared. I can't sleep. When I do, I feel like something is sitting on me, grabbing my neck and pressing tightly." Keith gasped for breath. "I can't seem to move. I feel helpless, as if I'm frozen. I'm not entirely sure if this happens when I'm asleep or half awake. This creepy thing on me, whatever it is, keeps choking me. It feels like I'll die any minute.

"I try to gather all my strength to push it away, but I can't. It terrifies me to the bone. I can hear myself screaming from the inside, but nothing comes out. I stay frozen for what seems like ten to fifteen minutes before I'm fully awake. And find nothing. Then I stay up all night, pacing in my room with the lights on. I get the urge to sleep again, but even the thought of this thing on my chest gives me nightmares."

I could see just talking about it was exhausting Keith, perhaps as much as undergoing the strangling experience.

"How often does it happen?" I asked.

"Every," he swallowed awkwardly, "night. Sorry—every night." Keith swallowed again. "Don't know why my mouth is always wet. It's like a swimming pool." He laughed in the face of adversity. "I don't understand, Mandira. I was hale and hearty a month ago."

"Did this all start before your last visit to the hospital, or after?"

"Um … I think after. Yes, definitely after. Why do you ask?"

"Just asking, Mr. Howard. Did you take the prescribed vaccine last time?"

"Oh, do you mean the rabies shots? Yes, I did—all of them. Do you think it's related to the raccoon bite?"

"Not necessarily," I fumbled. "This is for the form I need to fill out. I'm not a doctor, Mr. Howard, just aspiring to be. We have qualified staff here, and Dr. Green is a super-specialist. He will see you shortly. I have no doubt that you're in great hands."

Keith nodded.

The realization of getting carried away struck me. It was not my place to ask questions other than those in the questionnaire. I continued, "I don't want to bother you too much, but would you mind helping me with this form?"

"Not at all. Ask away," he returned, heaving a sigh of exhaustion.

*

After visiting Keith Howard, Green explained to his residents that the chances of rabies were minimal since he took all the shots. He still asked them to get his saliva sample tested to rule it out.

Briefly turning to me, he said, "Good work trying to

correlate anyway," and I was pleased to discover he had read my note at the bottom of the questionnaire.

Green suspected a sleep disorder called sleep paralysis. He explained that it generally happens between the stages of sleep and wakefulness. The patient feels conscious but is unable to speak or move their muscles. This can last between a few seconds to a few minutes. Patients may feel pressure on their chest or neck. They may also get a sense of some demon or a shadowy evil creature choking them.

This is a combination of two types of hallucinations: incubus hallucinations, which incite a feeling of suffocation, and intruder hallucinations, which involve a perception of a dangerous presence in the room.

I hated the word hallucination as it brought back bitter memories. For a second, it occurred to me that Green could be Hogdon—an evil chameleon disguised as another gentleman doctor. On second thought, it would be impossible for him to impersonate anyone in such a busy hospital in a populated area without getting caught. Jack had told me that bad keepers, aka daggers, thrived in deserted places.

"Keith Howard is experiencing something similar. Sleep paralysis can happen to normal people and is usually harmless, just bothersome when recurrent. What amazes me is that Keith claims to experience these episodes every night, which is uncommon, but possible."

Green instructed the residents to keep Keith under observation for another day and give sedatives to induce sleep as extreme exhaustion was wearing him down. He also referred him to a mental health professional to examine the symptoms of post-traumatic stress disorder (PTSD).

Green explained that PTSD was a mental health condition triggered by a terrifying experience, and that patients diagnosed with PTSD showed significantly higher rates of sleep paralysis. The doctor's conclusion made sense to me. A violent attack by a raccoon that chased Keith almost a mile could undoubtedly be a terrifying experience disturbing his mental health.

I had not worried about a patient so much before. At noon, I peeked into his room, hoping to see him sleeping due to sedatives. On the contrary, I found him pacing about the room with his shoulders slouching forward. I slipped away quietly before he saw me.

In the afternoon, the announcement startled me.

"Attention! Code blue. Medicine floor. Room one-oh-five."

The emergency staff immediately rushed to the room, and I followed. Nurse Dolma, responsible for restricting attendance in the room to essential staff only, let me stand outside the room.

Standing at the door, I caught a glimpse of Keith lying still on the bed, white foam bubbling out of his mouth while the staff performed CPR. It reminded me of my recent encounter with a red-eyed man on the metro train who had collapsed, throwing up foam.

I prayed to God for his life.

Twenty minutes later, Keith Howard was declared dead.

On my way home, I could not shun the visuals playing in my head of Keith greeting me with a feeble smile and asking, *"Mandira, haven't we met before?"*

Chapter Six

Dr. Steven Green called me to his office on my last day in the Internal Medicine department.

"So, Mandira, tell me: How has your experience on the floor been these past three weeks?" he asked, sinking back into his cushioned chair.

"I had a great time, Dr. Green. The staff here are warm and collegial. I've learned so much, and especially from you."

"You did?"

"Yes. I tried to absorb as much as possible during your rounds. Also, I liked the general work here. Like how we study files, follow procedures, empathize with patients, and make differential diagnoses. I wish I could stay for longer. This place is like a school for me with many teachers, and you're the headmaster," I said, instantly regretting my off-the-cuff remark in a bid to sound smart.

Green laughed out loud, and I quietly sighed in relief. His chilled-out demeanor was encouraging.

"That's new. Nobody has compared me with a headmaster before. Okay, good to hear you gained something. How would you assess your performance?"

"Well, I tried my best, Dr. Green," I returned, careful not to get carried away, "to fill out the questionnaire the way you had instructed me. I wish I could contribute more."

"Mandira, here's the thing. The shadowing students have the mindset of observing what we do so that they can apply the knowledge when they finally become doctors. Now, here's the difference: You observed everyone and tried to apply that knowledge in whatever little things you got to do here."

My eyes and ears were wide open, eager to know if he thought I did right or wrong.

"Mandira, studying medicine alone does not make you a doctor. You must think like one, and that's what you do. You have an analytical mind. I must say, I'm impressed. You managed to calm down a difficult patient that even our residents found tough. He was abusing the staff left and right but opened up to you. You extracted useful information from him, and he said good things about you."

Hearing those words, I struggled to keep the smile from my face.

"And that sleep paralysis patient … you tried to put the pieces together. Unfortunately, we couldn't save him. But you went beyond your form-filling task. You should be proud of yourself, Mandira."

Inside, I was dancing with joy.

"I'm going to write in this," he said, holding out the envelope, "that you're the best shadow I've had in years."

Green's words fell into my ears like Mozart's best symphony. Appreciation is the cherry on the cake of accomplishment.

Like a bee, I collected the nectar in the beehive without knowing its worth until then. Dr. Green's words— *"You should be proud of yourself, Mandira"*—splashed in my head for days like a fresh stream of water in a dry canal.

I returned to the Family Medicine department with renewed confidence, making Terry Henson curious for almost a week, evident from his frequent usage of, "Look at you!" when talking to me.

The following week, Terry's interaction with me suddenly reduced to monosyllabic responses, and it was my turn to become curious.

"Terry, you don't talk much these days. Is everything okay?" I asked one morning.

"Not much to talk about, Mandira, but so much to do. I'm swamped with work. I wonder what would happen to the hospital if I wasn't here."

"I understand, Terry. You're the backbone of the hospital. You're the secret behind the success of Victoria Hospital," I said, recalling Nurse Dolma and Sophie's Victoria's Secret joke.

"Why'd you say that?" asked Terry cautiously.

"Say what? That you're the backbone of the hospital?"

"No, the other thing." He gave me an odd look. "Did you hear anything?"

"Anything?"

"Anything about me?"

"About you? What'd you mean, Terry?" I asked innocently.

"Never mind. It's nothing."

"By the way, did you receive my feedback from Dr. Steven Green?" I asked, seeing to it that the conversation was not dropped.

"Yes, I did." The conversation picked up, but his face dropped. "I don't know what's in there; that envelope is for Lopez and Jalil to open." His expression said otherwise. "Look, Mandira. As I told you before. The floor rotation is just for experience. The doctors don't care for writing feedback."

"That might usually be so, but Dr. Green did write some feedback. He called me to his office and told me."

"He did?"

"Yes, and not only that. He promised me a reference letter for my med school application."

"Okay then! What do I know? After all, Jalil is the director of the shadowing program," Terry returned, sarcasm emerging in his tone.

"I was just saying, Terry. I know you know better."

"Look, Mandira. Confidence is usually good, but remember, it has two words: *con* and *confide*. Confidence is a *con* that you should not *confide* in too much."

I was no stranger to Terry's habit of twisting word meanings at his discretion. A month ago, he felt I lacked confidence. But my gaining confidence, so it seemed, was not making him feel any better. I wondered what would please him. Should I have cared to please him?

Oddly, perhaps inspired by Terry's word-twiddling, it occurred to me that the word *please* had the word *ease* in it. I hoped he eased up on me a little.

One person I certainly cared to please was Dr. Lopez. But looking at her face was like watching a castle's stone wall from the outside; you couldn't tell what was on the inside. She would answer my questions and nod with a straight face after my case presentation. I couldn't tell if my work impressed her.

Viru, citing his favorite proverb, *The well doesn't come to the thirsty; the thirsty must go to the well*, explained that I should ask rather than wait. However, asking for feedback was difficult as our brief interactions would be in group settings with Charlene and Ali.

Stealing a moment alone with her, I casually asked Dr. Lopez how I was doing on the pretense of attaching the questionnaire to the patient file in her office.

With a feeble smile she returned, "I can see you trying. You're doing as well as anyone."

Master analyst Viru dissected the vague feedback, zeroing in on the word *anyone*. Per him, the nature of positive or negative feedback depended on how she regarded *anyone* in her sentence. As always, his analysis did not help, as *anyone* could mean anything.

It turned out that only going to the well did not quench the thirst; your hand must also reach the water level.

I curiously sensed an air of indifference when shadowing other doctors. I noticed Dr. Ralph asking more questions, and every time I fumbled, he remarked that I should have known or prepared better. Dr. Kimberly hardly made eye contact while talking and often looked in a hurry to finish up with me. Dr. Kumar no longer seemed to be in a cheerful mood like before.

Out of nowhere, Dr. Herschelle declared that their assessment of shadow students was exemplary, unlike the

Internal Medicine floor, where internists were too busy to care.

I wondered what had changed since my return from the Internal Medicine floor: their view of me or my view of self.

One late afternoon I was absorbed in my computer, studying patient files which Terry had assigned me for the next day, when Dr. Jalil stopped by my office.

"Still working, Mandira?"

"Hi, Dr. Jalil. Good to see you." I instinctively rose from my chair.

"You're a hard worker. Do you often work late?" he asked, glancing at the offices of Charlene and Ali.

"Yes, sometimes, Dr. Jalil. Ali left just a few minutes back, and Charlene is on the floor rotation this week," I returned, feeling obliged to defend my colleagues.

"I see. How was your rotation on the floor?"

"I loved it. It was a great learning experience. I couldn't have asked for more. Thanks for sending me, Dr. Jalil."

Jalil smiled and asked, "Who was your supervisor?"

"Dr. Steven Green."

"Ah, Green. He is a good friend—a brilliant man. Anyway, don't be late home."

"Yes Dr. Jalil. You have a nice evening."

He said goodbye, and as he left, I considered that Jalil's unexpected gesture of checking on me cheered me up after a few stressful weeks at work.

*

"No, Mrs. Walker does not stop to talk to me." Viru stopped to gulp his glass of orange juice. "Now she waves from a distance and walks on."

"Why? Is she fed up with your jokes?"

"Fed up with my jokes? Are you kidding me, Mandy? She once told me my jokes made her day. It's your stupid dog that keeps growling at her and Tulip. She's afraid of him," Viru declared.

"At least you're back on time. I don't understand your urge to stop by to talk to every person on your way. Such a waste of time," I said, half-heartedly placing a jug on the table while gazing at Mom walking barefoot on the grass in the backyard.

"The word is *socializing*, Mandy. Civilized people do that. But thanks to your uncivilized dog that keeps scaring off all the other dogs in the neighborhood, I barely get to socialize with my morning buddies. I tell you, Mandy, we need to get him examined before people start complaining." He dipped his slice of toast in ketchup.

"Oh, c'mon, Viru; he's fine. He doesn't bite anyone. Perhaps he doesn't like you wasting time in the morning."

"Yes, his time is precious. Why don't we send him to Miami instead?"

"What time is your flight?" I asked irritably.

"I have time, Mandy. Let me eat my breakfast peacefully," Viru replied, munching his toast. "One thing I don't understand is why Tulip is wagging her tail around him these days. The more he gnashes his teeth at her, the more irresistible she seems to find him. She barely noticed him before and now she's eager for his attention. Wonder what could bring the standards of the supermodel dog to such low levels?"

"See! Now we know. Perhaps Caesar is displaying his machismo to impress Tulip. And it's working."

"Machismo. Really? I don't know what machismo has gotten into him. He's even shooing away the poor beavers and squirrels that are just minding their business."

After gobbling up every crumb of bread smeared with butter and ketchup and repeating his favorite phrase, *I tell you...* a dozen times, Viru left for a week-long business trip to Miami.

It was my final week of the shadowing program at Victoria Hospital. Charlene and Ali were back in the Department of Family Medicine after completing floor rotations individually.

We were much friendlier now. It felt like the shadowing program had started just a few days ago, but now we knew each other so well. We no longer interrupted or tried to outscore each other in front of the doctors, and lauded each other's efforts when they left.

I wasn't sure if we had developed a friendship or just an awareness that our fate was already sealed and that the last week would not matter in the outcome of the final feedback report.

I brought breakfast one morning for my work friends. Viru often said, "Do good and cast it into the well," which meant that one should do a good deed without expecting a reward in return.

One of these days, I needed to ask Viru about his obsession with this all-purpose well he mentioned so often as if dug right in our backyard. For Viru, it seemed all was well that ended up in the well.

Charlene relished the French toast with butter in the cafeteria, and Ali savored it with maple syrup. They couldn't seem to get enough of those bread slices soaked in beaten eggs and cream toasted on a frying pan with my favorite condiments sprinkled evenly.

Mom-made soft, sweet *laddus* melted in Terry's mouth, keeping his tongue from talking but not from wanting more.

Charlene said, "Yummy!" and Ali, "Delicious." Terry joined the words and coined a new compliment, "Yummilicious."

The week went on with the usual humdrum. Ryan continued with his usual lost self, only enjoying non-stop talking by Britney and licking from Caesar.

Licking would have also been agreeable to Tulip, who was no doubt confused why her charm had ceased to affect Caesar.

Of late, Mom was more relaxed but also curious, since she was no longer seeing Ryan and Caesar with the animals on the street at night. Like a child hooked on her favorite cartoon television channel, I would still find Mom glued to the window anticipating stranger things. I would laugh to myself, thinking her personal Netflix was out of order.

At some point, the things that had been stressing me out started to seem funny. Or, more accurately, when fresh worries surfaced, old troubles were suppressed. I think our problems never end. The existing ones feel alleviated as the new ones eclipse them. Our mind is a computer that stores eighty percent of worries in its hard disk and yet continues to stack up more.

The latest bug-causing sluggishness on my computer was the assessment result, which was due on Friday.

Reva's cheerful evening chats were like a gush of cold breeze in the scorching sun. Her happy-go-lucky attitude would rub off on me, causing a temporary getaway from my worries. I could see in her laughing eyes and rosy cheeks that she was on the best of terms with Timothy.

Her latest outing plan was our hot topic on Thursday evening.

"When did you come up with this idea?"

"This morning."

"This morning? Just like that? Have you two even planned it?"

"Yeah, we did. I told you we talked this morning."

"Revu, I don't like your last-minute adventures."

"Adventure? Mom, I'm not climbing Mount Everest, just hiking in the woods. And what's last minute? It's not like I'm going away for a week, like on one of Dad's trips."

"I can't let you go anywhere. You better ask your dad."

"Oh c'mon, Ma. Why bother him in Miami? Who is the boss of the house in his absence?"

"What do you mean, in his absence? Absence or presence, I am the boss of the house."

"Of course, you are the boss, Mom. Woman power!" Reva smiled hopefully.

We both knew she had succeeded in triggering me. Reva was well aware of Viru's pedantic approach to her plans. I was easier to persuade than Viru, who would bombard her with questions.

"Where is this hiking place?"

"It's not a place, Ma. It's a hike, starting at Canal Road, then all the way up to Driffin and back."

"And does Tim know the route? What if you lose your way?"

"It's on the map, Mother!" returned Reva, giving me a know-all teenage smirk. "Hiking trails have arrows for directions. Besides, Tim's friends walk in this area every other week."

"Who are these friends? Where do they live?"

"Ron and Nikki. I don't know. They live in Abbynton, somewhere."

"Have you met them? Do you know these people you're going with, Revu?"

"Mom, I know Tim. They are Tim's friends. He knows them well. I'll know them too when I see them."

"But, Revu…"

"Mom, please let me go. I know you're not fussy like Dad. You're much cooler," said Reva persuasively.

I took note of her growing art of manipulative flattery. I knew she would not consider even the winter breeze of Antarctica cooler than her dad, let alone me.

I eventually consented to Reva's hiking expedition, as I needed to get back to worrying about my big day.

Chapter Seven

I used to feel butterflies in school, waiting for my turn among the anxious crowd before the noticeboard to check the end-of-term examination results. I felt the same butterflies that morning, only they had grown in size and flight. As I settled opposite Dr. Jalil and Dr. Lopez in the conference room, I hoped they would settle down soon.

A file and a few papers were lying on the table with Jalil's arms resting around them, as if carefully guarding them. Dr. Lopez was also holding some papers and a file.

"So, Mandira. Your four-month shadowing program comes to an end today. How does it feel?" Dr. Jalil gave me a friendly smile.

"Well, Dr. Jalil, it feels like a learning journey I wished would never end. Victoria Hospital seems like a second home to me, and everyone is like a big family. I thank you and Dr. Lopez for giving me this opportunity."

I wasn't sure about them, but I impressed myself with my spontaneous speech.

"While we are at it, I think filling out the feedback form would be a good idea. Do you agree, Dr. Jalil?" Dr. Lopez chimed in.

"Perhaps we can do that later, Dr. Lopez?" he returned, then glancing at her again, changed his mind. "Alright, let's get the formality over with first. Mandira, could you take some time to fill this out?" he asked as Dr. Lopez took out the form and passed it to me.

I finished in about twenty seconds—a personal best— by checking "excellent" for all ten questions and glancing at the top two: *How would you rate the program?* And, *Did your supervisor meet your expectations?*

I could have done it in ten seconds if I hadn't had to pretend I was reading all the questions.

"That was quick, thank you." Dr. Lopez smiled, slipping the form into her file.

"Mandira, I have your final assessment with me," said Dr. Jalil. "The evaluation is based on the overall growth observed during this program. We collected feedback from all the doctors you shadowed. Our team sees scope for improvement for you in some areas. Now, I see potential in you. I do not doubt your capability to develop those skills."

While I struggled to decode the prelude, the conclusion was waiting in the following sentence:

"Mandira, I regret to inform you that you did not pass the program. I am sorry. We could see you tried hard, but sometimes it's not enough. This is not the end of the road. It's just the beginning…"

He kept talking, but I stopped listening after he announced my fate. Everything sounded distant, like someone garbling in the other room.

Several uncomfortable seconds (perhaps minutes) later, I noticed him sliding the papers he guarded toward me. The heading read: *Evaluation Report*. After my ears, it was now the turn of my eyes to strain.

Clinical judgment: Variable. Inability to discern urgent cases.
Data collection: Unstructured. Lacking interpretation of patient details.
Communication skills: Average. Difficulty in establishing empathy with patients.

I had finished the feedback form in twenty seconds, but this report took me twenty seconds to snail through each word. Spotting a strength among the bountiful weaknesses listed seemed like looking for a needle in the haystack. I didn't know I had that many shortcomings. The only two positive words were *punctual* and *professional*. So, according to the evaluation, I always arrived on time to do lousy work. And I was professional at accomplishing nothing.

The remarks at the bottom of the report made my eyes

dizzy.

Conclusion: Unsatisfactory. Failed in shadowing program.

Words hurt, but when written on paper and shoved in your face, they leave a scar. Unable to bear the lacerating words, I looked at Dr. Jalil and Dr. Lopez, who were waiting for my reaction.

"Sorry, but I don't get it. I got the impression from everyone that I was doing fine. I asked for feedback, and none of it mentioned any of this." I pointed at the report. "Dr. Kumar told me that I was handling patients calmly. Dr. Ralph and Dr. Herschelle … no one pointed out that I was rigid in my interviews. Dr. Green said he hadn't seen anyone like me in years and that I should be proud of myself. None of that is in the report. And Dr. Lopez, I thought you liked my presentation?"

Dr. Lopez reluctantly opened her mouth to speak when Dr. Jalil interjected, "Mandira, we can't discuss the verbal opinions shared with you by individuals. You can see the collective view of the team recorded on the evaluation points."

No words came out to reason with Jalil. He implied that the supposed appreciators I was referring to wrote the negative evaluation. A deafening silence followed.

"Look, Mandira, nothing I say will make you feel better right now. You're wise. I can only say that this moment right here is not life, just a part of it."

Just a part of it? I thought, *Easy for you to say, Dr. Jalil. For you, this moment is just a part of life. How would you know all the other parts I sacrificed, hoping to shine in this moment?*

Two years back, I had reproached Viru for not standing up to his employer when they gave him the pink slip. I believed they were unreasonable, and he needed to say it to their faces. Instead, he thanked them, which I felt was cowardly.

"Mandy, there's no dignity in arguing. Why make them feel that your entire existence depends on their mercy? It's a job, not the end of the world," he'd said, and I resented him for nonsensical preaching.

I felt myself in the same shoes, walking the same path. I signed the evaluation report, thanked Dr. Jalil and Dr. Lopez for their support, and walked out with a plastic smile.

When did I turn into Viru?

I wanted to run away from Victoria Hospital. My office, which would excite me every morning, had suddenly turned unwelcoming, and I didn't wish to stay even for a minute. The walls stared back at me, and the computer's black screen reflected my face.

With a heavy heart and light belongings, I walked to Terry's desk to hand him the keys. I stretched my face with an artificial smile, though deep inside, I wanted to burst into tears.

"Hey, Mandira! Look at you, you're all packed up to leave. How was the result?"

"I didn't pass, Terry."

"Aww, poor you. I'm sad for you," he returned with a forced look of disappointment. It seemed he had already known.

"Where are Charlene and Ali? Their office is locked," I asked, though not really caring.

"You don't know? They came at nine and left. Both passed."

"They passed?" With a pause, I said, "Good for them."

I thought nothing could hurt more, but hearing that they passed was like a final nail in the coffin.

People who think it's lonely at the top should notice that person alone at the bottom. Viru often said, "Be at your best in your worst time. Nobody deserves the pleasure of seeing you crushed."

I tried to remember those words, but that wasn't all. Terry would rub my failure on my face.

"I feel sorry for you, Mandira. Every batch has one person like you who doesn't pass. They come to me and ask, 'Oh, Terry, what am I gonna do now?'"

"They do? Well, I'm sure they eventually find something better."

"Unfortunately not, although I do my best to guide them. Remember the immigrant girl I told you about who didn't pass? The older one? She got so frustrated she went back to her country. By the way, what does your husband do? Does he have a stable job?"

"Oh, my husband? He's a project director. Senior management guy, you know? Always on business trips. He's in Miami this week. He's funny. He asks me, 'Mandira, why do you have to do charity in that hospital? I can find you a better place.' And I tell him, 'Viren, it's my hobby to give,'" I said animatedly.

Viru's saying was working. Terry looked curious. Perhaps my casual replies to his supposed concern for me didn't bring the desired pleasure he sought.

"Well, one cannot rely on their man's wealth. You gotta do some work. I felt bad when some people said you lacked confidence, despite trying hard."

"Who said that, Terry?"

"Now c'mon, Mandira, I can't name names. But you know what? You will be fine. You have a husband," Terry returned with a sarcastic smile.

Terry's fake niceties were starting to bother me. I decided to retort, "Well, people will be people. I feel bad when you work so hard for Victoria Hospital, and some people make fun of you. They call you Victoria's Secret, you know?"

Terry flushed crimson. "What? Who said that?"

"Now c'mon, Terry, I can't name names. But you know what? You and I will be fine. I have a husband, and you… You have Victoria's Secret!"

The pretense of my victorious marching out of Victoria Hospital left Terry sulking and mumbling something about Victoria's Secret. Viru would not appreciate my outburst at the end, but to hell with it! He was hardly an expert on any matter. What would a man who once searched everywhere for his earphones except his own ears know?

I vividly remembered a similar story in my second standard textbook. A man called Kutchu rummaged through the house looking for his glasses, only to discover that they had been on his nose all this time.

Who knew I would marry a Kutchu one day?

At home, melancholy engulfed me. Neither my comfy couch nor Mom's ginger and cardamom tea relaxed me. Medical school now seemed as distant a dream as the stepping stone to its entry had been. I couldn't understand how it came to this.

Why hadn't I ever considered failing the program as a possibility? Then again, how could I, after everyone's seemingly tacit acknowledgement and Dr. Green's vocal recognition of my work? Was it possible that Green actually gave me a bad review? But then, why didn't I get any indication from anyone except Terry?

I couldn't trust Terry as he had always been mean and belittling. Now, in hindsight, it seemed he had always seen it coming.

Crying over spilled milk wouldn't help, and another carton in the refrigerator would only fill up the belly, not satiate the appetite.

Tired, I retired to my room. Like in childhood, Mom, at my bedside, massaged my reeling forehead with her analgesic balm. I was still her little girl to her, and on this evening, I acted like one.

Mom had a collection of oils, balms, and lotions back home. They were manufactured from medicinal herbs. The forests were the home to the raw materials for medicinal and aromatic plants.

Besides richness, forests also stored mystery in their bosoms—like the mystery of that desperate female. I could still only see her back.

Her silky hair caught in the buffeting air scattered like the roots of a tree. Her loose-fitted top flapped like a clipped cloth in the windstorm.

The clueless trees stared. The suspicious leaves whispered. The anxious branches shivered. The nervous birds fluttered. And the hesitant bushes ducked as she sprinted past them all.

Her legs were giving up, but she wasn't.

I felt a strange connection with her, as if it were me.

Where was she running to, and what was she running from?

When it looked like even her extreme exhaustion could not stop her, the rock she stepped on slid and caused her to fall to the ground.

Helplessly groaning on the ground, she turned around, and I saw her sweat-soaked and horror-struck face for the first time.

At the top of her lungs, she screamed, "Mom!"

I opened my eyes and wondered what had just happened. I realized it was the same dream I'd had numerous times before, but this time I finally saw her face.

It was Reva.

Chapter Eight

The clock made me realize I had slept for five hours, though it hadn't turned dark yet due to the long summer days. I rose from bed with a headrush and walked barefoot to Reva's room, which I found empty.

"Mom! Where's Reva?" I asked, rushing into the living room.

"Munni, you're awake? I was going to ask you where she was. What time should she be home?" she asked, stirring the pot on the kitchen stove with a spatula.

"She should've been back by four. It's seven now," I returned, checking my cell phone for any missed calls or texts. There was nothing.

It was odd for Reva to be late and not inform me. Viru would say she always turned up before her recollection.

I tried calling, but her phone was off, which was unusual in itself. Reva never switched her phone off.

I called Tim's mom, Debra King.

"Mandira, Tim went hiking this morning with friends. He isn't back yet."

"Yes, I know, Debra. Reva went, too. They were supposed to be back by four. I can't reach her; her phone's off."

"Oh, I didn't know Tim went with Reva. That boy hardly tells me anything. Hang on, let me call him."

Debra put me on hold, but returned a few seconds later.

"Tim's not answering. They must be on their way back. Sometimes you don't realize your phone is ringing in your pocket when you're walking."

"Could you try again, please? I don't know why Reva's phone is off."

101

"Her battery might have died. But okay, I'll try again." She put me on hold again, but returned quickly. "He's still not answering. You know how teenagers are these days; they want to be left alone. 'Mom, I need some space,' he says all the time. I say, 'Alright, honey. I'll give you space, now don't come asking for the spaceship next!'" She chuckled and continued, sensing no reaction, "I'll let you know as soon as he returns my call."

"Do you mind me asking if Tim usually gets home late?"

"I wouldn't say late, but seven or eight is normal when he hangs around with friends. Don't worry about Reva. Tim's lazy but not irresponsible."

"Oh, I don't doubt it, Debra. Tim's a wonderful kid," I returned, realizing Debra probably wondered what the fuss was about my probing. "No problem. Let me know when you talk to him."

I didn't press Debra further lest she should think of me as a nosy mom. She could attribute her son's failure to answer his phone to teenage carelessness, but not me, especially when my long-standing dream had finally revealed the identity of the distressed girl.

I paced the living room, my heart pounding and negative thoughts running through my head.

Until that moment, doubt had not made its way through the cracks of the wall of trust about Tim's intentions for Reva, which I believed were nothing short of unadulterated love. But doubting was not going to help as much as tracking them down would. How could I do that?

Fogged by the terrible dream, it had slipped out of my mind that Reva and Tim had not gone hiking alone. Debra had no idea which friends Tim went with, but if I told her their names, she could contact them. Reva had mentioned them to me the previous evening.

Here's the funny thing about memory: When you wish to recall information most eagerly, it hides in the least accessible corner of your mind.

Two hours and many dreadful thoughts later, I called

Debra again, who now sounded concerned, since Tim was still unresponsive despite several attempts to contact him. When I asked her about Ron and Nikki, hoping for some lead, Debra dropped the shocker of never having heard those names. She added that they could be his Facebook friends with whom Tim often chatted.

I sank into the chair, and so did the heart in my chest. Reva had not met them before, Debra had never heard of them, and I wondered how well Tim knew Ron and Nikki, if indeed he had met them online.

One lesson I learned from my past encounter with evil Hogdon, disguised as a psychiatrist named Bob, was that danger could sneak into your life unannounced from an unexpected source. I dreaded another unwelcome entry in the form of Ron and Nikki.

Mom's pot was now off the stove, half-cooked food forgotten.

My cell phone on the table rang, and I leaped to grab it, hoping to see Reva's name on display.

It was Viru.

Upon hearing everything, he burst with anger at me. I wasn't sure if what upset him was me allowing Reva on a hiking trip, or the fact that I had not informed him before I did. But it didn't matter, I burst into tears anyway.

He cooled down in the next moment, realizing my frail state of mind. "I am sorry, Mandy. Not the time to lose it. It's not your fault. Don't stress out; we must hold it together. Reva is my supergirl; she always finds a way in adversity. She'll be fine. I know that," Viru comforted me, though he sounded more like he was reassuring himself.

After a thoughtful pause, he collected himself and said with renewed confidence, "Call 911 and tell them everything. Then call all of Reva's friends. Also, ask Debra to call Tim's friends, whoever she knows. And then…"

"Then I'll go to Canal Road."

"And do what? They didn't go by road to Driffin. No, no, Mandy. It's already ten. Don't go looking out in those woods. You don't know that place—there are confusing tracks and no well-marked trails. The last thing I want is to look for you too. Let me speak to Tom; he hikes all the time."

"I will go with him."

"Look, Mandy. We need smart thinking right now. Our top priority is to alert the police; they will act faster. I'll be on the first flight home. Till then, stay at home, please."

"Okay, okay. I'm calling 911."

"Okay, Mandy. Remember, keep your phone on. Any news, call me. I'll be back in a few."

Calling the emergency line, followed by visiting the police station with Tim's parents, Debra and Tom King, to file a missing person report, took a few hours. None of us could furnish details of Ron and Nikki. The police sprung to action, alerting all the stations in the vicinity.

Meanwhile, Elena and Britney kept Mom, Ryan, Ted, and Caesar company at our place. Elena fed the kids and Caesar. Mom wouldn't eat despite being on diabetes medication, as like all the other adults, she had lost her appetite.

After midnight, taking the matter into his hands, Tom hit the road with our neighbor Mr. Bergenza and a night torch. Tom didn't take me along, thanks to his telephone conversation with Viru a few hours ago. Viru joined them right after landing.

Up all terrible night, I repeatedly called Reva's phone with shaking hands, praying she would answer. I ran toward the door several times at the slightest sound, hoping she would show up smiling. But like sleep, the chance of my hopes and prayers coming true evaded me. Happy memories of Reva stashed in my head watered my eyes, and tears trickled down my cheeks in the dead of night.

By the first ray of light, police had launched a massive search operation. Helicopters hovered over the city. Multiple teams with expert hikers and search dogs had scattered all over, checking every track and trail between Abbynton and Driffin. The public was alerted of the missing teenagers by broadcasting texts, announcements on Abbynton news channels and FM radio, and reporting in the local newspapers.

Worn out, I sunk into the couch. Caesar sat beside me and slipped his head on my lap. I hugged him and sobbed weakly.

"Caesar, my child. I can't take it anymore. Help me. You have powers that we minners don't. You're not only our family; you *protect* our family. How can Reva go missing under your watch? I want my daughter back. I just can't imagine my life without her. Help me, please."

Caesar, in an assuring gesture, licked my hand. But assurance was all I had been given since last night, to no avail.

I realized how deeply Ryan was affected by his sister's disappearance when I found him in Reva's room, teary-eyed, crouched on the floor. Ryan would rarely wake up by himself in the morning, and displaying emotions to him was akin to a miser flashing cash.

Before I could embrace him, the phone rang, and I hastened down to the living room to answer the unknown caller.

The voice at the other end stopped my heart in one moment and charged my veins with a current in the next.

"Mom!"

"Reva! It's you! Oh my God, my Revu! Are you okay?"

"Yes, I'm okay, Mom," Reva returned weakly.

"Where were you? We were terrified! Where are you?" My knees suddenly buckled in relief, and I had to grab the chair.

"At a gas station … near Norville," said Reva with effort.

"Norville? That's far! How'd you get there? What happened?"

"Mom, I'm exhausted. My mouth's dry. Take down the address and fetch me. I feel like I might pass out at any minute."

"Pass out? Why? Are you alright?"

"Mom, I can't explain on the phone." Reva's voice became more feeble with every word.

"Okay! Just a sec." I sprang forward to grab a piece of paper attached to the refrigerator with a magnet, and Mom appeared with a pen before I could look further. I scribbled down the address and said, "Don't worry, Revu; Dad and I are rushing right now to pick you up. Is anyone with you? Is Tim there?"

"No. Just this guy at the station. Hello? Excuse me?" Her tired voice cracked as she raised it. "Talk to my Mom, please. I'm lost. Here, please."

The man from the gas station who had mistaken Reva for an unstable village girl told me that her tattered clothes were covered in mud, and she had bruises all over her body.

After ensuring the gentleman helped her with water and cookies and simultaneously informing Viru, who was still wandering with Tom somewhere in the woods, I hit the road for the hundred-kilometer drive to Norville.

Forty minutes later, I was partially relieved by Viru's call stating that Reva was safe with him. Despite her weary state, my brave girl was helping the police with information to locate Tim. Fighting off tears from my sleepy eyes, I stepped on the gas.

An impatient forty-five minutes later, choking back tears, I was finally united with my daughter at Norville Hospital.

*

Late afternoon back home, a pale-looking Reva described the horrifying ordeal she had gone through on the hiking trip.

According to Reva, Ron and Nikki were funny and charming, and they gelled with Tim and Reva well. Ron had been introduced to Tim by mutual friends as a hiking enthusiast. Tim had met him only a few times with his other friends around Driffin, but they often chatted on social media. Tim was impressed by Ron's hiking adventures and the pictures he posted online. Nikki was Ron's girlfriend.

Ron persuaded them to take a new route he and Nikki had explored on their last trip. There were no designated trails, but Ron claimed to remember the way by heart.

After walking for an hour in the woods, Ron excused himself into the bushes to answer nature's call. When he did not return in ten minutes, Nikki went looking for him. Both disappeared, leaving Reva and Tim stranded.

Half an hour of hurtling through the woods in a helter-skelter fashion and shouting anxiously at the top of their voices in vain made Reva and Tim realize they were on their own. After struggling with the bad signal, navigation on their phones indicated that they were somewhere on the outskirts of Driffin, far ahead of the initially planned spot.

Suddenly, a roar startled them. They looked around nervously until Reva pointed in the direction of rustling twigs and trembling bushes at a visible distance.

A head emerged from the thicket and fixed piercing golden yellow eyes on them.

It was a tiger.

The fearsome tiger roared again, louder this time. In that moment, Reva froze like a deer caught in the headlights.

Tim grabbed her hand and let out a blood-curdling, "Run!"

They ran together through the rough terrain, trampling the thick grass, scattered twigs, wild shrubs, and cluttered gravel under their feet. Like the prey desperate to escape the predator, the desire to live was trying to break free from the jaws of death. Tim did not once let go of Reva's hand in the hair-raising race for survival.

But fate had other plans. They stumbled upon a narrow, steep path where they had to move single file. Reva paced ahead, closely followed by Tim.

One miscalculated step on the edge of the track cracked

the fragile lump of soil under Tim's feet, tripping him down the slope deep into the dense thicket.

Reva stopped abruptly and screamed, "Tim? Tim! Where are you?"

She could not spot Tim from the edge. Still, she was almost ready to jump after him.

"I'm okay! Keep running, Reva!" Tim's muffled voice echoed from the bushes.

"Are you okay? I'm coming down to you!"

"No! Don't come down. I'm going this way. Don't stop, Reva! Run!"

Before she could think, the beastly tiger appeared out of nowhere and pounced on her. How she instinctively ducked down, narrowly escaping its razor-sharp claws, was beyond her.

The steep, uneven path proved to be a boon to Reva this time as the large wild cat lost control and skidded a few meters down the slope, only to be blocked by an aging tree.

While the raging tiger struggled to climb up, thanks to its weakened grip on the moist soil and slippery plants, Reva sprinted like a horror-stricken deer.

She ran like never before, treading the random, seldom-trodden, lumpy, bumpy paths of the jungle of Billaria.

She ran like the girl in my dreams.

The farther she ran, the nearer the roaring seemed. Exhaustion would have knocked her down if a rock in her way hadn't.

She lay on the ground, her trembling legs having given up, every ounce of energy depleted, and there was no narrow track to pave the way for another close shave. There was no escape. The savage beast had a clean shot.

The tiger would have pierced its fangs into Reva's flesh had something unexpected not happened. Another animal, perhaps a leopard, violently thrust the tiger when his salivating jaws were inches away from her neck.

Dizzy from fear and fatigue, Reva watched the spine-chilling struggle between the two beasts with blurred vision before passing out.

"What happened then?" asked Viru. His curiosity was burgeoning in Reva's momentary silence.

"When I opened my eyes," said Reva, "I saw the tiger's mouth just a meter away from me. It was all blood-stained, and I could see its huge teeth. I sat up, I think in shock, but I was so dizzy that it took me a minute to realize that the tiger was lying dead on the ground. Then I looked around and noticed a dog sitting under a nearby tree."

"A dog! Wait, didn't you say there was a leopard?"

"Yes, I thought that before, but there was never a leopard. The dog resembled a leopard. I figured it had attacked the tiger and saved my life."

"A dog killed a tiger?" Viru was confused. "Are you—"

"What did it look like?" I chimed in.

"White fur with black spots. It was a large dog, Mom. I haven't ever seen a dog that big before."

Tormon! I almost said aloud. If any dog besides Caesar could dare to grapple with a ferocious tiger, it had to be one of the four dogs of his D-Force. And who better than Tormon, Caesar's trusted top commander, to do the job?

I looked thankfully at Caesar, who was relaxing on the chair as if saying, *"I told you. Nothing will happen to Reva under my watch."*

Reva continued to tell us what had happened. It was getting dark, but she didn't know the time as she had lost her phone. Initially, she was scared of the dog, which was covered with blood from fighting the tiger. But it remained calm, sitting under the tree. After some time, it came closer and lay beside her. She felt safe in its company and soon went back to sleep.

She had no idea how long she slept, since she was so exhausted. Eventually the sun's rays filtering through the trees fell on her face and woke her up. Reva described how every single part of her body was aching when she woke.

She found the dog sitting at the foot of the tree, gazing at her. When she rose from the ground, the dog started walking and she followed it. She had no idea where it was going, but felt she had no other option but to walk behind it. The howling sounds of the wild animals in the dense jungle terrified her. Still, she was confident that that dog could take on anyone who dared come near.

"After walking for God knows how long, we crossed a river, and I drank almost a bucket full of water," Reva explained. "Then we set off again. Eventually, I spotted a gravel road and realized the dog had helped me out of the jungle. It watched me cross the road toward the gas station. I could see it watching me for a while, and then it disappeared."

"Disappeared?" asked Viru, sounding disbelieving.

"Yes. Perhaps it went back into the jungle while I was talking to the guy at the station? I wish I'd hugged the dog and thanked it for saving my life, but it didn't cross my mind at the time," uttered Reva as she lay on the couch, her speech slurring more and more with tiredness. "Mom, will they find Tim? I'm worried about him."

"Hopefully, honey. We're in touch with the cops."

"Tell the cops I'll come with them to find him. Maybe I can show them where we separated."

"I'll tell them. You go back to sleep now."

"Will he be alright, Mom?"

"Of course, dear. I bet they'll find him soon."

"Mom…"

I leaned toward her, but she just mumbled something unintelligible before dozing off.

"She doesn't seem to be thinking right. Perhaps it's due to some medication they gave her at the hospital?" Viru whispered. "How can a dog kill a tiger? Even if we assume there was one giant dog stronger than a tiger, why would it save Reva? And then walk her out of the jungle?"

"So are you saying Reva is lying?"

"I didn't mean that, Mandy. But this story doesn't make any sense."

"Not everything has to make sense, Viru. Miracles

happen. God finds ways to save their favorite ones."

An hour later, Viru received a call from Mr. Bergenza. The cops had recovered the body of Tim in the jungle of Billaria.

A rainfall of tears soaked my cheeks as I stared helplessly at a serenely sleeping Reva.

Rohit Dharupta

AUTUMN

"Mayhem"

Chapter One

The fall had fallen. Nature's journey from bright summer to gloomy winter had taken a temporary detour to its colorful gardens. In this magnificent exhibition, the deciduous trees with red, pink, orange, and yellow leaves stood tall on the bed of fallen leaves like models in colorful gowns posing on the red carpet.

That year, the fun and frolic of the fancy fall were marred by fret and fear. Zoophobia—the fear of animals—was gripping the entire world. Wild animals were becoming increasingly violent, and contact with humans within the wilderness, however superficial, mostly resulted in brutal animal attacks. Morning walkers attacked by raccoons; tourists ambushed by packs of hyenas; tigers violently striking safari vehicles; and lynching by lions, bears, boars, and bison had become common news headlines. Hiking trips, trekking expeditions, voyages into the woods, or journeying through the forests were growingly proving a walk into the lap of death.

The people in towns and villages situated at the borders of forests or in the foothills of mountains lived in constant fear of animal aggression. Children were barely let out in the late afternoon, and the adults, mostly armed with weapons, would prefer someone's company to accomplish their necessary evening errands. The cities and towns far from the wild were generally considered safe havens, but not free from isolated incidents.

Animal attacks were not just limited to humans, but also to each other. The forests were becoming battlegrounds of ugly brawls between frenzied beasts. Their murderous rage would only stop when the flesh and bones of their opponents were riven asunder.

Seasoned hunters had stopped wildlife hunting for fear of falling prey themselves. Governments were shutting down wildlife sanctuaries, national parks, and safari tours in the wake of the attacks. Illegal deforestation activities, illicit timber trafficking, and the theft of forest resources had reached an all-time low.

Some self-professed experts called it nature's retaliation against humans for destroying the wild. Others felt the animals were avenging humans for meddling with their food chain and natural habitats.

Some soothsayers predicted the world was doomed, and that like many creatures since the advent of Earth, the human race was due for extinction soon.

Scientists made a discovery that had, for the most part, put the various doomsday theories to rest. It was a virus called *rages* that they had named after its main symptom: rage.

Rages drew some similarities with rabies, but was far more hostile. It made its way through the nerves of the infected animals into their central nervous system and attacked the brain, thus making them delirious. The virus progressed slowly but, in a few days, replicated proportionately. At its peak, the infected animals, like wrathful beasts, wandered aimlessly, savagely tearing apart mammals that came their way.

The worst part was that the rages virus was contagious, and like rabies, it survived by moving from one body to another, transmitting through animal saliva.

Some evidence suggested that the rages virus most likely originated in hyenas. Several theories claimed that raccoons had started it. Nothing could be substantiated.

The more important question, however, was how to contain the rages spreading in the wild like wildfire by infected animals biting healthy ones.

Though the rages' reaction to animals and humans differed in the sense that infected humans did not go on a biting spree, the conclusion, in either case, would be the same: miserable death.

If not killed instantly by a ferocious animal attack, the humans would brace themselves for an agonizing departure from life in a few days. The symptoms began with general anxiety and panic attacks involving sweating, abnormal breathing, accelerated heartbeat, chills, and choking sensations. The condition would soon turn into one or more phobias and extreme irrational fears of situations, places, objects, or living or imaginary creatures. The symptoms would worsen when the virus attacked the brain, causing a lack of appetite, nausea, sleeplessness, and excessive exhaustion, and by that point the end was just a matter of time.

In hindsight, one could conclude that Keith Howard, the patient admitted to Victoria Hospital after a raccoon bite, was infected by the rages virus, which led to his tragic death.

Prevention is better than cure. This quote suited when the cure was an option to consider.

Rabies shots were ineffective for rages. The leading pharmaceutical companies were burning the midnight oil to invent vaccines.

Governments around the world were on high alert, devising strategies to tackle this new crisis. All eyes were on the forest departments deploying heavy forces to control and contain this menace in the wild.

Alongside this public tragedy, there was also a personal one afoot. Two years back, it was fall when I watched my daughter fall in love. I wondered how it was that grief befell her this fall.

Two months had passed since Tim's demise, but sadness had not left Reva's eyes even momentarily. She ate little, talked less, and pondered abundantly.

My girl, who once giggled wholeheartedly at Daddy's jokes, would now half-heartedly acknowledge his deliberate effort to make her laugh. At times, she would be so lost at the dinner table that Viru had to repeat his punchlines to attract her attention, to which she sported a superficial smile. Lately, the sole purpose of Viru's humor was to bring back the twinkle in Reva's stony eyes, and he would not give up on his favorite distracted cheerleader.

On the fateful day when he was chased by a bloodthirsty tiger, fate separated Tim from Reva when he tripped down the bushy slope and rammed his head into a rock. The blow proved fatal, as he died on the spot a few minutes later. He had perhaps anticipated his end and insisted that Reva keep running, giving false assurance to her about himself. Even in his last moments, he put Reva's safety above his own life. Such was a gem my daughter had found herself, only to lose forever.

In the darkest hours, when they went missing, I had suspected Tim's intentions for Reva, but that boy bore no blemish of malice toward anyone, let alone for his dearest Reva.

Upon my insistence, Mom had canceled her plan to return to India after my shadowing program. I needed Mom's shoulder to cry on and wished Reva would feel the need for mine. But the dam of shock had barricaded the flood of emotions. Reva confined herself to her room, mainly lying listless in bed. Mom's belief that she would come around with time seemed a false assurance.

Though one late afternoon, startled by loud wailing, I hastened to Reva's room.

Clinging to Ryan, Reva was sobbing inconsolably.

Upon seeing me, she clasped me in her arms and cried her eyes out. "Mom, I miss him! I miss Tim so much. Day, night … I can't stop thinking about him. Why, Mom? How could I leave him there by himself? It's all my fault. Why didn't I jump after him?"

"You didn't know he was hurt."

"I should've known, Ma. I could have saved him."

"You couldn't have, honey! Nobody could have."

"Then I should've died with him."

"Don't you ever talk about dying, Revu," I said, choking

back tears. "What would happen to us? Your dad? Ryan? See how sad he is to see you like this!"

Reva wrapped one arm around Ryan.

"Tim was a brave and noble boy. God also needs good people around him," I continued.

"I needed him more. More than God! He has many good people. God is unfair. God is cruel, Mom."

Reva lay glued to my chest for a long time. Sharing had finally closed the distance created by several weeks of grieving alone.

I wondered why the floodgates had suddenly flung open, outpouring emotions hitherto held back. Looking at the papers on the side table, I realized Ryan had pulled off a miracle. It was the application forms for admission to Abbynton International Academy for the following year's session. After downloading and printing them, Ryan had asked Reva's help to fill them out. The innocent gesture perhaps brought back the fondest memories of Tim, causing the volcano of suppressed feelings to erupt.

For Ryan's sake, Reva had stayed at Saint Augustine school, putting off Tim's wish to join him at Abbynton School by another year.

As fate would have it, Reva would not join Tim the following year either.

Chapter Two

The night when Reva and Tim went missing during their hiking trip, Mom saw Caesar and Tormon at the foot of the lamp on the street. As they stood silently for about a minute before disappearing from her magical sight, Mom noticed bruises and blood stains on Tormon.

She didn't know what to make of this seemingly calm meeting that felt oddly rattling as she watched from the window. Mom told me about it a few days later.

After Reva had mentioned a white dog with black spots, making an inference that Caesar had masterminded Reva's rescue plan with the aid of Tormon was easy. Even Mom could deduce it based on what she knew about Caesar and his D-Force by then. The intriguing part, however, was that Mom had established the factual details of something I could only have concluded based on logic. Not only had she witnessed the interaction between Caesar and Tormon that very night on Saint Thomas Street, but she also spotted Tormon's injuries from the clash with the tiger.

As if our lives weren't miserable already, the investigation into the case led by the confused authorities made it unbearable.

From their summoning Reva and repeatedly questioning her, it seemed they suspected her of pushing Tim down the slope. I could only imagine how traumatic the inquiry about her relationship with Tim was for Reva at this time of grief. The investigating officer, Peter Wilkinson, was keen to know if they had any fights or arguments before Tim died.

The story of a dog killing a tiger and leading Reva all the way through the forest to the gas station was hard to digest, even for Viru, let alone the scrutinizing Wilkinson. But nothing deterred Reva from cooperating with him.

The world was not kind to the people who survived a harrowing experience that the others accompanying them could not, and for that reason.

Unable to bear the loss of her son, Debra did not speak to any of us for weeks. Even if she had blamed the entire world, one could not think it unreasonable for a mother whose child meant the world to her.

Eventually, the light of new evidence put the unwarranted suspicion to an end: a trail of shoe marks left by two people being chased by a tiger in the woods, and the discovery of the mangled body of the tiger in the jungle of Billaria. The site revealed a fierce struggle between two animals. They discovered the paw marks of what they called the "other animal," giving crutches to Reva's version.

Peter Wilkinson still found it hard to believe that a giant dog with paws larger than an average dog could hack a powerful tiger to death. The tiger, infected by the rages virus, was another alarming revelation. Thankfully, Reva had escaped the attack unscathed and tested negative for the virus.

Officer Wilkinson and his team could not trace Ron and Nikki. They recovered Ron's number from Tim's call history, and the last location of his phone showed someplace in Billaria before permanently losing contact. Digging Ron's social media profile and questioning Tim's friends did not unearth his whereabouts. Some had met Ron casually, but none seemed to know Nikki.

As time passed, the chances of tracking down Ron and Nikki became slim, as did the odds of the incident being just an unfortunate accident.

Following Reva's struggle to deal with Tim's demise and the affliction of the investigation, the principal thing now occupying my mind was the possibility of a conspiracy at play. I could sense something cooking up, a plot beyond Officer Wilkinson's comprehension.

One person I knew could help with my predicament, but

that person would only show up when he needed me, not the other way around.

I had made up my mind.

One morning, shortly after Viru had left with Caesar, I quietly walked out of the house, down the street, and stood under the lamp. My face and exposed feet in rubber slippers felt the autumn chill, and my thin sweater barely shielded my shivering body against the sneaky breeze. It oddly struck me how the lamp caught by Mom's divine vision in the night could witness many queer occurrences, including Ryan and Caesar's inexplicable assembly.

It was not long before the familiar figure I was waiting for emerged from the soft curtain of fog. Samantha waved at me and gave me her usual bright smile.

"Hi, Mandira! How are you? It's good to see you," she said, jogging on the spot.

"Likewise, Samantha. I'm fine. I was looking for you."

"Me?" returned young Samantha, amazed.

"I need a favor from you," I stated, too pressed for time to make any small talk.

Samantha stopped jogging. "Tell me. How can I help?"

"I need to see Jack. It's urgent."

"Jack? Who?"

"Jack, the keeper of Shloka!"

"Sorry, Mandira," she said after a confused pause, "I don't know any Jack. And what's Shloka? Some workplace?"

"Are you saying you don't know Jack?"

"I don't."

"C'mon, Samantha. I know the secret of the other worlds and how you keepers keep them in order. I wouldn't be looking for Jack if I hadn't run out of options. I must speak to him."

"I'm sorry, Mandira. I wish I could help, but nothing you're saying makes any sense. I don't know what you mean."

My ears caught Caesar's muffled barking, though my

eyes were yet to catch a glimpse, thanks to the fog.

"Listen, Samantha, I gotta go. I don't understand all the fuss about this secrecy. But hear me out, Ryan will not participate in The Meet if Jack doesn't see me soon. No way am I giving you people permission to exploit my son if you continue to keep me in the dark."

I hastened back toward the house.

Two years ago, Jack had told me that Samantha was one of the keeper soldiers deployed to watch over my family. Per Jack, the keepers of Rudram—the local organization of Loka, headed by Caesar and unknown to the mortals—mingled so perfectly with us minners that nobody could tell them apart.

Samantha's exchange of pleasantries with her heartwarming smile always cheered me up. However, there had been no indication that she was on a mission. We had never had a conversation like today, and I had not imagined it to turn out to be the way it did. I wondered about the remote possibility of Samantha being an ordinary girl heading for Mount Mary like every other morning until I popped up and uttered what she had perceived as the garble of an unstable woman. I reminded myself that Samantha's impression of me should've been the last trifle to bother with then.

Back at the house, I found Reva standing in the kitchen area.

"You're up, Revu?" I asked, acting casual.

"Where were you, Mom?"

"Just took a quick walk. It's cold. Is Grandma up, too? She should wear a cardigan today." Without looking at Reva, I walked to the glass door. Mom, as usual, was strolling in the backyard.

"You weren't walking, Mom. I saw you from the window, standing on the sidewalk. And then you were talking to that jogger girl. What was it about, Ma?" Reva said.

"Oh, that was a casual greeting, Revu. Hello, hi… What

else would I talk to her about?"

"I saw you. You two were engaged in a serious conversation."

"Nah, nothing serious. Were you spying on me?"

"Ma, please. I'm not a child. You got upset with her about something. Why don't you tell me?"

"Reva! I'm your Mom; I told you, and that's it. I don't need to explain anything to you," I returned in a stern tone, thinking it was the only way to get out of the uncomfortable conversation.

Just then, Viru walked in with Caesar, looking in a good mood for a change.

"Hello, amigos! You're all awake?" While removing his shoes, Viru noticed the silence. "What's with the heavy atmosphere?"

"Mom sneaked out of the house to talk to the jogger girl. When I asked why, she snapped at me."

"I told her I needed fresh air. That's all," I said.

"Honey, if you need fresh air, you can walk this burden every morning," Viru said, pointing at Caesar. "You can get air in abundance."

"So you're spared of the only work you do in the house? Never!" I retorted.

"Okay, okay! Listen, Revs—your Mom's a complicated woman." Stealing a glance at me, he corrected, "Did I say complicated? I meant intelligent. She sometimes gets overwhelmed with our troubles and needs space; that's it. So let her sneak out as long as she comes back."

Viru put his arm around Reva's shoulder. "Come. Let's leave your Mom alone and make me some honey lemon water. Look at your Grandma getting fresh air, walking barefoot on grass. They're looking for variety even with the fresh air. Mom likes the fresh air at the back of the house and the daughter at the front. I tell you, your Mom and her folks are a bunch of queer people."

They quietly chuckled together as they walked away.

Intentional or not, I was glad Viru had managed to

distract Reva. Putting a smile on her face again made him seem like a superhero who had regained his temporarily lost power for cheering up his darling daughter.

Sometimes, I felt Viru noticed peculiarities in my behavior and actions, though I could not tell if he regarded them as mere idiosyncrasies. For the most part, he acted ignorant and hardly enquired if I was up to something.

On the other hand, Reva would be persistent when she set her mind to something. She had always suspected me of hiding some secret from her. After the last incident, I believed she had sensed a supernatural element behind a large dog rescuing her from the fierce tiger in the wilderness and guiding her to safety.

"Why would a dog I have never seen before save me?"

The question troubled her for weeks. She would ask me about it, clearly having the impression that I knew something about the dog. When I expressed ignorance, she would look into my eyes as if catching a lie. The seeds of doubt had rooted in Reva's mind, and she would not let go of a matter that involved the tragedy of her dearest Tim.

I didn't want to ruin her normal life by dragging yet another family member into this supernormal world of fear and uncertainty. I felt content with Reva and Viru's ignorance and sometimes wished it had been the same for me.

Moreover, I had many questions begging for answers. Samantha's denial had left me in a quandary.

Chapter Three

Days crawled into nights, and nights would budge reluctantly into days. Despite being stripped of their treasure, the resilient trees would continue welcoming by spreading colorful carpets of leaves around their feet. But the rude leaf blowers would chuck away the last ounce of beauty, rendering them naked and lonely.

Like trees, loneliness besieged me regardless of the treasure of my family around me. The ocean of uncoordinated thoughts had immersed me. My mind felt wrapped in blotting paper, barely letting external conversations seep through my internal dialogue.

At the dinner table, I would nod and smile at Viru's rambling and jokes without grasping the intent or content of the subject. Viru would make no mistake of thinking I had become agreeable to him lately. He knew me well enough to tell the difference between attentive and distracted.

Reva only talked monosyllabically to me after my snubbing her for enquiring about my conversation with Samantha on the street. I made her favorite rice pudding twice in one week, but its sweetness did not alleviate her bitterness.

One morning, a muffled knocking at the window woke me up. A few dazed and confused moments later, I realized that heavy raindrops were sporadically tapping the windowpane. The glowing clock at the side table conveyed I had slightly overslept compared to usual. Viru had already left for a walk with Caesar.

I drew back the curtain to witness the window's welcome to its favorite guest—the morning light—keeping the unruly intruder—the rain—at bay.

Through the hazed windowpane, I noticed a silhouette on the street. I wiped the windowpane with my sweater cuffs, but the obstructing raindrops sticking and dripping down the pane continued to blur the image of what looked like either a person or an animal.

Unable to curb my curiosity, I opened the window, and the unwelcome rain almost gave me an untimely shower. Heedless of my drenching head and face, I looked out of the window down to the street.

The person in the black cloak and hat gazed directly at me from under the lamp.

A spark went down my spine. It didn't take me long to recognize him by his uncanny appearance and queer posture.

"Jack!" I almost cried out loud.

In the next moment, I grabbed my raincoat and dashed down the stairs, forgetting to shut the window behind me.

In the living room, slipping hastily into my sandals, I was about to throw open the front door when I saw Reva staring at me from the kitchen. Like the trip unit breaks the circuit to stop the flow of electricity in the event of excess current, Reva's piercing look broke the sudden tide of excitement that had overcome me.

"Reva, you're here! Um, I didn't see you," I said, wiping the trickling water and guilt off my face with my hand. "Thought I'd take a walk in the rain. It's refreshing, don't you think?" I asked with an abashed smile.

Reva fixed her eyes on me without saying anything. In that moment, I realized how a person's silence could embarrass you more than their words. Their inquiring could help you excuse yourself from an awkward situation with the aid of argument, but silence would leave you no choice but to either justify your actions or storm out shamelessly. Reva would not give me a reason to argue.

I sheepishly grabbed the door handle, then dropped it. "Although now I think it's probably not a great idea.

Walking in the rain can be tempting," I said, jerking the sandals off my feet, "but like I always tell Ryan, you can fall sick if you get wet. You must be thinking I should practice what I preach. I must set a good example for you kids. So, I'll go up and make my bed instead. You carry on, okay?"

I could sense how ludicrous every word I spoke sounded as I was talking. Reva's eyes continued to follow me from the kitchen as I walked up the stairs.

In the bedroom, I rushed to the half-opened window. Jack was gone. And the streetlamp, thoroughly rinsed and alone, looked as dejected as me.

After Viru left for the office and the kids for school, I remained in bed for a while, watching the raindrops bursting like tiny water balloons on the window. Now and then, I would stand by the window hoping to find Jack smiling under his pointed nose, but in vain.

The rain brought back old memories. I remembered how, two years ago, everyone around me didn't wake up one morning, and I was panicking on the street. Clueless and crestfallen, I had sunk onto an ancient bench in a small park near Saint Thomas Metro Station. Then, Jack appeared from nowhere and shook my entire comprehension of the world—or rather, *worlds*.

The thought of Jack stuck in my mind like chewed gum on a woolen scarf. Without thinking twice, I rose from the bed, slipped into my raincoat, and stormed out of the house.

A few minutes later, drenched in rainwater and sweat, I stood next to the soaked bench, which was dripping water streams from its sides. Due to the pouring rain, there was hardly anyone in the park. The cruising cars were sloshing the stagnant water on the nearby street.

I sat down on the wet bench and waited.

While waiting, every second felt like hours. Just when I began to perceive my instinctive decision as a meaningless whim, I heard a voice from behind.

"Hello, Mandira!"

"Jack!" I exclaimed. "Finally, you showed up. I had begun to feel stupid out here."

"Stupid? Mandira, you're one of the smartest minners I know. See, you knew you'd find me here."

"Well, I guessed."

"So, tell me. How are you doing?"

"How do you think I'm doing, Jack, rinsed like a dish by this cloudburst, sitting on a wet bench? How come you always appear from behind, regardless of the direction I sit in? I remember sitting the other way last time."

"Well, Mandira, I'm sure that question is not why you were waiting here for me."

"Absolutely not; it's just an observation. I have plenty of serious questions for you."

"I look funny, but I'm a serious keeper. So, shoot."

"First, tell me: What's with this secrecy? Why did Samantha express ignorance about you? Even when she was aware I knew about both of you."

"What did you expect from her? She's following the protocol. Samantha is a keeper, a part of the Watch Force of mon cher Caesar. The keepers of Loka play the role of silent contributors. They must serve without disclosing their identity to minners, not even you. The minners should continue with their delusion of operating independently. I will say this: It was not fair to blackmail Samantha."

"*Fair?* Don't even get me started on fairness, Jack. Would you have shown up here had I not blackmailed her? And it's not blackmail. Make no mistake; I will not let Ryan participate in The Meet if I'm kept in the dark. I don't give a damn about your secrecy and protocol."

"I respect your feelings about Monsieur Ryan. I'm an insignificant employee of the honorable institution, Kendram. We have no authority to decide on protocols; we simply follow them. Since I have authorization from the chief, I'm here to answer your questions."

"Oh. Did Chief Joseph send you to see me?"

"Not really. The chief has authorized me to see you

when I think it necessary."

"I see. Thank you for realizing the necessity. Tell me, Jack: Was Sebastian, the homeless man I would meet at the metro station, really Chief Joseph?"

"I cannot answer a question about the chief's identity. I can only say I always appreciate your intelligence."

"Thank you," I said, understanding the answer. "I want you to know that I miss Sebastian. I would feel more confident if I saw him again."

"I would say *amen*."

In the last few months, a plethora of questions had bugged me, with every new one seeming more pressing than the former. In my imagination, I'd had several encounters with Jack, asking a series of genuine questions and receiving fabricated replies. But now that Jack was sitting next to me, it seemed the rain had washed away the order of my questions, and I didn't know where to begin.

I noticed Jack had learned new vocabulary, perhaps thanks to Professor Lingua Franca, and kept his old mode of addressing Ryan and Caesar as *monsieur* and *mon cher*, respectively.

"Jack, the tragic incident with Reva and Tim has boggled my mind. No matter how many different ways I look at it, it still seems an evil design conspired against them rather than an unfortunate accident."

"Why do you think that?"

"Well, first off, Tim's so-called friends Ron and Nikki led them to some uncharted hiking path and then disappeared. One could think that this tiger might have also attacked them. But the cops could not find any trace in the entire jungle. Not only that, nobody knows much about them, who they were, and where they came from, not even Tim's friends."

"You're right, Mandira. It was a plot. Remember I told you about the corrupt keepers working against the institution's principles? We call them daggers. These daggers don't follow any protocol and operate secretly from secluded places in Loka, Shloka, and Parloka. The good keepers of Kendram (in Shloka and Parloka) and Rudram (in Loka) work hard to keep these daggers away. Ron and Nikki were daggers. Ron slyly managed to make this thing with Tim. What is it called…"

"Friends?"

"Not really."

"Pals? Buddies?"

"No, a better word."

"Make contact?"

"Acquaintance is the word. I have worked hard on minner language, Mandira."

"Go on, please." I didn't need a thesaurus at this time.

"And then Ron disguised himself as a hiking enthusiast, persuaded Tim to join him on the trip, and deliberately took the wrong way, leading Reva and Tim astray. It was all part of the daggers' scheme. The purpose was to leave them stranded in the jungle."

"So, they become some wild animal's food?"

"Exactly."

"Tell me one thing. Who was the target? Tim or Reva? Be honest, please."

"I'm a keeper, Mandira; I tell everything honestly. The real target was Reva. Tim was just a means to gain access to her."

"Oh, dear God." I held my sopping forehead with a wet hand. "Why? What has my poor girl done? She doesn't even know daggers exist! I kept Reva and Viru out of this paranormal hidden world so they would be safe."

"Mandira, by living an ordinary minner life in Loka, you don't realize that you have the most precious jewel in your possession, Monsieur Ryan. Keepers have never been fascinated like this by anyone before. Your family has automatically become the center of attention, the most coveted. And as it happens, great attention attracts both civil and evil equally. Evil means nothing but harm toward the precious and anything associated with them. But there's

131

nothing to worry about as long as we have brave keepers. Any attempt to harm you or your family will be crushed."

"Oh really? Like you people crushed the attempt on Reva's life?"

"Yes. The Watch Force did. Don't you know? Mon cher Caesar's top soldier, Tormon, saved Reva and brought her to safety. Tormon is no ordinary keeper dog. Forget some minner animal; no dagger could come close to Reva under his watch. I have no doubt you and your family are safe."

"Jack … Tim died, my daughter almost got killed, and you say we're safe? Tim and Reva were walking with two dangerous daggers in the jungle, and you say they couldn't come close to them under Tormon's watch? Why did you keepers let it happen in the first place?"

"Had Tim not died due to an unfortunate accident by falling down the slope, Tormon would have saved him too. Mandira, you must understand that the daggers are also keepers—bad ones. They are clever and cunning. The good keepers of Loka do an efficient job of keeping them from interfering with minners. But like weeds, they sometimes creep into the highly secure zones. And then there are less guarded zones where the daggers… What's that word?"

"Live?"

"Not exactly."

"Are found?"

"No, the places where daggers, um…"

"Bloom? Blossom? Flourish? Survive?"

"Thrive. Thrive is the word I was looking for. Professor Lingua Franca advises me to always use the best words. The daggers thrive in high mountains, thick forests, uninhabited deserts, or abandoned places."

As much as I wished to dwell on dragging my family into danger, I couldn't afford to waste the opportunity to clear the confusion that had kept me up for several nights. Jack's appearance, like the downpour, was brief and rare, and my questions were abundant. Besides, his manner of response had changed in the last two years to the point of almost being annoying. Jack had perhaps taken Professor Lingua Franca's lessons more seriously than needed.

Before, he would keep it simple, although confusing me with the wrong usage of words, thus making me feel better for correcting him. Now, he seemed to be eyeing perfection, refusing to settle for anything short of the most fitting word, even if the synonym had conveyed the message. All the vocabulary I threw at him seemed inadequate.

"Mandira," continued Jack, "you must not worry. Your family is safe. The D-Force, Tormon, Shuru, Aaj, and Kal guard you constantly."

"Shuru, Aaj, and Kal?"

"Yes. Shuru is the black dog. Aaj and Kal are the brown twins. With them around, nobody can dare cause you any harm."

"Jack, I thought the only enemy after my family's life was that dagger, Hogdon. And his prime target was Ryan. Are there more? Do you know who could be behind the plot against Reva?"

"I cannot tell for sure, but the keepers of Rudram are looking for a few dagger suspects."

"Do you think those suspects could be somehow associated with Hogdon?"

"Could be. The dagger activities have significantly increased since Hogdon disappeared."

"Disappeared? What do you mean?"

Hogdon, the wicked son of Chief Joseph, desired to succeed him as the next head of Kendram, the organization controlling the affairs of Parloka, Shloka, and Loka. The chief never trusted him for the top job due to his immoral practices and surprised the selection committee by suggesting Ryan as a contender. Enraged, Hogdon conspired against Ryan by misleading me, disguising himself as a psychiatrist.

Jack told me that he was tried at the apex court of Kendram, not only for interfering with the family of Ryan—the prime contender for the next chief—but also for attempting to kill us. There was no escape for Hogdon, as Jack himself was a witness to his crime. Hogdon was stripped of his responsibility in Parloka and imprisoned at the behest of Chief Joseph. However, Jack delivered a shock by revealing that Hogdon soon managed to escape with the help of his influential sympathizers in Parloka and had not been traced since, despite several attempts.

"Oh, my God! The evil that tried to kill my family and almost destroyed the entirety of Loka is roaming free?"

"Not roaming free, Mandira. He's hiding," said Jack, rising from the bench and standing in front of me.

"And you still say he could be the one? Who else could plot to kill my daughter if not him? After all the mayhem, the least I could expect from you people was to catch him."

"Mandy."

"What?"

"Mandy!"

"What, Jack?"

Annoyed, I looked up. Jack stepped aside, and I could not believe my eyes.

Drenched in water, Viru was staring at me with an astonished expression.

Chapter Four

I had barely expected any passerby, let alone Viru, to notice me on the bench in the park talking to air (Jack would be invisible to anyone else). I had a false notion of privacy, having concealed myself in the cloudburst as if sitting behind a pane of frosted glass.

Viru, visibly miffed, did not speak to me in the car and went straight up to our bedroom as soon as we arrived home. Moments of nervous pacing in the living room later, I went after him.

"Viru, how come you came home early?"

Viru made no reply.

"Viru, are you going to give me the silent treatment now? What were you doing in the park?"

"Mandy, tell me which question is more relevant. What was I doing, or what were you doing in the park?"

"I just went for a walk and sat on—"

"Mandy, please. I have no interest in hearing another lie. It's pouring outside. Not a single person is out there, and you were sitting in that deserted park blabbering to yourself."

"Viru, I was stressed out. It felt suffocating at home, so I thought the rain would help me vent my frustration."

"Could you not give me that malarkey? A few days back, Reva saw you sneak out of the house into the street and yell at the jogger girl. This morning, Reva told me you almost stormed out in the rain and flushed in embarrassment upon seeing her. I was worried and couldn't focus on work. So, I came to find out if you were doing okay, and look where I found you—soaking in the park."

"Viru, c'mon." Sitting beside him, I gently touched his

hand, but he pulled it away.

"No, Mandy. Don't you realize the trauma our daughter is already going through? Your weird actions are only aggravating her pain. I'm all ears if you're ready to speak the truth. If not, please leave me alone."

Viru had spent much of our married life making light of my troubles with his lame jokes. If anyone could trigger his sensitive side, it was Reva. What bothered him that day was not my wandering per se, but the effect it had on Reva. Viru had made a resolve, but I wondered if knowing the truth would resolve anything for him.

"Viru, remember two years ago, I would see a person that others could not, and I thought it was a hallucination?"

"Yes, I do. Some weird old man. You were consulting a psychiatrist."

"Yes. That weird old man is for real. His name is Jack."

Like an open book flipped page by page, I opened up to Viru. A chapter about the existence of the sleep world called Shloka and the world of the next life, Parloka.

Another one on the highest organization unknown to humans, Kendram, with Chief Joseph at the helm and the keepers maintaining the order of the worlds.

Then Joseph projecting Ryan for the top job and his devil son, Hogdon, after our blood and determined to wipe away our world, Loka.

The local body of Kendram called Rudram operating in Loka, headed by Caesar with its keepers guarding secretly by mingling perfectly with the living beings (minners).

And finally, a plot hatched by the bad keepers called daggers against Reva, foiled by the good keeper and Caesar's deputy, Tormon.

A few hours had passed by the time I finished. The rain had long stopped outside, yet Viru was all washed out in the bedroom. Nothing I had said before in our sixteen years of marriage had drawn his attention for three hours.

At last, he broke his silence. "Mandy, are you reading novels?"

"What?"

"Are you reading fantasy novels these days?"

"See, that's why I didn't tell you!" I exclaimed in vexation. "I knew you wouldn't believe me. You wanted the truth; I told you everything. Now you don't believe me. I bet jokes are popping up in your head right now."

"But, Mandy, how can you expect me to believe this figment of the imagination? It's like making up a story. A script of a Hollywood sci-fi thriller."

"Oh yeah? How would you explain a large dog coming out of nowhere to save Reva by killing a tiger, watching her all night in the dense forest, guiding her the next day to the gas station, and then disappearing? How? Or do you think your daughter is also making up a story? A Hollywood sci-fi thriller?"

Viru became thoughtful.

"Reva is convinced that there was something supernatural about her rescue and believes I have the answer. That's why she keeps spying on me. Tell me now, should I tell her all of this?"

"No way, Mandy. Don't mess up her mind with this story. I know what happened with Reva is hard to explain, but let's be practical here. There can't be some unknown worlds and aliens controlling us. There's no scientific evidence of such a thing. We love Ryan and want great things for him. But imagining him to head some otherworldly organization is ridiculous. Don't you know his challenges? Our kids are not part of some grand alien politics. Forget the world; even in this neighborhood, we are the most ordinary family. And you think invisible aliens have chosen us to rule some imaginary universe?"

"Ryan. Not us. And definitely not you," I blurted. "You're only chosen to make jokes that nobody finds funny. I didn't tell you this to convince you. I told you because you were sulking in the bedroom like a baby. I don't care if you believe me or not. But don't come again to me saying, 'Mandy, I'm all ears if you're speaking the truth.'"

Caesar appeared at the door and meekly sat on the threshold.

"Mandy, I would consider the tiny possibility of all this being true, but when you say this dog—this stupid dog, who runs after squirrels—is some sort of a king…"

"Not king, the head of an organization, Rudram."

"Yeah, whatever. So, apart from running around in the house, he's also running an alien organization? Where's the headquarters of his organization? In our house? In the living room? Give me a break, Mandy. Why am I even discussing this?" Viru walked out irritably, almost jumping over Caesar.

He returned a few minutes later.

"Mandy! Did you say the old alien guy was there when I came to fetch you in the park?"

"First, stop saying alien; they're *keepers*. Yes, Jack was there. He was standing next to you, smiling."

"Oh really? Smiling? Did you say cheese?" returned Viru and walked out again, leaping higher over Caesar and mumbling, "The head of Rudram is sitting on the floor. Why don't you get his throne?"

I would not call it a futile exercise, as although Viru did not believe me, the sharing did relieve me. I felt lighter, as if heavy clothing had been removed from my soul.

Viru struggled to take kindly to the big revelation for a week or two. His way of expressing denial and disbelief, much to my annoyance, was joking more about it. Caesar, whom he referred to as "Head," became the prime target of his jokes.

Every morning after their walk, Viru would test my patience, recounting Caesar's mundane activities. For instance, he would say, "Mandy, our esteemed head peed on a car tire today. Shouldn't he use a toilet in the chalet? Would you appeal to him?"

He would also improvise with wordplay, like, "Mandy, the head of Rudram was barking at a crow today. Think it had come from an alien world? I thought our head was losing his head. Almost gave me a headache."

Reva became curious upon overhearing the overuse of the word head, but Viru downplayed it with another joke, something like, "I can't make head nor tail of this dog's mischief." He was careful about raising any suspicion in her mind.

By denigrating Caesar for his ordinary dog whims, Viru alluded to my account as utterly preposterous.

When I outrightly rejected his advice to consult a psychiatrist, Viru, to my amazement, started making jokes about it, too:

"Mandy, would you consult a psychiatrist for your alien delusion? Oh, wait, you already have—an alien psychiatrist."

To stop comedy, one must pay no heed to the comedian. My first hand experience of living with a mediocre comedian came in handy. Seeing none of his jokes landing, Viru soon got busy with his work again and occasionally broached the topic in private on a serious note.

I wondered why I had bore the burden of guilt for two years by keeping it from him. I could have told Viru long back; he would have used jokes and sarcasm to reject the whole idea, and we would have moved on.

*

Lately, my subject of worry was the signs of indifference in the endearing friendship of Ryan and Britney. They no longer seemed to be talking, and Ryan, like his every other feeling, would not share anything with me. He would spend all his time with Caesar in the house after school, and Britney had stopped visiting. I wondered if the friendship that blossomed after years of bold Britney's perseverance and timid Ryan's silent admiration for her was withering away.

Though I always felt Britney was fond of Ryan, I knew things could change growing up, given their distinctive personalities. Whereas Britney could make friends with strangers effortlessly, Ryan tended to push away even the people who cared for him.

Britney was hanging out more with Ted, who seemed to advance in psychological development rapidly. The untimely loss of an older sibling is akin to the premature end of the younger's childhood. Tim's demise had transformed the eleven-year-old from a talkative to a sensitive boy. Unlike before, he spoke gently and listened patiently to Britney. I hoped nonchalant Britney's newfound likability for Ted would not deprive reticent Ryan of the only friend he had other than Caesar.

I often thought about my meeting with Jack in the park and wished it had not ended abruptly, thanks to Viru. Many questions still lingered in my head that could have been answered. I had quietly visited the park a few times, hoping to see him again, but to no avail. Knowing Hogdon was at large, most likely conspiring against my family, gave me sleepless nights.

When up all night, I would suppress the urge to see Mom, my only confidante, for fear of drawing the attention of Viru and Reva. While Reva believed I had a key to a secret door of mystery, Viru thought I spun wild fantasy novels in my head.

I would talk to Mom at length during the day in the absence of the two spies of the family. Mom, witnessing the inexplicable visuals herself, would believe everything I told her. Though I had deliberately kept the account of Hogdon from Mom for fear of frightening her, she had a notion of evil designs at play.

One morning, I noticed Mom was lost in her thoughts. Though she had been mostly quiet and thoughtful lately, I could tell by her dropped activities when her thoughts were bothering her. Stress would prolong Mom's routine of rising from bed, walking in the yard, washing, and eating without her realizing it.

After everybody left, I made her a strong tea with extra

ginger and cardamom and sat beside her on the couch.

"Tell me, Mom. What is it?"

"What is what, Munni?"

"What's the matter? What's bothering you today?"

"Mmm. Well…" Mom sipped her tea thoughtfully.

"Don't think of lying to me, Mom. I know there's something."

"It's those visuals at night, Munni. I don't understand why I see them. I keep thinking the universe is giving me some messages through those visuals that I must decode. It bothers me when I don't see anything for days, and when I do, it bothers me more. I await these visuals only for them to agitate me. I feel like a prisoner in my mind with pieces of puzzles thrown at me that I cannot assemble."

"Mom, Jack would have told me that day had Viru not butted in. But I promise I'll find out. You look tense this morning. Did you see anything last night?"

"Yes. I saw Ryan and Caesar under the lamp and bears on the street."

"Bears?" My heart skipped a beat.

"Yes, bears. Hundreds of them gathered all over."

"What were they doing?"

"They weren't doing anything except for the one standing closer to Caesar. That bear was shaking its head."

"Shaking its head?"

"Yes, violently. Like this." Mom shook her head. "Whatever it was doing, it didn't look pleasant. And then…"

"Then what?"

"Suddenly, it turned its head and looked right into my eyes. As if angry with me for peeking out of the window. I got scared."

"Then?"

"That's it. They all disappeared."

"What did the bear look like? Was it black?"

"I think so. It was dark. All of them were dark-colored and big. I can't forget the stare it gave me. It was frightening."

I was terrified by Mom's mention of an angry bear; it reminded me of a horrifying encounter two years ago with one such bear, Duma.

"Mom, did you notice anything strange about that bear? Like red eyes or only one ear?"

"Well, its head was turned sideways when it was looking at me. I couldn't make out from that distance, even if it faced me. But why do you ask, Munni? Do you know any bears?"

"Nothing. Just asking."

Mom gave me a confused look. Like every chapter of this unfathomable world, I would keep her in the dark about another dark character, Duma.

Chapter Five

The freshly fallen snow felt like I was stepping on a spongy bed of cotton spread evenly, exhilarating the child inside me. Cheerful couples in their warm, colorful coats strolled together hand in hand. A family walked by, with a gleeful girl wearing a Christmas hat holding her dad's hand and two overjoyed little boys trotting ahead, oblivious of their Mom exclaiming with motherly concern.

Another happy family of four marching forward, all wearing noticeable long snow boots, giggled while licking soft, snow-like ice cream cones.

Shops were decorated with lights as if welcoming a newlywed bride, and the streetlamps appeared like a series of white spots in the air. In the sky, stars, like distant houses, twinkled light, and the nearest neighbor moon shone brightly. Downtown was abuzz with noises of laughter.

Suddenly, the streetlights, looking like orderly placed glowing beads threaded along an invisible cord, started going off, one at a time.

The hustle and bustle of the town dwindled. The snow melted away in the darkness, as did the shops on both sides, and a black smoggy cloud eclipsed the moon.

I could see the child that I previously felt inside me. I could not tell if it was a girl or a boy, but it felt like my reflection, standing alone in a strange place, never seen before.

The next moment, the area turned into a graveyard and a sea of tombstones appeared like ghostly crops in a barren field, ready for harvest.

A scream from far away broke the unsettling silence, terrifying the child, who shrank in fear. Another scream, louder this time, was heard from another direction, followed by multiple heart-wrenching screams from all around.

Horrible dark shadows started to appear in the air. One could not tell if they were for real or if those incessant screams had taken the shape of creepy figures in the child's mind.

The child ran wildly between the tombstones, arbitrarily changing direction like an aimless peg of Chinese checkers, chased by the shadows that screamed, inching closer every second.

When the exhaustion crept up and the lungs gave away, the child stumbled on something soft. A hand emerged from the dark, resting on their shivering back.

It was then that I woke up and, a moment later, came to my senses. I wiped the sweat on my forehead away and felt the beads of perspiration under my arms trickling down to my back as if I was worn out from sprinting in my dream.

Thinking of the frightening dream occurring for the second time in a few days gave me shivers. The last time my frequent dreams of a damsel in distress rushing through the forest ended in an actual tragic incident with my daughter. I feared that this latest one was another premonitory dream warning of a future event.

The last few months had been difficult, and I wondered how much more testing time was ahead of me. I now missed the time when I shadowed at Victoria Hospital along with Charlene and Ali, supervised by the inspiring Dr. Steven Green and entertained by the charming Nurse Dolma and bubbly receptionist Sophie.

Although it wasn't any less a challenging experience, thanks to the admin coordinator Terry Henson's meanness, the teaching head Maria Lopez's toughness, and the program director Adam Jalil's declaration of my unfavorable result, it was still all part of a human experience I could handle. However, the fear and uncertainty caused by the involvement of the unearthly actors—or aliens, as Viru would teasingly call them—was hard to deal with.

A gentle tap slowly opened the bedroom door.

"Who's there?" I called, fumbling for the lamp switch in the dark.

The room lit up, and I saw it was Caesar, now sprawled on the floor next to the bed, moaning gently—his well-known morning signal.

"Caesar? But honey, it's only four!" I said, looking at the clock.

Viru was away in Miami on a two-day business trip. He would generally take Caesar for a walk around five a.m.

If he were an ordinary dog, as Viru perceived him, I would have ignored his request. But around four-fifteen, Caesar and I hit the road in the dark for Mount Mary Hills.

As we padded along with almost no walkers around at this time, I noticed the gloom in the cemetery bordering the gravel road that stretched deep into the thicket. I avoided looking at the hundreds of rows with thousands of tombstones for fear of reminding myself of the nerve-wracking dream of the child stranded in the graveyard.

Walking up the sloped sidewalk lit by streetlights, I saw movement on the road at a distance. Ignoring my yelling, Caesar suddenly charged toward the two skunks crossing the road.

Before he could pounce on them, the skunks disappeared at the shoulder of the road. Upon closer inspection, I realized they had emerged from a drainage culvert hole on one side of the road and slipped into the other.

Of late, Caesar's animosity toward animals, including his once dearest Tulip, was beyond me.

At the top of the hill, we walked on the leveled ground across the lake. Only our stepping on the fallen, dried red leaves and Caesar's heavy breathing broke the silence of the atmosphere. The duck family huddled together in the middle of the lake seemed to be enquiring about our trespassing on their property, disturbing their resting time.

Oblivious to our surroundings, Caesar walked faster than usual and headed toward the adjoining children's park.

"Caesar, no! We're not going there," I yelled to no avail, reluctantly following him.

Walking past the swings and the open slide, Caesar stopped by the whirl spinner near the spider web climber.

"What is it, Caesar? Why are we here?" I asked.

"You are here to see me, Mandira."

I turned around and saw a figure emerge in the dark from behind the climbing rock.

"Jack! It's you. I'm so glad to see you again," I said as he acknowledged me by removing his hat and exposing his bald head.

"I'm happy to hear that, my lady. And thank you, mon cher Caesar, for helping me. It's tough to have a private conversation with you, Mandira, away from minners," he said, smiling under his conspicuous nose.

"Well, at least I know now that you people communicate with each other."

"We do. The keepers of Loka, Shloka, and Parloka always communicate when needed."

"Tell me one thing, Jack. Why didn't you warn me when Viru came to the park last time?"

"How could I? The keepers don't interfere in minners' lives, Mandira."

"Oh really! But they can conspire against a minner's daughter, almost getting her killed. Right?"

"Sarcasm. I know minners use it to mock someone. I meant *good* keepers, Mandira. We don't associate with daggers in any way. They are like weeds on barren land, popping their ugly heads up occasionally, only to get trampled over."

"Well, calling bad keepers you don't associate with daggers doesn't change the fact that they are messing around with our lives."

"Mandira, we got interrupted last time, so here I am again to answer your questions. I hope you won't spend this time arguing about good and bad keepers. It's a matter of time before the first ray of light hits Loka and the minners come this way."

"I don't care about minners, I just hope Reva doesn't come looking for me. She doesn't trust me anymore, and I'm sure you won't warn me even if she stands behind me listening in to our conversation," I returned, sitting down on a bench.

Saying I didn't care about people I often saw on morning walks was a bit of a stretch to back my argument. Why would I like to be seen talking to apparently nobody, making a complete fool of myself?

Without wasting the precious predawn moments, I got straight to business, asking Jack about Mom's strange sightings on Saint Thomas Street at night.

"Mandira, when the chief proposed Monsieur Ryan's name to the committee of Kendram for his successor, I didn't doubt his wisdom for once. But I was curious how he chose an innocent little minner over the qualified and competent keepers of Parloka, including his own son. Watching Monsieur Ryan closely over the last few years has only strengthened my belief in the chief's judgment. I also realized it's not just him; the genius runs in the family. Your Mom has a rare gift of vision called *drishti*. She can see the keepers at work."

"Keepers at work? Could you elaborate, please?"

"Of course. Remember I told you about the keepers of Rudram? If they wish to, they can become invisible to minners' eyes by concealing themselves behind the air. They can't hide from Monsieur Ryan, though. He can see all the keepers. But for the most part, they impersonate the minners of Loka so well that they cannot tell them apart. However, living like minners is not the purpose of their being in Loka, nor is doing mundane chores their work. Their actual work gets done at times when the minners' activity is minimal. Your Mom's drishti gives her a glimpse of the head of Rudram at work," said Jack, pointing at

Caesar casually sitting on the grass.

"Do you mean Caesar works at night after we fall asleep?"

"Yes. He performs his duties of Rudram, and your Mom, through her power of drishti, catches sight of his meetings."

"But she sees Ryan too."

"That's because Monsieur Ryan joins him in the meetings with keepers… What's the adjective for those keepers?"

"Good?"

"No."

"Bad keepers?"

"No, no. Those important ones."

"High-profile?"

"Um…"

"Renowned? Prominent? Eminent?"

"*Distinguished* keepers. Yes, that's the right word." He grinned. I would have asked him how my synonyms didn't fit his description had there not been a pressing confusion in my mind.

"I don't get it. According to you, Mom sees Caesar joined by Ryan conducting meetings on Saint Thomas Street. But I've checked and seen them snoring in sync, never leaving the house at night. How can they be present in two places simultaneously?"

"Because they are not. They are only in one place— Jantar."

"Jantar?"

"Exactly."

"No, you don't get it. Mom sees them on the street. Outside!"

"I get it, Mandira. Let me explain. I hope you remember your conscious journey with me through Jantar two years ago. Do you? Let me refresh your memory anyway. When the minners sleep in Loka, they unconsciously journey to a new world, Shloka, via distinct territories called Antar,

Jantar, and Mantar. Jantar is the most obscure place of all. Its unique positioning enables it to connect with Loka.

"You'll be amazed to know that Jantar has many spots that coincide with Loka, like common contact points. In other words, one can also be on Loka by being in those spots on Jantar. These are also called 'keeper zones,' used by the keepers to watch over Loka. One such zone coincides with Saint Thomas Street, where Jantar meets Loka. It's the headquarters of Rudram, from where mon cher Caesar handles his operations.

"So, with her power of drishti, your Mom can see the activities of the keeper zones. She thinks Ryan and Caesar are on Saint Thomas Street when, in fact, they are in Jantar at a keeper zone that coincides with Saint Thomas Street," Jack explained.

"So technically, when Caesar and Ryan are in Jantar at a keeper zone that coincides with Saint Thomas Street, Mom can see them through her drishti?"

"That's correct, Mandira. I couldn't have said that better in one sentence."

Unfazed by his compliment, I asked, "But why is Ryan involved in this? I'm guessing Caesar is doing some important work at night."

"The two are inseparable, Mandira. Monsieur Ryan has a natural aptitude and inclination for this work. And who better to assist than his best buddy? Chief feels the experience in administration of Rudram will prepare him for Korsi—I mean, The Meet."

"I haven't given my consent for The Meet yet, remember? And shouldn't you be consulting me before involving Ryan in Caesar's administration?"

"We would if we had involved him. He does it with free will. Unlike minners, Monsieur Ryan makes the conscious journey to Shloka, aware of his surroundings. We don't restrict his movement."

I resisted the urge to dwell on Ryan's involvement in Caesar's affairs without my knowledge, lest I should derail my focus on gaining knowledge. I also felt guilty about caring less for Caesar, whom I had raised like my third child. I knew it was a rare and limited opportunity to clarify matters that had deprived me of many nights of sleep.

"Okay, Jack, about Mom's drishti: why does she see only for a minute or so?"

"Good question. That's because drishti develops over time. Hers is not fully developed yet. She sees the keeper zone in a flash, like a glance of their meetings."

"Hmm. Speaking of meetings, Mom saw hundreds of bears gathered in the latest one. She said one of them looked angry."

"I'm glad you asked this question, Mandira. It is one of the reasons why mon cher Caesar and I wished to see you."

"Why, was it that angry bear, Duma?"

"Duma? No! Duma is an exiled dagger, Mandira. He was barred from attending any keeper meetings long back."

I let out a relieved sigh at hearing this news.

"Okay, I will need to give you some background to understand this. Remember I told you once about three main parties representing Rudram, headed by keeper-bears, keeper-dogs, and keeper-humans?"

I nodded, and he continued, "Other keepers join either of these parties. Mon cher Caesar, the leader of Rudram, is from the keeper-dogs party. His mother, Meena, became the first female and the first one from the keeper-dogs party to head Rudram. Before her, the keeper-bears had dominated the leadership position for centuries. They still enjoy the status of the most powerful party.

"Thanks to the bitter history between the feisty Meena and nasty Duma, these two parties aren't on excellent terms, although they work together. Billa, the angry bear your Mom saw the other night, is the leader of the bears. He has a firm hold on the keeper-bear party and is very demanding. He was never happy with Monsieur Ryan's involvement in Rudram, but the chief's fear kept him quiet. Now he's almost revolting due to your Mom's drishti."

"Mom's drishti? But why?"

"Because he feels Rudram's top-secret affairs are getting exposed to minners, the last thing any keeper would like. He is demanding that the headquarters be moved to another zone in Jantar that doesn't coincide with Saint Thomas Street, evading Mom's drishti."

"And there's a reason not to do that?"

"Mon cher Caesar strategically chose this zone for the headquarters of Rudram to make it the most secure spot of Loka. He is not ready to compromise your family's safety. So, he has a request for you. You must stop your Mom from using drishti to peek into Rudram's affairs."

"Stop Mom from peeking? Isn't that an odd request, mon cher?" I questioned, addressing Caesar, still sprawled on the grass and red leaves.

"Well, that's the only way to keep the zone and disgruntled Billa from rebelling. Rudram cannot afford acrimony with bears, especially in these times."

"In these times? Now, there is more to it, Jack. What is it?"

"Ah, you caught me. Do you carry an opener, Mandira? The worms are all out of the can."

Chapter Six

Seeing Jack had given me the false impression that he had waited for me in the wee hours to clear my head. This balloon of misconception soon deflated upon realizing his occupation had brought him to me, and not care for my mental peace. I wondered if those keepers rode on the non-stop rollercoaster of emotions like us minners. Perhaps they didn't, but my Caesar was undoubtedly an exception.

"Tell me, Jack. What did you mean when you said Rudram cannot afford bitterness with bears, especially in 'these' times?"

"I said acrimony with bears."

"Sorry if the word bitterness conveyed the opposite meaning for your bear connection," I returned, slightly annoyed by his unnecessary correction. "But I'm asking about 'these times,' if indeed you said those words."

"Alright, Mandira. I'll have to give you a quick background about daggers to understand this. When a keeper—whether from Loka, Shloka, or Parloka—is proven guilty by the top courts of defying the order and guidelines set by Kendram, they are called daggers.

"The elimination of daggers is rare in Kendram unless the crime is heinous and criminal beyond repair. The standard punishment is sending them into exile. In Loka, the daggers usually survive in deserted places, high mountains, or thick forests. If life in exile changes them for the better, they are accepted back into the keeper community through a rehabilitation program and given low-key responsibilities.

"Now, here's the important thing. Daggers are offenders with keeper powers that they can use for destruction. To avoid this, they are injected with *elizer* before casting them out."

"Elizer?"

"Yes, elizer is curse water. It's like a drug that causes harmful effects. When injected, the daggers lose both power and willpower. The effect of the elizer drug and loneliness together makes them dormant. They spend their banishment wandering in oblivion."

"That's great. So, they can't cause harm to us— I mean, all minners?"

"Yes, exactly."

"I hope you drugged that devil Hogdon and the dangerous one-eared bear Duma."

"Not them. They were the source and origin of the dagger menace. Before them, there were only good keepers. The practice of elizer punishment started recently when the nefarious activities increased."

"This isn't making me feel better, Jack. The originators of the problem are still powerful and absconding."

"I think the right phrase is *at large*. And I'm afraid this will not be a feel-good account."

Certainly not, I thought, *when you fixate on correcting my words constantly. One of these days, I must meet your language teacher, Professor Lingua Franca.*

Two years ago, I had liked correcting Jack's wrong word usage. Not only had he deprived me of the pleasure, but now he annoyed me by objecting to my proper word usage.

"About a year ago," Jack continued, "a disgruntled scientist of Parloka, Dr. Dhingra, stole the recipe and samples of elizer. He secretly worked on the chemical formula to reverse its effects. The dagger Dhingra developed an anti-elizer drug in his secret laboratory and shared the formula with his corrupt associates in Parloka, Loka, and Shloka. The bad news is that many daggers have cured of the effects of elizer."

"What do you mean, cured? Have they regained their evil powers?"

"Yes."

"Please tell me, Jack, you have captured those daggers again."

"Some of them. Many are still at large."

"And Dr. Dhingra?"

"At large."

"My God. You're telling me your so-called prison of elizer is broken, and the criminals are at large? A large number is at large!"

"Not to worry, Mandira. Our best keepers are looking for them. They will track them down soon."

"Like you have hunted down Hogdon and Duma?"

"They are clever. Not all daggers are shrewd like them."

I shook my head in disappointment.

"I have more to tell you, Mandira."

"There's more? Go on, rip the band-aid off. Cripple me with affliction."

"When a weapon meant to control wrongdoing falls into the wrong hands, there are repercussions. Not only did Dr. Dhingra restore the daggers' powers by developing an anti-elizer, but he also supplied stolen elizer samples to his associates.

"Now, here's how twisted dagger minds are. In Loka, they spilled elizer in the ponds, rivers, streams, and puddles in the wild forests. Upon drinking the contaminated water, the traces of elizer were transmitted into minner-animals. The infected animals became violent due to the effect of elizer and started brawling with the healthy ones, thereby transferring the contagious elizer."

"Wait. Are you talking about the rages virus that is spreading in the jungles where the animals go crazy, biting each other and eventually dying?"

"Yes."

"That's not a mysterious virus, but your elizer?"

"That's correct."

"So the daggers caused the rages virus?"

Jack nodded. "They did."

"Oh, God. Why would they do that? What have poor animals done to them? And it's not animals alone! They have also found this virus in humans." I remembered the case at Victoria Hospital where poor Mr. Howard had died miserably.

"Yes, the humans bitten by infected animals get elizer traces transmitted to their bodies."

"That's horrible! Why don't you find a cure and heal them all? If a bad scientist can make an anti-elizer, I'm sure you have some good scientists who can do that too."

"Of course we have, Mandira. The top keeper scientists are on it. But it's not easy. Elizer was never meant to be used on minners. It affects them differently, and its composition in a minner body is complicated. To find a cure for minners and to give them all the antidote is a challenge for keepers."

"Does that mean you're helpless? You've no solution right now?"

"I wouldn't say helpless, but the only solution, for now, is to contain the infected animals in the wild and minimize the spreading. You won't believe how efficiently mon cher Caesar and his keepers of Rudram manage this humongous task. They work tirelessly to protect healthy animals and humans from infected animals. It's a challenge for Caesar as the daggers take advantage of the chaos. Disguised as infected animals, they assist in worsening the situation in the jungle."

"God bless my Caesar," I returned, looking at Caesar, stretching and yawning lousily on the ground. "But the thought of daggers responsible for what I regarded as the rages virus until fifteen minutes ago makes me feel unsafe."

"You don't have to feel unsafe. Mon cher Caesar has it covered. He's so paranoid about your family's safety that he doesn't even let normal animals come close."

That explains his behavior toward other animals, including Tulip, I thought. *And thankless Viru calls him the Tasmanian devil. Even his affection for Tulip doesn't stand in the way of his devotion to his family.*

Seeing me lost in thought, Jack continued, "As I told you before about mon cher Caesar, your top protector is a member of your family. He lives with you. He will stand like a wall before you in the face of any danger."

I nodded, gazing gratefully at Caesar, who was casually scratching his back with his hind leg.

"I don't know if it's any help, Mandira," said Jack, "but I feel compelled to share this information. After all, I am told to gain your trust, to build with you that thing, what minners call..."

Tired of suggesting words that he rudely rejected, I offered no help in guessing this time.

"Ah, rapport! So, one of the associates of Dr. Dhingra, who helped spread elizer in Loka, was recently captured. And you know him."

"I know him?" Looking up at Jack I asked, "Who?"

"He worked at Victoria Hospital. You knew him well and talked to him."

"At Victoria? Who? Terry Henson?" I uttered the first name that came to mind.

"Not him. He's just a normal minner."

"Then who? I can't think of anyone meaner than Terry."

Jack seemed to test my curiosity, deliberately withholding his next words.

"Dr. Adam Jalil," he said eventually.

"What? Dr. Jalil? The program director? I don't get it!"

"Let me explain. As I told you before, part of a keeper's job is to blend with minners perfectly by living and behaving like them. When in disguise, they must perform minner duties with utmost honesty. Jalil was one of Rudram's keepers. Turns out he was a dagger sympathizer secretly involved in Dr. Dhingra's convoluted plot."

My eyes were wide open with shock, as if I had forgotten to blink.

"You wouldn't believe the role you unknowingly played in busting this grand elizer conspiracy," continued Jack.

"Jalil was believed to be a trusted keeper. But the Intelligence Agency of Rudram (IAR) became alert when a minner doctor, Steven Green, from another department, complained to the hospital authorities about your failing the program. Jalil's role raised suspicion, as Green had given you an excellent evaluation. As is common with minners, the hospital authorities downplayed the matter. Still, IAR discovered that Jalil had ignored Green's feedback and used his influence over other doctors to rate you poorly."

"Unbelievable! I did feel my evaluation wasn't fair. But Dr. Jalil? Why would he do that? Even if he was, as you said, a dagger sympathizer, what purpose could my failing of the shadowing program serve him?"

"Mandira, you forget that you're the mom of the projected successor of the Chief of Kendram. The loyal keepers in Parloka already regard yours as the first family, a status sore to many dagger eyes.

"Also, the IAR investigation revealed Jalil's connection with the dagger boy and girl that misled your daughter Reva into the jungle of Billaria. It seems that Jalil was distracting you from paying attention to Reva so that the dagger designs ushering her to Billaria to become the prey of the elizer-infected animals could be accomplished. They conspired to make it look like an accident.

"Further inquiry revealed that he was one of Dr. Dhingra's agents involved in the elizer racket. He distributed the anti-elizer and elizer to daggers of Loka, helping them heal and cause harm, respectively."

"Jalil rigged my evaluation to distract my attention from Reva? To get her killed?"

The reminder of the tragic event had blanked my mind, and my ears heard nothing Jack said after the mention of Reva.

"Yes. But there is nothing to worry about. He is now in keeper custody."

"What now? Will you give him the same dosage of elizer that he was distributing?"

"I think that's sarcasm, so no reply is warranted."

"I don't believe it. Your optimism is appalling. You people are a mess! You pose as our protectors, but others in your clan are trying to destroy us. Destroy my family! I wonder if our Loka would have been better off without caretakers like you. I don't know how many more dagger sympathizers are out there impersonating minners, meddling with their lives. It's…"

Familiar music distracted me. Jack pointed at my cardigan pocket, and I noticed it was my phone ringing. I answered the call.

"Mom, where are you?"

"Um, Mount Mary, Revu. Walking Caesar."

"It's six forty-five, Mom! What's taking so long?"

"Oops. Caesar took me to the park; I lost track of time. I'm coming back."

"I'm late for school, Ma. Ryan is still in bed. Grandma is alone in the kitchen."

"Sorry! On my way. I'll be home in a jiffy. Caesar! Gotta go, honey."

Walking hurriedly with Cesar, I glanced back at Jack.

"I can see you're upset, Mandira. But I don't doubt that keepers will manage this untoward trouble," he assured me.

"Self-created."

"What?"

"You spend so much time looking for the perfect word, but missed this time. *Self-created* is the fitting adjective for trouble here, rather than untoward."

I didn't look back. The sun was out, and so were the morning walkers, peering curiously at my animated chatter.

Chapter Seven

The thing with tornadoes or tsunamis is that onlookers get mesmerized by the magnitude, like deer caught in headlights, believing they are safe from peril. They realize the ugly jaws of destruction have caught up when the tidal waves or whirlwinds sweep them off their feet. The rages virus, as the world knew it, was like a tornado or tsunami begging for swift action rather than dumb attention.

Like the worst deluge beyond the dam's control, rages could not be contained in the wild. Before this unsettling realization could sink in, violent animal attacks became an everyday affair in villages, towns, and cities. Wild animals across the world were crossing the limits of dense jungles and thickets at an alarming rate, causing mayhem in populated places.

Delirious tigers, lions, hyenas, wolves, dogs, boars, bears, raccoons, and other animals roamed on the streets, attacking each other or humans they encountered on their way. When not discovering living things to tear asunder, the deranged beasts banged on parked vehicles, streetlamps, dividers, and trees, damaging private and public property. Fear engulfed humankind.

Humans had not learned much from the previous pandemic besides announcing a lockdown. The streets became deserted, and walks became a distant dream. People locked themselves in their houses. They risked going out only for emergencies or to buy groceries or medicines in bulk, careful not to step out of their vehicles. Terror loomed in the air.

Though late, the governments acted by gunning down savage animals found in the open. Others died in bloodthirsty battles or from the effect of the virus. Authorities directed people to drop off their domestic animals at designated shelters to avoid getting them killed. Establishments knew that slaughtering wild animals spotted in inhabited areas was not the solution, as more monsters, like reinforcements, crossed the borders of jungles every hour.

A war of survival had broken out between humans and animals. Governments across the globe were contemplating eradicating the problem from the source, which meant erasing the entire animal kingdom in the wild.

The victims that didn't die instantly from the animal attacks but got infected with the rages virus through their bites flooded the hospitals. They paced about restlessly, hoping for respite from their inevitable death.

Alongside being gripped by fear and anxiety, several phobias developed among the infected. One that stood out was somniphobia—the fear of sleep. The virus victims could not doze off for more than a few minutes, fearing a choking sensation. Exhaustion would soon suck every ounce of life out of them.

Schools resorted to online classes, and businesses survived on the work-from-home model. Unable to step outside, people turned to social media to vent their anger and outrage. The internet became a substitute for the real world. From criticizing governments' inaction to suggesting numerous methods for mass murdering animals, the virtual space became flooded with hate mongering executionists. The empathetic animal lovers, urging the exercising of restraint toward sick animals, were shut off by the jobless online trolls.

Amid this unusual battle, a war of words broke out between human rights and animal rights activists. Hate and mistrust were at their peak, as were the online surveys and polls, fueling the fire.

The World Congress of Medical Science made a significant breakthrough, among other research centers.

The scientists declared that physical activity was the primary reason for the rages virus replicating exponentially, attacking the central nervous system in a matter of days. In other words, prolonged resting could significantly reduce the proliferation of viral agents in the infected bodies, helping the autoimmune system to fight them. Minimum activity would not cure the disease, but delay succumbing to death by many months.

Through lab work, scientists proved that a day's inactivity in an infected animal calmed them, putting the brakes to their biting spree and potentially helping to stop the virus from spreading.

The problem was the virus encouraged physical activity by making individuals anxious, terrorized, and sleepless. Sleeping pills and other sedatives were ineffective in inducing sleep.

Anesthesia became the top-searched word on Google. Top pharmaceutical companies burned the midnight oil for large-scale anesthetic manufacturing. The demand for anesthesia, the only known boon for infected humans, outweighed the supply.

Leading countries collaborated in large-scale chloroform production and sprayed the targeted jungle areas through aerial routes.

All these measures were beneficial but insufficient in the wake of the virus spreading like wildfire.

Only I knew the truth about the rages virus—that it was caused by the drug elizer, developed by the keepers and meant to debilitate the daggers. But the unscrupulous daggers had outsmarted the virtuous keepers, causing havoc among the innocent minners. Nevermind the ignorant minners—even the mighty keepers seemed helpless in the wake of this disorder of the world.

*

Three weeks had passed since my meeting with Jack, and I

reflected on my outburst toward him and the keepers.

Good and evil have existed for as long as existence itself, be it prehistory, ancient, the Middle Ages, or the modern era. Selfless and selfish, fair and fear, we and I, light and dark; these traits are the motivators and instigators of good and evil, respectively. One is born in the heart, while the other breeds in psychology and circumstances. How could I expect to have good keepers without the prevalence of evil daggers? Blaming good for the existence of evil is akin to doing a disservice to good.

"Mrs. Bergenza gave up her cats. She's not a Catwoman anymore," announced Viru, walking into the bedroom and breaking my train of thought. It took me a moment to switch from a meaningful reflection to a meaningless deflection.

"Hmm."

Sensing my disinterest, he continued, "And Mrs. Walker is not a dog walker anymore. She handed over Tulip."

"Viru, I've told you many times, we are not giving up Caesar to the welfare shelter. I'm his Mom."

"Mandy, if you say that, I automatically become his dad. I care for him, too. They are killing all animals. I can't take him out anymore."

"As if you're allowed to go outside."

"Exactly. I'm fed up with picking up his shit in the backyard. Dads don't clean their children's shit forever. I risk my life every morning for him."

"You don't have to risk your precious life for Caesar. I'll clean it up from tomorrow."

"That's not the point, Mandy. Animal welfare folks keep warning people, asking them to submit their pets. Don't you watch TV? Your stubbornness could get him killed. He's not safe here."

"There's no place safer than his house. Ryan and Caesar are inseparable. Don't you get it? Besides, Caesar doesn't need your protection."

"I see now. You still think he is some head of the alien

world. What was it called? Ah, Rudram!"

"Hush, Reva will hear you."

"She's downstairs. C'mon Mandy. Our dog is just a dog. Not even a superior one. The lowest IQ dog in Abbynton. He's no head. One can only associate him with the word head by calling him a knucklehead."

"I've told you before, Viru—you don't have to believe anything."

"One of these days, we need to publish that crazy fantasy story playing in your head so that you can move on with real life. The life where wild animals are mauling humans and their pets."

"For God's sake, Viru. Give me a break from your sad jokes. Work-from-home has made you so annoying."

"But you're unbelievably pleasant," exclaimed Viru, storming out of the bedroom. Walking down the stairs, he mumbled something about Disney characters being in the house.

I lay in bed thinking. Like elsewhere, Abbynton was placed under curfew. The news had been full of wild animals' aggression and crackdowns by the authorities globally. However, Saint Thomas Street was quiet, and I knew why.

Viru wouldn't understand he was in the safest house on the planet thanks to the family member he wished to drive out. If his narrow mind could create room for the possibility of Caesar's greatness and selfless service to his family, picking up shit once a day wouldn't hurt. To Viru, Caesar was just a nuisance, now more than ever.

Upon my persuasion, Mom stopped using drishti to watch the activities of the keeper zone at Jantar, which coincided with Saint Thomas Street. I would be the last one to increase Caesar's challenges, especially during these testing times and after knowing the opposition leader of Rudram, the keeper-bear Billa, had objected to Mom's snooping in keeper affairs.

I sometimes wondered if there was any point in being

blessed with a power one couldn't use. Then I would ponder if watching keepers doing something you barely understood was a useful superpower. The closest comparison I could draw with drishti was watching the National Geographic's night reels on mute, except for an appearance from my son in the frame. Also, the animals of Nat Geo could not gaze back at their viewer.

Unable to use one power, Mom busied herself in invoking another—the power of prayers. She spent her mornings in front of Lord Shiva's statue that she had brought with her and installed in a corner of the house, chanting mantras for peace and well-being.

Reva had been easy going since she was very young. Or perhaps I felt so, as going was always tough with Ryan. I often felt guilty about paying little attention to Reva due to my primary focus on Ryan's challenges. But she never complained. I was glad that she was raised well and had rarely been the subject of my worries.

However, things had changed since Tim's passing, and I worried a lot for her. Reva spoke normally to me and played along with her dad's jokes, but she was not at all the same.

Scarred skin heals faster, but the scarred heart of an adolescent needs more than a bandage. They say time heals the worst wounds. I believe time shoves wounds beyond repair into a corner, like old files, by stacking up fresh trifles in our minds. Though rarely accessed, the old files, eating dust, remain at the back of the mind like a permanent blemish.

Reva felt responsible for Tim's death and distracted herself by becoming immersed in her studies. She never complained.

How could I help my girl, who since her early years had learned to deal with her problems alone because her Mom had been chiefly occupied with her brother?

The best I could do was to tell her everything she suspected me of hiding. However, Viru was against telling her any part of what he thought was a fictional fantasy worth publishing. I wouldn't care much for Viru's opinion had I believed dragging her into the mystery world would do Reva any good. Even if she believed me, I feared knowing Tim became the victim of a plot solely designed for her would torment her more.

I rose not only to separate from my bed but also from inconclusive thoughts. Standing by the window, I watched the unsettling calm of Saint Thomas Street in the clear morning light, which would previously have been abuzz with people.

Nowadays, public movement was restricted to emergencies, accompanied by emergency response teams. Patrolling vehicles with armed police officers would occasionally take rounds and deliver online-ordered groceries and medicines to households.

My eyes searched for my daily dose of reassurance.

Perhaps I overstayed in bed, I thought.

Seeing Samantha always gave me the comfort to endure the rest of the day. Especially since the lockdown, seeing her jogging to Mount Mary became part of my morning routine, as I knew she was only visible to me.

I noticed a black squirrel spring down a tree and cross the street. A shot was fired, and the squirrel succumbed at the shoulder of the road. The patrolling vehicle cruised ahead.

My heart sank. Another life destroyed in order to save lives.

Lacking the desire to look outside any longer, I turned around and headed to the adjacent room. Sunk in the ruffled duvet was my boy, making no effort to overcome his known addiction—sleep. Next to him lay another sleeping beauty, the head of Rudram, whom Viru called knucklehead.

Ryan's alarm went off for the tenth time, and without opening his eyes, he hit the snooze button yet again. Before, the joint effort of the alarm clock and Caesar, fresh from his morning walk, would wake Ryan. But since the lockdown, lethargy had set in thanks to no more rushing to get on the school bus.

Now the joint effort was between Ryan and Caesar against the persistent clock. If Ryan missed, Caesar would come to the rescue by tapping on the clock's head, putting off its jarring notes for another ten minutes.

Turning off the alarm, I decided to let them doze a little more, thinking the head of Rudram, assisted by the potential head of Kendram, must be attending to otherworldly chores somewhere in Jantar, Mantar, or Shloka. Although, their open-mouthed snores alluded to an attempt to escape their morning chores in Loka.

I found Viru and Reva glued to the TV in the living room, their mouths open, but for a different reason. I was about to ask them why when the tired-looking newsreader grabbed my attention.

"Just past midnight, the residents of Driffin were brusquely awakened by noisy growling and howling, and witnessed the horror of their lifetime. Lions, tigers, bears, wolves, gorillas, bison, and many more wild animals went on a rampage, destroying everything in their way. Thousands of bloodthirsty animals that had crossed the nearby jungle of Billaria barged into houses by breaking doors, shattering walls, and smashing windows.

"The savage beasts mercilessly mauled innocent inhabitants. The casualties identified so far are in the thousands, with the death toll rising to three hundred and twenty. The hospitals caring for the severely wounded are at capacity, and the authorities are setting up several first-aid camps.

The Driffin Police Department, backed by the nearby stations' forces, did its best to save the residents by killing scores of raging animals. The matter, however, remained out of control until the army joined hands with them in the early hours of the morning and launched a massive rescue operation.

"Such was the delirium among the animals that despite being shot multiple times, they continued to destroy every obstruction coming their way and ambush each other until their last breath. Presently, the situation is tense but under control. Gunshots are still being fired by authorities, ensuring that animals hampered by severe injuries and fatigue do not resurrect.

"Driffin has been completely sealed. Given the increased risk, law enforcement agencies are on high alert, and army troops have been deployed in neighboring cities Weldon, Hamlin, and Abbynton.'

Chapter Eight

It was Diwali. The Festival of Lights symbolizes the victory of good over evil. However, with the waging war of animals among them and with humans threatening to eradicate several species globally, if not all, the evil designs seemed to get the better of good intentions.

Every year on this day, we would throw a bash for our neighbors and Viru's colleagues after days of meticulous preparations. For the first time in my life, confined to the house, neither the meaning nor the means to celebrate the festivities seemed appropriate.

The world had become an immense prison with every family under house arrest. Those who didn't have houses were held captive in shelters.

Upon Viru's insistence, we decided to celebrate the occasion with limited resources in extraordinary circumstances. I busied myself with Mom in the kitchen while Reva volunteered to mop the floor.

The two heads—as Viru would sometimes call Ryan and Caesar to annoy me—did not contribute much. I assigned Ryan the task of dusting the bookshelf, which he finished, or perhaps didn't, in two minutes before he whisked off to his room with Caesar.

Viru took up the task of decluttering our storage boxes. He collected all the articles that seemed useful but had never been used in a large Ikea bag.

He took out my best party dresses from the old suitcases, asking me if he should throw them away. When I refused, he teased me by asking when I had worn them last time, to which I stumped him with a counter question: "How many parties have you taken me to?"

When it came to the shoe rack, Viru discovered around ten empty boxes on the upper shelf, allowing him an opportunity he wouldn't miss to lecture me.

This was why I never trusted Viru with any household work. He would either do a lousy job or become overly efficient, thus finding faults in how it was previously done. Viru would take a cleaning job upon himself once a year and act as if it was the only real cleaning done in the entire year. I wondered how his colleagues tolerated him at work.

After the elaborate cleaning job that Viru made a fuss about as if he had cleaned the entire neighborhood, we offered prayers to Laxmi, the goddess of wealth and prosperity.

The day progressed with humdrum until evening knocked on the door, and along with it, Elena and Britney. They came through the glass door in the back after crossing the short wall separating our backyards.

Viru entertained the only guests we could afford during the lockdown with anecdotes I had heard—rather, suffered through—multiple times.

He told them about his childhood back in India when he would accompany his father to buy firecrackers on a Diwali morning. Every year, they went to the local shopkeeper and Viru would pick one or two boxes of his favorite firecrackers, like flowerpots (*anar*), ground spinners (*chakri*), garlands (*ladi*), sparklers (*phuljhari*) and other crackers (*patakhas*). The shop owner would list the prices of the items in the blank space of a newspaper. Viru's Dad would then list new prices in the space next to each item, discounting the original by twenty to twenty-five percent. After a long, spirited conversation on each item, they would finally agree on a new total.

Viru later observed that they could save time by simply negotiating on the total rather than individual items, giving them a similar result. But such bargaining would not satisfy either of them. Viru's Dad said, "The shopkeeper inflates the price of each item, knowing I will make my own list. So, I need to fix the problem at its root."

Viru's Dad had a sense of humor quite like his son's.

Everyone relished the food. Elena complimented me, and I passed the credit where it was due: to Mom, our head chef.

Enjoying *rasmalai*, Mom's special evening dessert served by Reva, Viru animatedly shared another Diwali recollection:

"You know, Britney. When I was your age, on Diwali evenings, my Mom kept the boxes of sweets the neighbors and friends gifted on the table. I'd light one firecracker outside, come inside and have a bite of my favorite sweet, and go out and light another one. I'd go on for an hour or two. The following morning, my Mom would find boxes with half-eaten sweets of different kinds."

"Wow. You were a naughty boy, Mr. Sharma." Britney chuckled. "My mom would never let me do such a thing."

I thought Britney had heard this story before, as Viru was the king of repetition, barely keeping track of his audience, but Britney always enjoyed his accounts as if listening for the first time. She even asked him to tell the stories she had previously heard.

Though Ryan barely engaged in any conversation, I could sense him feeling left out at the table, thanks to the silent treatment from Britney. Eating cold *rasmalai* would not alleviate the effect of the cold shoulder Britney gave him.

Later, in the kitchen, Elena helped me wipe the cleaned dishes dry and we caught up on the latest gossip that had lately become a rare commodity.

"I called Mrs. Bergenza last night. She is really depressed," said Elena.

"Why, what happened?"

"She had to give up her cats. That woman lived for her cats. She loved them, perhaps more than Mr. Bergenza.

She's taking medication."

"Poor lady. You don't realize when pets become family until they're gone."

"She told me that Mr. Bergenza said they should adopt a child."

"Adoption at this age? They must be kidding."

"I can't say. Mr. Bergenza is a funny man. He told her they wouldn't have to give up a child as they leave anyways when they grow up. Perhaps he was just trying to lift her spirits."

"That's a unique way to lift spirits."

We both chuckled.

"What about Caesar? Do you…" Elena trailed off.

"I don't know. I can't imagine Ryan without him. Viru keeps nudging me," I said, glancing at Caesar sitting on the couch.

"I know. We all love Caesar. I've no idea how they treat them in those shelters. I hate this situation."

We finished drying the plates and soon after, Elena and Britney sneaked back to their house from the backyard, as the gathering was prohibited in the lockdown.

*

Something woke me up. Viru, next to me, was up too.

"What was that?" I asked.

"Don't know. I heard a sound. A loud thud, perhaps," Viru returned, confused.

I turned on the bedside lamp, and the darkness softly melted away in the luminescence. The clock, tired from sitting steadily on the side table, struck two-fifteen. Sitting up, I strained my ears.

"Do you hear that?"

"What?"

"A galloping sound. Like horses running on a dirt road far away."

"I don't hear horses. I hear something else, like the wind

blowing."

"Wait, I hear something else."

"What?"

"Sort of muffled grunting. It sounds like it's coming from the house," I returned.

"Mom! Dad!" shouted Reva. A growling sound followed.

Viru and I jumped from the bed and rushed to the living room. Reva stood barefoot at the foot of the stairs, looking nervous.

I looked behind her, and my heart skipped a beat.

It was Caesar, standing in the living area. His demeanor was bold and different. His eyes fumed in anger, and his growl felt like it was coming from his gut. His brown fur, interwoven with light gray, gave him an unbelievably muscular appearance in the dim light. He looked bigger and stronger. He was no longer our docile buddy Caesar, but a scary, formidable force. Only once before had I seen that fearsome side of Caesar.

"What the hell is he up to?" asked Viru.

I just watched our dog curiously.

"Caesar! Caesar! Stop it!" yelled Viru.

Caesar didn't stop. His growl became louder and more menacing.

"Stop it, you idiot! You'll wake everyone." Viru advanced forward, but I held his hand to stop him.

"Wait, Viru. Stay back."

"What for? We have to stop him!"

"We can't stop him. Stay where you are. He's doing it for a reason."

"Yes, he's gone crazy! That's the reason. I told you, Mandy! I told you, this dog is trouble. We must give him up before it's too late. He will kill us or get us killed. But you never listen to me. You don't—"

"For God's sake, Viru! Shut up!" I shouted, and Viru gave me a bewildered look.

"Mom! Come here! Come to this side," I said, seeing

Mom exit her room. "Reva, stay where you are."

Everyone followed my directions.

Viru was perplexed, perhaps more by my commanding voice than Caesar's growl.

I carefully stepped forward. "Caesar, honey… What is it? What's going on?"

Caesar snarled louder and stomped his feet on the ground.

"Okay, okay!" I stepped back and looked around from floor to wall to ceiling. I noticed the sliding glass door facing the backyard was half-open. I recalled I had closed the door when Elena and Britney had left.

Before my thoughts could process more information, a large dog entered through the glass door. My eyes widened and my mouth dropped open upon seeing the familiar figure. Three more dogs followed him through the open space. A strange mix of fear and relief overcame me as if jelly blended with whipped cream.

The dog with a white coat and black spots stood next to Caesar. The second dog, with a black coat, positioned itself on his other side. The remaining two brown-furred dogs also fell into line. The large dogs of the D-Force—Tormon, Shuru, Aaj, and Kal—and their average-sized master at the center now faced the front door.

"What the hell?" exclaimed a visibly shocked Viru. "Who are these giant dogs? Where'd they come from?"

"I know that one!" cried Reva, pointing at the white dog. "That's the one who saved me! He saved me from the tiger, Ma. He's the one!"

"I know, honey; I know. He's Tormon. They're all with us. They're here to protect us."

"What'd you mean, protect us?" Viru squeaked.

"Where's Ryan?" I suddenly realized he was missing. "Reva! Go wake Ryan and bring him down here. Hurry!"

Reva remained starstruck for a few moments, gazing at Tormon, and I had to yell at her again before she dashed upstairs to fetch Ryan.

The five charged dogs growled at the locked front door of the house.

"Mandy, what do you mean, they're here to protect us? Who are they? What's happening?"

"Stay behind them, Viru! We are under attack!"

Chapter Nine

There comes a time when one's pride and wisdom get shredded into pieces of naivety. Their arrogance of understanding is sliced into chunks of ignorance. What they thought was logical sounds like a joke, and what they proclaimed as obscure no longer seems as such.

The incomprehension of the actual world I lived in had struck me years ago, and for Viru, it was about to happen.

The five dogs standing in a row in the center of the living room continued to stare and growl at the front door.

"Mandy, what do you mean, we are under attack? Who's attacking us?"

"No time, Viru! Stay behind Caesar and the dogs, and don't move!"

Viru became clueless and speechless before me, perhaps for the first time.

A loud bang on the door made me shake with fear, and Caesar snarled furiously. Moments later, another strike flung the door open, almost breaking it.

Silence fell in the room, and I felt the weight of it on my chest. All eyes were fixed on the open door, as if glued there.

A big, scary head emerged from the darkness. His eyes widened with rage, and mine dilated with horror. His nostrils flared with fury, and mine gasped for air.

The next thing I knew, the giant bison was charging at us. He met with a hurdle as he got stuck in the narrow door, almost cracking the walls on either side of the threshold. Infuriated by the obstruction, the bison descended a few steps back to attack with intensified force.

He was sure to demolish the entrance this time, but didn't realize it was not the only blockade. My eyes were so fixated on the bison that I didn't notice one of the brown dogs leaping into action until he appeared at the door, blocking my view. Such was the force with which the dog slammed into the bison that both toppled down the steps, crashing into the recycling container.

I heard the sounds of a violent clash between them outside the house. The noise of jumping, thumping, crashing, and cracking rocketed my curiosity and anxiety. At one point, I got a glimpse of the dog tumbling down, but he sprung back up the very next moment.

Jack had told me the brown-furred twins were called Aaj and Kal. I could not tell which one was fighting the bison, but in my head, I named him Aaj.

While Aaj brawled fiercely with the bison twice his size, the other four remained unmoved from their spots in the living room. It didn't take long for me to realize why they left their buddy alone outside to grapple with the wild beast. He was not the only enemy that night, and the battle was just warming up.

"Reva, I asked you to get Ryan!" I yelled, noticing Reva standing frozen on the stairs.

"He wouldn't wake up, Mom! I tried!"

"What? Did you try hard?"

"Very! Holy moly! What the hell?" cried Reva, steering my attention back to the door.

A pack of five hideous hyenas burst into the house, and their shrilling screeches terrorized Viru.

"Oh, my God! What's happening? Hyenas in my house!" Viru shrieked, moving closer to me.

The other brown dog, Kal, pounced on them. Three hyenas retreated a few steps while the other two attacked from behind. Displaying lightning agility, Kal swerved swiftly, shoving back the other hyenas.

The noisy hyenas kept charging from all sides, aiming for any part of Kal's body they could until they succeeded. Two hyenas dragged his leg, the third knocked him down, and the fourth and fifth bit his thighs and back, cutting into the flesh with their pointed teeth.

I wondered if and when Caesar, Tormon, and Shuru would step forward to assist their friend struggling on the floor by the bookshelf. The first twin, Aaj, had also not returned, and the howling noises indicated that the bison was not the only beast outside he was fighting with presently.

I was optimistic about a well thought out keeper-dogs strategy in place behind this unique battle and hoped they were not simply leaving each other alone to die.

I was pondering the twin dogs' plight when my worst fear came true.

A bear emerged before us.

My heart sank. I'd had several terrifying recollections in the past two years, but nothing came close to the nightmares one bear had given me. The anxiety, like unwanted company, would not leave me for days after seeing that ugly bear, irrespective of them being only dream encounters.

It occurred to me that my house's entrance had suddenly transformed into a door from hell, with wild beasts stepping into my living room one after the other. The fuming bear strolled around confidently, as if he owned the house and I was just a tenant overstaying my lease. His locked gaze with Caesar indicated it would be the clash of the titans.

I realized that the bear didn't look exactly like Duma. For one, he wasn't pitch black like Duma, but dark brown instead. And most importantly, he didn't have an amputated ear. But then the daggers were nothing short of immoral chameleons, more than capable of changing colors and growing back an ear. Moreover, his size and demeanor were akin to Duma.

I watched the creature, my disquieted mind unsettled with the thought that it was indeed Duma, slightly transformed, and likely for the worst.

While walking like a boss, he briefly moved his eyes from Caesar and directed his murderous gaze toward us. I felt Mom's trembling hand clasping my wrist tightly as she whispered in my ear.

I realized the look was meant for Mom, and it reminded her instantly of one of her drishti encounters. The bear we were facing was not Duma 2.0. It was Billa, Caesar's adversary at Rudram, head of the opposition party of keeper-bears.

Until then, I only knew about a handful of daggers gone rogue. But the thought of keeper factions warring shook me to the core.

"Mandy, are we going to die?" Viru asked softly, standing close behind me.

I hadn't imagined such a time when Viru would seek answers from me on a subject that he had ridiculed before as my fantasy novel in the making. I had no answers, and upon realizing the bizarre turn of events, my hopes to escape alive had dwindled, too.

Viru's scariest dream, as he often talked about, was in his childhood, of a man repeatedly uttering two words to his face: *titch button*. His biggest fantasy, perhaps, would be cracking the funniest jokes, getting the audience to roll on the floor laughing. By that standard, Viru was witnessing something beyond his wildest dreams or fantasies, a sight he would not venture into his imagination, let alone experience in reality.

Our pet, whom Viru had perceived as a nuisance, was, in a true sense, the only barrier in the way of an ever-closer violent death. He watched Caesar thrust himself into the gravest peril to prevent our likely perish. The dog he often called worthless was grappling with a massive bear twice his size and strength.

Although Billa's incredible power was evident, given his enormous size, his agility was menacing. Anyone watching an ordinary dog fighting a belligerent bear would regard it as a non-contest, however I had hope, considering I was privy to Caesar's lightning speed from his clash with Duma two years ago. But young Billa, it seemed, was superior to Caesar in this department.

Every time Billa pinned him down by his large paws, Caesar would slip out quickly, scratched all over by his curved nails, only to be strangled again. In several quick moves, Caesar repeatedly squeezed the bear's neck between his jaws, but was unable to cut his teeth into the thick skin each time, leaving the beast unscathed. Despite every distinct move Caesar attempted, Billa seemed to get the better of him.

In their violent struggle, the table broke and the chairs cracked, followed by the toppling of the couch, and then the TV came crashing down.

Amid Caesar struggling against monstrous Billa, Kal became overpowered by the pack of noisy hyenas. Biting all over his body, the nasty hyenas dragged Kal out of the house.

There were also no signs of the return of Aaj, who was perhaps still fighting the snorting bison outside. Tormon continued to be an onlooker, and Shuru had disappeared. I was seriously concerned with their coordination and strategy.

To make matters worse, at that moment another beast entered the house—the one I dreaded the most.

His pitch-black coat glistened, long canines protruded from his mouth, and his only ear flapped. His fuming red eyes scanned the entire area, then rested on me with disgust.

I shrank in fear. Duma looked precisely the same as when I saw him two years ago, though perhaps uglier and scarier.

Viru, Reva, Mom, and I huddled together in the kitchen—the farthest corner possible from the living room, or for that matter, the battleground—like a bunch of sticks tied by a rope.

Duma took his piercing gaze off me and fixed his eyes on the top of the stairs. Though obvious, it had not occurred to me until then that those beasts were not focusing on us mortals shuddering and juddering in the kitchen. They were here to harm Ryan.

Seconds later, Duma headed resolutely toward his target, while my palpitating heart considered a heart attack.

A fragment of hope arose when Tormon blocked Duma at the first step. Duma roared with anger, and a bloody scuffle started.

Tormon was a combination of strength and aggression. He was a formidable force before Duma, less in size but not in courage. Every time Duma laid his hideous paws on Tormon, he would be forcefully thrust back, as if he had touched a barbed wire.

Months ago, in her moment of distress, Reva had seen Tormon pouncing on a tiger, knocking it down. Though, thanks to extreme exhaustion, she was unable to keep her eyes open for long to watch the fierce battle, discovering the tiger lying dead upon returning to her senses was a testament to Tormon's potential. She trusted her savior would once again rise to the occasion, defeat the one-eared bear, and demolish all the other beasts.

Reva had known since her first encounter with Tormon that he was no ordinary dog. However, she was yet to witness how extraordinarily brutal Duma was.

Duma's savagery was on another level. Duma showed how the initial seconds of the brawl were just a warm-up for him when he flung Tormon in the air in one moment and plonked down firmly on the floor in the next.

Tormon scrambled to return to his feet but could not escape Duma's tight grip. Taking complete control, Duma clobbered Tormon by repeatedly striking his head with his paws, diminishing his chance of rising again.

Watching Tormon lying listless on the ground, my last shred of optimism had been tattered, and so had Reva's only hope. The brave warriors fought fervently, but the enemy was powerful, predominant, and prepared.

Intoxicated by the arrogance of an easy victory, Duma headed toward his real target, expecting no other hurdle.

Though I didn't qualify as an obstacle in his way, let alone an opponent, there was no way this beast would lay hands on my son without crushing his mom first.

I desperately leaped after Duma like an eagle, knowing full well my prey was indeed my predator. Halfway up the stairs, I managed to grip my hands into the fur of his back, shaking him violently. In the next moment, I watched the massive monster lose his balance and fall down the stairs, crashing back into the living room.

A mother makes the finest warrior when protecting her child.

I wondered if I had proved the expression right.

The expression held firm to its ground, though I could not take the credit for Duma falling down the stairs. As when the temporary haze of confusion and misconception cleared, I noticed an angel, bright as light and white as milk. It was a wolf snarling atop the stairs. He had leaped up from the living room and landed straight in the hallway, forcing Duma thunderously off the stairs.

The wolf jumped down before Duma could recover from the fall, landing on his chest. The white beast squeezed Duma's neck between his jaws, cutting its sharp canines through his flesh. Duma roared in pain.

The black dog, Shuru, reappeared. He stood next to Tormon, who was still lying drained on the floor, making a slight effort to move. Apparently, Shuru had fetched this white angel, bringing a new wave of hope into the room.

I could recall Mom's mention of a wolf in one of her drishti encounters. The intriguing characters from her heavenly vision were causing mayhem in my living room.

Duma, who had looked invincible only moments ago, didn't stand a chance against the mighty wolf. Trampled and battered, he had lost the will to fight before losing the fight itself.

Such was the infectious energy from the wolf that Caesar had suddenly sprung back onto his feet, and Tormon picked himself up with great effort. Billa's confidence had lowered, and so had his speed.

The tables were turned—not to mention the one overturned, lying broken in the corner. My eyes lit up at the positive development, though my body was still frozen on the stairs, thanks to the hair-raising action around me.

The one-eared and two-eared daggers were receiving a third-degree beating. At one point, the wolf and Caesar thrust Duma and Billa so hard that they banged into each other, and Reva almost clapped with joy.

Duma sprang back to his feet faster than Billa and roared, angrily by lifting his forepaws. The wolf snarled back at him and howled louder at the ceiling.

That was it. Duma neither roared in response, nor did he make any attempt to charge again; instead, he retreated a few steps and turned around. Billa followed him.

The wolf and Caesar didn't chase them as they exited.

I kept gazing at the dark space behind the rectangular door frame, fearing they would barge in again with reinforcements. But perhaps the wolf's presence was too intimidating for the beasts to dare enter the house. Only the twins, Aaj and Kal, hopped back inside with a triumphant demeanor.

Tormon, Shuru, Aaj, Kal, and the wolf huddled around Caesar in what looked like a victorious bonhomie.

Suddenly, a chorus of noisy howling broke out in the backyard.

Chapter Ten

Months back, Viru had laughed off my two-year-long ordeal that I had shared with him, ascribing it to a figment of my imagination. I was relieved of the burden of keeping a secret from him, but would have felt better had Viru attached a little significance to the extraordinary revelation.

Over time, I had made peace with the fact that Viru would remain in the dark, despite having precious information the entire world lacked. I never imagined a day when the unknown actors of the undisclosed world would cross paths, giving Viru and Reva a glimpse into the impossible. This snippet of an unfathomable experience would forever change Viru's perception of me and the world.

As the Wolf and the D-Force surrounded Caesar in the middle of the messed-up living room, Viru, Reva, and Mom gathered around me near the stairs. Nobody spoke a word. We all stood there watching the cordiality among the good Samaritans.

Suddenly, howling sounds filled the temporary silence. I saw hundreds of tiny white bulbs glowing in the backyard. My eyes didn't take long to adjust to the dark outside, realizing that the seeming swarm of fireflies were the shining eyes of wolves, howling in chorus at the sky. I had not encountered wolves before; they also looked larger than I knew wolves to be.

Moments later, the white wolf and the dog army—Tormon, Shuru, Aaj, and Kal—walked out of the sliding glass door, mingling with the pack of howling wolves.

The noise was not limited to the backyard; there was

uproar at the front, too. I was curious to know but fearful of stepping forward. Then Caesar, as if reading my mind, plodded forward, and I gathered the courage to walk behind him with Viru, Reva, and Mom following me.

I had not seen such a sight before; nobody had, except perhaps Mom in one of her drishti visions.

The passage, street, sidewalks, gravel road—every inch of space outside my house—was filled with animals. Lions, tigers, elephants, giraffes, zebras, horses, rhinos, chimpanzees, bears, camels, and deer all huddled together. The trees were laden with innumerable birds and owls.

Bark, bellow, bleat, bray, chirrup, croak, growl, meow, moo, neigh, roar, snarl—all resonating sounds blended into one loud rumble.

I was speechless at the remarkable display of unity and strength. There was no sign of Duma, Billa, and other raging beasts grappling. Perhaps they had escaped upon seeing the flock of animals surrounding my house turn into a fortress.

The thunderous noise by the crowd dropped abruptly when they caught sight of Caesar at the door, as if their leader had taken center stage to speak.

"Dear God! What the hell? Are they going to attack us?" mumbled Viru, freaking out a little.

"They won't. They're the good guys. Our saviors," I returned calmly.

The leader did not deliver a barking speech, nor did the audience break into roaring applause. But I could sense Caesar's eyes addressing them and a thousand hearts seconding every unspoken word.

An overloaded, weak branch cracked and fell off, temporarily breaking the silent communication, and hundreds of birds fluttered off to a nearby tree, alighting on a firm branch. And then, in the blink of an eye, the sea of animals vanished—the street, the gravel road, and the sidewalks, abuzz seconds before, were now deserted.

I turned around. The wolf and the dog army had disappeared along with the pack of wolves from the backyard. Silence fell all over again, only broken by the random sounds of the distant shots being fired.

"What the hell happened? Where did everybody go?" Viru cried.

"I don't think they went anywhere. They are around. Just not visible."

Just then, a ringing startled us. Reva answered hesitantly, then handed the phone to me. "It's Elena. She's terrified."

"Elena!" I said, taking the phone from her. "Yes … yes. Calm down. They're gone. Yes, all of them. Yes, I checked. There're no animals outside. They left. Did they bang on your door as well? Ah, okay. Nothing to worry about now. We're safe. Come over with Britney."

The sounds of many sirens grew louder.

"Yeah, I hear that. Oh, did you call 911?" I walked back to the door. "Oh my, police vans."

A caravan of thirty or forty police vehicles followed by ambulances, loaded with glowing beacon lights rotating like mad dogs chasing their tails, cruised into the neighborhood, two or three stopping at each house. Looking at the number of cars, the entire area had probably called 911.

A car and a van pulled into our driveway, and a group of armed cops hopped out.

"Everything okay, ma'am?" one officer asked, looking around at the broken branch blocking the sidewalk, overturned flowerpots, displaced slates of the front yard steps, and the cracked front door.

"Yeah, officer. We're fine," I returned, unsure what the appropriate response was.

"Where are the animals?"

"They ran away."

"All of them? We saw a lot on our way, but the noise mainly came from this area."

"And the complaints," another officer said.

"Perhaps your sirens scared them off."

"Quite a ruckus happened here, looks like." The first officer stepped closer, peeking inside the topsy-turvy living room.

"Yes. Quite."

In the next moment, he pulled out his gun.

I sprang back to cover Caesar with my body. "No! Don't shoot! He's a pet dog."

"Step aside, ma'am!" he said sternly. The second cop also dashed forward with his gun.

"No! Promise me first that you won't shoot."

"We've gotta take him."

"Take him or take him down? What are you doing?" yelled Viru.

"Take him. Away."

"Where?"

"With us."

"But why? He's the one who saved us. He fought with the wild animals," Viru pleaded.

"That's why, sir. He might have caught rages. We must test him for the virus. We can't let him stay here; he needs to go to the hospital. Stand back, please."

Viru's change of heart toward Caesar was evident from his persistence. However, it was futile to argue with the cops, who were already confused by the sudden disappearance of the animals. We complied.

Caesar did not budge initially, until I whispered in his ear, "My dearest warrior, go with them, but stay with us."

With that, Caesar quietly walked into the cage. The cops gazed at me like I was some queer woman babbling nonsense.

I wished they knew their guns were mere toys that could not battle a force like him. And no cage could keep him against his will.

Refusing Viru's request to accompany Caesar, they slipped the cage into the trunk of their van. I would worry about the safety of an average dog taken away by the cops under such circumstances, but not the head of Rudram, who was protecting us and the entirety of Loka.

The cops helped temporarily fix the door and arranged

a security van to wait outside the house, then left with Caesar.

As soon as the cops left, a dreadful thought crossed my mind, and I hastened back inside. I found Ryan fast asleep in his room.

Running my fingers through his hair, I shook him gently. "Ryan! Wake up, honey!"

He didn't budge.

"I tried, Mom. He wouldn't wake up," said Reva, standing next to me. Viru gazed from the door.

I started to worry when Ryan remained motionless, yet breathing, despite several attempts to wake him.

"Is he okay, Mandy? What are you thinking?" Viru asked.

"Where's Mom? Mom!" I called.

Mom's weak and tired legs had by now also followed us to Ryan's room.

"What is it, Munni?"

"Mom, I know I forbade you to use drishti, but we must find Ryan."

"Find Ryan? Well, he's right here!" chimed Viru.

"Can you help, Mom?" I asked, ignoring Viru.

Mom nodded, so I opened the window, and Mom looked out.

"Any idea what your mom and grandma are up to?" Viru spoke softly to Reva.

"Not at all. Looking for Ryan's twin, I guess?"

A minute passed, and Mom shook her head.

"Try again, Ma. Focus on the lamp."

Some uneasy seconds passed, and suddenly, Mom's eyes widened.

"What's happening, Mandy?" Viru peeked out of the window. "It's a lonely street."

"Shhhh."

My shushing confused Viru more, but he at least stayed quiet this time.

About thirty seconds later, Mom's eyes went back to normal, and she said, "I saw Ryan, Munni. He was sitting."

"Under the lamp?"

"No, someplace else. Like a workshop or a factory. Wheels were rotating."

"Wheels?"

"Yes, large grinding wheels all around him."

"Grinding wheels? What grinding wheels?" Viru cut in.

"Did they look dangerous?" I asked.

"Yes. They looked like big crushing machines. Many machines," Mom returned.

"And Ryan? How was he sitting? Was he tied to something?"

"Can't tell. It lasted a few seconds, but he wasn't moving."

"Mandy! Mother!" Viru tried to get our attention, but I was too focused on what my mom was saying.

"I must find him. He could be in trouble," I mumbled.

"Mandy!" exclaimed Viru. "For God's sake, could you tell me what's going on? How can Ryan be sitting somewhere? He's sleeping here."

"Viru, had you paid attention when I told you everything, you would know," I returned, annoyed. "There's no time to explain now. Stay with Reva and Mom. I'll bring Ryan back soon."

"But…"

Without wasting a moment, I lay beside Ryan on his bed, praying the shortcut method Jack had disclosed two years ago during the crisis would still work.

While Viru, Reva, and Mom gazed at me in confusion, I slipped my arm under his head, supporting it like a pillow, and clasped his hand with mine.

An uneasy minute later, the silence broke into a sudden jerk, and the great fall began. It felt like the bed had entered an elevator dug deep into the earth. I didn't open my eyes, fearing returning to the origin or losing my way to the destination.

After descending what felt like infinite levels, the imaginary elevator finally halted.

I hoped to see a strikingly blue sky, as I had before. Instead, my eyes exposed me to the most familiar sight from countless sleepless nights and hopeless mornings that I could paint in my imagination at any time. The wooden-crafted ceiling, identical in all the bedrooms. I was still at my house on the bed beside Ryan, surrounded by everyone looking curiously at me.

"It's not working," I said to Viru, who was still just looking at me in bewilderment.

Removing my hand from under Ryan's head, I sat up. Everybody was still staring at the pillow I had shared with him.

"What is it? Do you see something here?" I asked, scanning the pillow closely.

Reva said something to Viru in a hoarse voice that seemed to come from miles away.

"What did you say, Revu?"

Viru returned with an equally deep and distant voice.

It was then I realized they could not see me. Or perhaps a better explanation, given the pillow gazing, was that they could see me lying on the bed but not sitting up. As shown in the movies, everybody observes the body while the soul separates and moves around.

I nervously wondered if I was dead. Did I goof up the transport procedure to Shloka and land in Parloka instead? But Parloka ought to be another place altogether. Why would I still be at my house? My baffled mind debated these questions.

I wandered around my house from room to room, aware of my feet touching the floor, like a toddler mindful of her first steps or a learner driver conscious of the foot pedals.

Heading downstairs, I could not find the slightest sign of the damage that had happened shortly before. The living room looked spotless, like the ones displayed in furniture showrooms. The house looked immaculate as if the years of living had not depreciated its quality. I wondered if I had time-traveled back to when we first moved into the house.

I opened the brand-new front door. It was still dark outside, but strangely bright at the same time. There was no security van or guard in the driveway. The neighboring houses, including Elena's, the street, the sidewalks, and the gravel road next to the street looked picture-perfect, as if everything had been constructed simultaneously and finished yesterday.

I walked out and crossed the street. Stepping onto the gravel road, I could not tell why, but an instinct made me head toward Mount Mary.

Walking past the oak tree, I noticed a black squirrel, identical to the one shot dead the other day, darting along a branch.

"Hello, Mandira!" A voice, neither hoarse nor distant, broke the calm of the very bright night.

"Jack! Is that you?" I exclaimed.

"Yes, my dear. Welcome to Jantar."

Chapter Eleven

Seeing Jack felt like a stranded person in a wild forest finding company, or someone on their deathbed getting a last-minute lifeline.

"I'm so glad to see you, Jack!" I smiled. "Did you say Jantar? How come? But wait! First things first"—my smile faded at the sudden thought—"I must find Ryan! I think he's in trouble. Do you know where he is?"

"Monsieur Ryan is fine. Relax. Take a deep breath," returned Jack, noticing my overwhelmed state of mind.

"Are you sure?"

"I'm a keeper, Mandira. It's either a yes or no from me. We don't use weak words like *maybe*, *perhaps*, *possibly*, or *think so*. He is fine. Come, I will take you to him. This way."

"This way? Did Ryan go to Mount Mary?"

"If you say so. To the Mount Mary of Jantar."

"How is this, Jantar? Didn't Jantar look like a magical land with white sand, gem rocks, et cetera?"

"Yes, that's another part of Jantar, down south. You saw a small park last time. Jantar is quite large. This is a secure keeper zone. Remember I told you about the spots where Loka coincides with Jantar?"

"Oh yeah, you told me about the common contact points! So, this place is Jantar coinciding with our street?"

"Yes."

"Unbelievable! This looks exactly like our place, only brand new. It might be a silly question, but I want to know the science behind it."

"Simple. Imagine a rough sphere wrapped in irregular foil. At many points, the foil comes into contact with the sphere."

"The irregular foil is Jantar, and the rough sphere is our Loka."

"Absolutely! See, you figured it out before I finished."

"Wow! Sounds like an analogy of a Ferrero Rocher chocolate wrapped in crumpled foil. I can't believe there is a carbon copy of my neighborhood in Jantar. Last time, you blew my mind by showing me the mysterious world. And now this spot where Jantar meets Loka. You make me feel like an insignificant human whenever I meet you."

"How can you be an insignificant human when you have known something the minners will not know in their lifetime?"

"If you say so. However, I don't know what to do with this knowledge. It's like a drop in the ocean of your mystery world. My life is a riddle I can't seem to solve. You pushed me into this maze, and now I can't find my way out."

"You think so? And I thought I was helping you find your way. It's all about perspective, Mandira. The way you see things."

"See things! See, that's the problem. I see things, my son and Mom see things, and now even my husband and daughter have seen things. We see things we aren't supposed to. Savage things, gunning for our blood."

"Well, quite obviously, Monsieur Ryan sees things. He was chosen for big things. You see things because the rulebook would not permit involving a minor in Kendram's affairs without his Mom's blessing. As an insignificant employee, I cannot speak for it, but I'm sure Kendram did not intend to involve anyone else from your family. Your Mom has a gift of drishti. And your husband and daughter would not see anything if it wasn't daggers' doing. I agree you were never supposed to see what you saw tonight."

"So you know we were almost killed by those beasts tonight?"

"Nobody can kill you on mon cher Caesar's watch."

"I know Caesar will die for us. There's no match for his loyalty. But the cops took him."

"Yes, I know." Jack smiled under his pointed nose.

"I was horrified to see Duma barge into my house. My house! And you say nobody can kill us. Were they all daggers?"

Jack nodded.

"But the other bear was Billa, if Mom was right. Wasn't he?"

"Yes."

"Isn't Billa a keeper? A responsible opposition leader of Rudram? Why would he attack us? Didn't you say only daggers were our enemies?"

"Well…"

"Caesar and the D-Force did everything they could, but we wouldn't be alive had that white wolf not saved us. Who is that Wolf? I haven't seen him before."

My head was like a pot of boiling water, with questions popping like bubbles, not knowing which one to address first, and Jack was a mind reader.

"Mandira, as always, you have many questions, and I will answer them all, but the answer to your most important question is in there."

Occupied by unanswered questions, my emotionally drained brain didn't realize we had arrived at the lake, and Jack was pointing toward the nearby chalet.

Humans believe the brain continues to be active during sleep, helping to restore physical, mental, and emotional health. I hoped the trip to the Mount Mary Hills of Jantar with Jack would do some healing as, technically, I was sleeping back at my house.

The chalet was a broad, old wooden house with a sloping roof and a flat, cemented front yard. When walking Caesar to the lake in the mornings, I would barely notice this old house except when I needed to use the restroom, the only utility I attached to its existence.

Jack and I entered Jantar's chalet from one of the multiple doors, where he claimed all the answers to my questions were present.

As expected, the huge hall stretched before us, almost empty other than the beautifully handcrafted benches in the middle. To our right opened the passage to the familiar spot that addressed nature's calls.

I followed Jack up the spiral stairs, which I had not taken much notice of previously. We arrived at a dimly lit reception area, where the only furniture was a white desk, an unoccupied black swivel chair, and a broad wooden cabinet.

Jack stared at the cabinet, perhaps spelling out a secret code in his mind, opening its doors automatically. Without a word, I stepped into the cabinet behind Jack.

In the next moment, I wobbled, feeling my feet slightly sinking into the floor, which had turned soft. At the same time, a white light flashed in my eyes.

When my eyes adjusted to the day-like brightness, I found myself in the open field of fine white sand that stretched as far as I could see under the bluest sky ever. Far away, where the sky and ground met, it appeared even bluer, as if a boy with a highlighter drew a line along a painted piece of paper to demarcate between two colors.

The image I had in mind from my previous visits to Jantar of countless sand particles glittering like powdered white gold finally came alive.

"Jack! How did we land here from the chalet?"

"The door we entered was a shortcut to one of the many design laboratories of Sir Lockman Keyhole."

"Lockman Keyhole? That locksmith? Didn't you tell me he designed high-tech locks and keys last time?"

"That was just a little introduction I gave you. Sir Keyhole is not a locksmith but a legend. He does much more than locks and keys."

"Okay, but where's the laboratory?"

"There." Jack pointed to a door frame hanging in the air a few inches above the ground. Neither a door was attached to the frame, nor any wall or structure to support it. I had left the words *normal* and *practical* at my house before heading for Jantar, so I quietly followed Jack to the empty door frame, curious but not surprised.

As soon as I stepped through the frame, I was greeted by the most pleasant surprise of the night, breathing heavily and wagging his tail vociferously. Yelping with joy, I hugged Caesar tight.

"Now I know why you chuckled when I talked about Caesar."

"Funny that you thought minner cops could take him away," Jack returned.

"Did he escape?"

"He doesn't need to. He's on a doctor's table right now in Loka. Those minners think he is unconscious from their drugs."

When my excitement settled but Caesar's playfulness did not, I noticed we were in an enormous dome. Large spherical containers, resting a few inches above the ground, were placed in a circle along the dome's walls equidistant to each other. Silver-plated pipes joined the white containers hanging in the air, making it a gigantic pearl necklace.

Many other high-tech-looking machines caught my attention, but my jaw dropped upon seeing the giant wheels rotating all over the dome.

Out of the hundreds of wheels, some were glowing brighter than others. Looking closely at one of them, I realized the wheels were not actually rotating. On a strip bordering the wheel's circumference, countless lions and tigers, looking like live toys, were walking steadily in a clockwise direction. This collective walking strangely gave the illusion of rotating wheels.

"This looks like the place Mom saw through her drishti. Ryan must be around here somewhere."

"Yes, he is. There." Jack pointed to a corner where Ryan sat on a black chair behind a white desk, like the one I saw on the chalet's first floor.

Anticipating my motherly instinct to run to my son, Jack quickly added, "Don't interrupt him just yet. Monsieur Ryan is busy doing a crucial task."

"Crucial task? What crucial task?" I returned, choking back tears. The separation of a long, exhausting night had intensified my longing to hold Ryan in my arms.

"He is altering the order of the world."

Jack waved his hand, and a transparent screen appeared before us with data bursting and flowing in an alien language.

I only partially understood the task after several curious questions and Jack's vague descriptions and usage of confusing unknown terms.

Each wheel logically represented the physical trip of an animal species from Loka to Shloka via Antar, Jantar, and Mantar and back. An individual starting from any point on the wheel's circumference completed the cycle when they returned to the respective point, or in other words, the total time they spent in the world of sleep.

Apparently, Ryan was working on a supercomputer with a transparent screen, trying to move some of the wheels. How he could operate such a complicated machine was beyond me. He had selected some stationary wheels, and that's why they glowed, depicting selective animal species. He was attempting a never-before seen feat to force them clockwise by altering their logic.

Since the animals moved clockwise with a fixed speed, Ryan's motive behind moving the wheels in the same direction, roughly by half their speed, was to delay their roundtrip time to return to the starting point. Since the relative speed of the animals with respect to the moving wheels became half their original speed, their total cycle time would double. In a nutshell, Ryan was trying to keep selective animal species in the sleep world for a longer time, almost double their average time, thus delaying their return to Loka.

Why is Ryan trying to change the order? I asked myself.

"Mandira, remember I told you about the corrupt

scientist Dr. Dhingra, who was responsible for infecting minners with the cursed water, elizer, which was originally invented to tame the daggers?" prompted Jack.

I nodded, encouraging him to continue.

"The contagious drug, elizer, which minners believe is a virus, rages, makes many animals hysterical and violent. They infect more animals by going on a biting spree and ultimately succumb to injuries, exhaustion, or the proliferation of drug agents inside their bodies.

"Elizer causes anxiety in minners that encourages high physical activity levels, leading to faster propagation of elizer agents in their bodies. The infected minners keep landing in Jantar to embark on the journey to Shloka, but the effect of the elizer creates a mental force each time, pulling them back to Loka, resulting in sleeplessness. So, they continue to be awake and delirious.

"After performing several experiments in the lab, Monsieur Ryan has found the solution to apply to the glowing wheels. There will be two benefits of setting these journey wheels in motion. Moving the wheels at the desired speed will aid the journey by creating a forward mental pull, offsetting the backward force by the elizer, thus keeping infected minners steady in Jantar.

"Secondly, the extended time taken to complete the cycle will help the bodies lying in Loka to heal, thereby slowing the propagation of elizer. They won't be aggressive anymore after waking from a long, relaxing sleep. No more biting would mean stopping the elizer from spreading to healthy minners. Also, the infected minner animals will gain time due to slower spread within their bodies. By then, the permanent cure will be on the way."

Amazed by my son's genius, I asked, "Why did Ryan choose some of the wheels?"

"He only chose the aggressive animal species, not all. They are mainly responsible for the widespread infection."

"Okay, for the species he chose, wouldn't setting the wheels in motion impact both the infected and non-infected animals?"

"Yes. But the only impact on non-infected animals will be a long, restful sleep."

"Don't tell me those animals will have long sleep hours for life."

"Not for life. Just this one time. Monsieur Ryan will program the algorithm so the wheels stop moving after one cycle. The sleep cycle will return to normal after that."

"Jack, seeing and hearing all this is making me nervous. What is Ryan doing sitting here? How does he even understand this alien technology? Shouldn't someone supervise him? Where's your Dr. Lockman Keyhole?"

"Relax, Mandira. Nothing here is alien for Monsieur Ryan. He has known this lab since he was a little boy. He would break the journey to Shloka and come running this way. Seeing his curiosity, Chief Joseph permitted him long ago to watch Dr. Keyhole work in his labs. Monsieur Ryan gained the chief's trust after he smartly managed the last crisis. You witnessed the standoff at Shloka's gates, didn't you? Then what? He was promoted from shadowing to assisting Dr. Keyhole. Mandira, you talk about supervision. What you don't know about Monsieur Ryan is that he's so good even Dr. Keyhole consults him sometimes from Parloka."

"Okay, even if Ryan knows what he's doing, shouldn't Dr. Keyhole be making these changes?"

"The cycle of wheels was designed by Dr. Patchman Sinkhole, legendary scientist and the genius architect behind the vision of Shloka. He was also the father of Lockman Keyhole. Keyhole is an expert who maintains it. He doesn't have any authority to manipulate the order. Only the chief has this authority, but you know his integrity doesn't allow him to alter the order. Still, he understands that sometimes, to fix the order, you need to break one. Monsieur Ryan has the blessings of the chief, an evolved brain, and no qualms to break the order for good. So, who do you think is the best person?"

Imagine you hear about a scientist named Lockman Keyhole, whose father was a visionary called Patchman Sinkhole, and the next generation would probably be named Ditchman Drillhole. You probably wonder if you are being subject to an elaborate joke performed by a bunch of pranksters. Then you see your son, declared unfit for technology by his schoolteachers, trusted by the creators of the supercomputers of the life cycle. In this context, the "Hole" family no longer seems buffoon-like.

Jack suspected the chief's estranged evil son, Hogdon, was the mastermind of the elizer menace aimed at destroying Loka. Hogdon's whereabouts remained unknown, and his role unestablished, but Jack believed he still controlled the daggers through secret orders.

The news of Ryan trying to save Loka again enraged Hogdon, who ordered his barbaric soldier Duma to launch an audacious attack on Ryan to stop him. That explained Duma's barging into my house along with his dagger kindreds.

Duma brainwashed malleable Billa by instigating fear of losing the opportunity to lead Rudram forever if Ryan became Kendram's chief. Alluding to the bond they shared, Duma insinuated that Ryan would declare Caesar the permanent leader of Rudram by bending the rules of Kendram. That was enough for power-hungry Billa to switch sides and join Duma.

Thankfully, most keeper-bears, otherwise loyal to him, didn't support Billa, and none of them joined him in the criminal act, or else it would have led to an all-out war between the keeper factions.

"Jack, you told me keepers could be invisible at their discretion. Then why did those daggers barge into my house, openly appearing when they could attack us invisibly also?"

"They could not," Jack returned. "Keepers or daggers can be invisible when they want to be, but if they wish to interact with a minner, verbally or physically, like attacking

Monsieur Ryan in this case, they must take on their minner form to do so. Keepers in invisible mode are harmless like the air in the atmosphere."

"Okay, and who was the good samaritan wolf that saved us and forced Duma and his accomplices to escape?"

"That's Assar, the wolf leader. He is a keeper, feared by enemies and revered by friends. Wolves are nomads. They don't join any factions, nor do they associate with Rudram. Assar was close to Meena, Caesar's mother, before she became Rudram's leader. When Duma, the leader of the keeper-bears, eliminated Meena, who was pregnant with Caesar and two other puppies, Assar was enraged. He chased him, but Duma managed to escape. Duma is Assar's biggest enemy, responsible for the loss that he considers personal. He and his wolves help Caesar and the D-Force when needed. Duma is terrified of a face-off with Assar. There is a … very … interesting …"

Suddenly, the glowing wheels started flickering terribly and Jack's voice became vague, interfered with by more faint voices in my head. The lab began to shake as if hit by an earthquake of magnitude ten, and I felt like I would tumble to the floor at any moment.

Seconds later, I opened my eyes and found myself surrounded by the enquiring faces of Viru, Reva, and Mom. Ryan was awake next to me.

I blurted the first thought that crossed my mind:

"Did Ryan finish the job successfully?"

WINTER

"Vengeance"

Chapter One

Whether filled with noise or vacuumed by silence, darkness is far from comforting. But the absence of light becomes menacing for a child alone in the middle of a graveyard. Add to this grass blades piercing out of the soil, getting bigger rapidly, like a fast-forwarded montage of grass growing over months condensed into seconds. The moon and the stars seemed to have disappeared, as if some wicked thief had stripped the sky of its embellishments.

A distant scream followed by several more in quick succession, inching ever closer, made the child shudder, perspiring in the winter night.

Topping off the blood-curdling scene were the dark shadows in motion visible on the thick grass, scattering the blades wherever they advanced.

It was hard to fathom why those visuals played before my eyes and in what way the present chilling circumstance connected to me. At times, it felt like I was that child.

The petrified child ran desperately from the creepy shadows that were seemingly closing in from all directions. The spreading roots of the trees, the ballooning shrubs, and the growing grass seemed to conspire to cling, curl, and squeeze the child.

When the legs surrendered, the worn-out child stumbled on the thicket and was grabbed by a pair of hands, unsure if they were going to protect or harm the poor thing.

Those hands looked remotely familiar. It seemed like I had seen those rough, dry-skinned hands before, but when and where, I could not tell. The familiarity was such that they looked like my own hands, only more wrinkled and sundried.

I woke up dripping with sweat and wondered again why I kept seeing this dream. The beautiful, snow-laden locales filled with Christmas trees and lights switched to horrifying visuals of a child in a graveyard with the instantaneity of changing a TV channel.

Like before, my mind did not present me with any logical explanation for this. Viru had already left with Caesar for a walk, though it was still dark outside due to the long winter nights. So I lay in bed, spinning my thoughts.

I often thought about that fateful night when the devil Duma and his accomplices had attacked us, then when I slept my way to Jantar and witnessed Ryan's unprecedented experiment, and later abruptly woke up after he pushed the execute button.

I discovered the following day that all the minners around the globe which had been sleeping had suffered a forced awakening around that time.

The news of our family mysteriously escaping unscathed despite being attacked by dozens of savage animals supposedly infected by rages became a subject of nationwide attention. Accounts of thousands of animals appearing briefly in the Saint Thomas neighborhood of Abbynton went viral.

Two days later, some even bigger news delighted me immensely. The violent animals causing havoc around the world had become dormant and drowsy. The incidents of rages-infected animal attacks reduced drastically. I was on cloud nine after realizing that Ryan's attempt to save the world by temporarily altering the sleep cycle of animals had produced the desired result.

Theories cropped up to explain this pleasant occurrence of ruthless animals turned restful. Some said the extreme exhaustion composed them. Others claimed that sleep eventually caught up despite the insomniac nature of the virus. The religious bodies believed that the Gods had shown mercy on humans. After noticing the easing off of the virus reproduction in the infected animals, scientists stated that the virus had mutated to a less aggressive form. However, they struggled to explain what led to this overnight transformation.

Ten days later, it rained. Not just a brief local rain. It rained cats and dogs for days and nights. The gods of showers poured non-stop on the entire world for three days. The earth became a sponge ball soaked in a bucket of water.

Days after the deluge, another news story swept the world. The rages virus had mysteriously vanished among the already hibernating animals.

Scientists around the world were rattled, grappling to explain one phenomenon after another.

Jack had told me that manipulating the cycle of the wheels of Jantar would tame the aggressive animal species, but not cure them. It occurred to me that the unusual rain for days across the globe healed the infected animals. Perhaps the keeper scientists had made a breakthrough against elizer; while the bad elements had spread elizer by contaminating water, the good folks countered by circulating anti-elizer through rainwater. Drinking medicated water restored the animals' health.

I was not the only one to crack the code of the mysterious cure; the pharmaceutical companies did too, claiming they used a bunch of compounds from natural resources to invent vaccines. It was not hard to guess that the only natural resource used was rainwater.

To avoid exceptional attention on us after the dreadful night, we stuck to a simple narrative: Two wild bears barged into our house and caused havoc before being driven out by our brave dog.

The chief investigating officer, Peter Wilkinson, remained suspicious about our connection with extraordinary dogs. He could not fathom a miraculous rescue in the family yet again by another dog after Reva's horrifying Billaria adventure. Caesar's examination report puzzled him, as it revealed several external injuries but no transmission of the rages virus from supposedly infected bears. Officer Wilkinson had no clue they were not wild animals infected by rages, but vile daggers infested by rage.

It took us two weeks of trouble to finally gain back Caesar's custody after he was subjected to rounds of curious testing.

Given the circumstances, the house insurance agencies had almost stopped covering damages caused by animals. However, because of the high visibility of the case, they agreed to partially cover the damages.

Two months had passed since the nightmarish night. The wild animals in the wilderness were composed, and the domesticated animals were cozy in their houses.

The world was charming again in a mundane way, and people were back to their humdrum lives. Except for two still over excited people—Viru and Reva. They had heard all my otherworldly anecdotes of the past two years almost five times, with all characters learned by heart, but their curiosity would not fizzle out.

Since Ryan's birth, Viru had given me undivided attention only occasionally. I could not blame him entirely, as I had drowned myself in worrying about Ryan's progress, and all I talked about was him. Discussing any other topic with Viru would seem trivial to me.

Over the years, Viru formed a habit of monotonously nodding when I spoke. I could tell he wasn't listening but continued as I had to get things off of my chest, even if it meant talking to a robot. And when the robot occasionally responded, I knew he was partly listening to find fodder for his jokes.

Lately, Viru paid exceptional attention when I talked, when I was about to speak, and even when I did not utter a word. I could, at times, sense him randomly gazing at me and grinning when caught. It felt like my courtship period with Viru had returned.

Reva treated me like a rockstar. Now that the cat was out of the bag, she no longer begrudged me for being secretive.

Her new favorite subject had outweighed the ones from school, and she would spend hours discussing with her fellow student (Dad), and clarifying her doubts with her teacher (me). The spark in her eyes that had been missing for months returned. Perhaps the big revelation had helped her see Tim's passing in a new light and taught her to no longer hold herself responsible. I hoped she would finally move on from her tacit grief.

Viru also had a change of heart for Caesar. He would wake up ahead of time to walk Caesar to the Mount Mary Hills and refused when I occasionally offered help. He would not rush him back to the house like before, even if he became late for the office as a result.

He didn't complain about his conduct either. On the contrary, Viru would proudly share how Tulip, the Cinderella of dogs he previously considered out of Caesar's league, found him irresistible and how it upset Mrs. Walker.

Caesar showed neither aggression nor any ludicrousness toward Tulip, like before. Mrs. Walker, who once considered Caesar unworthy of even sniffing Tulip's behind, was bemused by his newfound attitude and Tulip's docility around him. Caesar had become a known figure in the neighborhood for the daredevilry he displayed against dangerous bears, though it was perhaps still not enough in the eyes of Mrs. Walker for her self-professed daughter, Tulip.

Viru would wonder why Mrs. Walker fancied some imaginary prince for her daughter, who had already set eyes on the Rockstar King of Rudram. With the missing Caesar-deprecating humor, Mrs. Walker no longer found Viru funny.

Although Mom had not ceased to worry about things in general, her demeanor seemed relatively relaxed lately. Her drishti did not present her with much action that could raise concern like before. She would now find Caesar under the lamppost hanging out with his buddies Tormon, Shuru, Aaj, and Kal, or occasionally holding silent meetings with a few amiable-looking keeper animals, as opposed to the mass meetings she had witnessed before. Her gifted vision would no longer spot Ryan accompanying Caesar in Jantar's replica of Saint Thomas Street, seemingly indicative of restored normalcy. She was now planning to return to India.

Ryan, my unsung hero who saved the world yet again, continued to live a mundane, nobody life, devalued and denigrated by his peers, teachers, and therapists. To them, he was different, incapable of blending with societal norms. One could not blame them as their comprehension of capability was guided by preset standards and unawareness of the otherworldly existence.

Those who matter do not judge you; those who do should not matter to you.

I was delighted that the two who mattered most were proud of Ryan. The love for Ryan in the eyes of Viru and Reva had blossomed as affection blended with respect. They would discuss how greatness was always bound to kiss Ryan's feet and how they had foreseen it long before the biggest revelation of their lives. They would support their claim of noticing his extraordinariness by citing instances they had not mentioned before.

Viru would spring a step further, attributing the credit to his self-proclaimed exemplary genes. Reva, for a change, would not support her dad's unsolicited claim, arguing it had to be Mom's, if genes indeed played a role. To her, Mom and Grandma were the actual sources.

Reva was intrigued by her brother's hidden genius and tried to initiate conversations. However, his sister's bantering and curious questions would not draw a response or reaction from Ryan. He acted as if he was oblivious to the feats he performed in the magical world of sleep.

Viru and Reva would barely acknowledge the risks involved with the great powers. Viru would say, "Superman and his family cannot waste time worrying about their safety as they have more significant missions to accomplish." With such examples, he would deliberately tag himself with Ryan as if he also had a role in the grand scheme.

The gossip in the neighborhood doing rounds about me had taken various shapes and forms over the last two months. The latest one Reva overheard from a bunch of enthusiastic kids was that the Indian lady performed black magic to attract wild animals into the neighborhood.

I did not care much about anyone's perceptions of me, except Elena's, whose aloofness bothered me. After the fateful night, she became reserved and never asked me anything. Our communication had reduced to mere salutations or occasionally transactional interactions.

Of all the things, the pensive sadness visible through Ryan's shining eyes bothered me the most. Others would not notice, but when had a mom's radar of care missed her child's unexpressed woes?

Ryan would not speak of it, but I had a fair idea. Ryan's emotions were like coconut water shielded by the covered kernel, never overflowing or spilling. The only person capable of jiggling water inside the nut was Britney. Her affinity for Ted and indifference toward him hurt Ryan.

Britney had been obsessed with Ryan when she was a little girl. Every afternoon, she would walk up to Mrs. Bergenza's house and wait for Ryan. When she spotted his school bus, she would barge into my house and excitedly announce with her endearing lisp, "Mithes Thelma, Lyan hath come."

She would then stand at the door and provide me with a spirited running commentary of the bus stopping at two other houses, followed by Ryan getting off with Reva at our stop. I would deliberately stay inside to acknowledge her funny yet adorable status updates.

She would then join Ryan and Reva for their afternoon snacks, missing no opportunity to engage Ryan in her non-stop prattle until her mom sought her. Ryan, as usual, would not respond, but his aloofness barely discouraged Britney.

I hoped Ryan would change one day, and never thought time could affect any change in Britney. But life would not be painful enough had there been a guarantee attached to fulfilling our wishes. Contrary to my expectations, Ryan remained reclusive, and Britney became evasive.

Britney could touch a chord within Ryan that I didn't know existed. As Ryan's family, including Caesar, we were always there to support and care for his needs, but without Britney, he was like a fish alone in an aquarium.

Chapter Two

"How about the golden one?"

"The golden one?"

"Yes, the new one I got you on your birthday. Remember? It has a neck scarf and those black zig zag laces you love so much."

"Oh, that gold dress? Do you realize when you bought it? Before Ryan was born. You call a twelve or thirteen year old dress a new one? What would you call an old dress, then? The romper Mom bought me when I was born?"

"See, you don't like my jokes but make similar yourself. Couples who live together joke alike. Thanks to me, your standard of making jokes is rising."

"Viru, it's 'the families that eat together, stay together.' Don't twist a saying as per your convenience. And my standard would be falling, not rising, if I were joking like you."

"Joking once a month doesn't make you funnier, Mandy. You should see how Tom and Jerry crack up at my jokes every morning. They don't call me Fun Viren for nothing. Do you know what Jerry said the other day? 'We could not have survived in this company without your jokes.' Being funny is an art, and consistency is the key to nurturing any art."

"Alright, Mr. Artist. Save your comedy for them. By the way, you joined this company two years ago; they've been there for ages. How did Tom and Jerry survive before without you? By chasing each other? Who nurtured this art form for them?"

"Another joke within a minute? I tell you, Mandy, I nurture humor not only at work but also at home."

"Viru, can we stick to the dress selection, please? I don't know if the golden dress fits me anymore."

At the mere mention of his sense of humor, Viru could lose focus on any subject at hand, however pressing. The topic of discussion was picking an appropriate outfit for our anniversary outing, and Viru contributed by suggesting the oldest present he had given me.

Every year, we went out for a family dinner, but this time, Reva had insisted we go without them, like a dinner date. The idea of going out with my dated date seemed outdated initially. All these years, it never occurred to me that Viru and I could use an occasion by ourselves. The idea of celebration to me was another effort to ensure our children had fun.

After rummaging through my inadequate wardrobe with Reva for almost an hour, trying to match one thing with another, we ended up picking Viru's golden dress and bore the pain of seeing a smug expression on his face.

I readily agreed to Reva's recommendation, outrightly rejecting Viru's restaurant suggestion despite liking it better. I would not give Viru another opportunity to gloat over his smart choice-making, and certainly not on the same day.

Looking dapper in a purple satin shirt and black trousers, Viru drove downtown. We got lucky with parking on the street near our restaurant as the car occupying the space moved out seconds before.

The courteous hostess showed us the spot Viru had reserved by the window with the twilight view of the hustle and bustle of the cold street.

The restaurant was sparsely occupied. In front of me were a beaming elderly couple and a giggling family of four, and to the left was a metal reserved sign sitting on the tabletop.

A waiter wearing a smile and a bright shirt greeted us and lit up upon seeing Viru.

"Viren!"

"Simon!"

"Shut up!"

"You shut up!"

"Why are you here?"

"I work here!"

"Do you? I didn't know you guys worked undercover, too."

Simon chuckled. "No, no. Surd & Lay fired my agency. I was on the bench for a few days. My contract was ending, so I changed jobs."

Surd & Lay Limited was Viru's previous company that had sacked him, too.

"Wow. Wonder why they still call it Surd & Lay. Absurd & Lay-offs sounds more accurate," said Viru.

Simon laughed again, noticing me only because my reaction to Viru's joke lacked intensity.

As if reunited with a long-lost brother at a fair, Viru had almost forgotten me. He finally made an introduction:

"Meet my wife, Mandira. Mandy, this is Simon, my colleague and friend. He worked with me at Surd & Lay in the security department."

"This man cracks me up every time. I wonder how you live with him."

"Well, I try," I returned.

Seeing Viru's excitement, I nodded my ascent to Simon's recommended wine, and he stepped into the bar area to fetch it.

Viru enthusiastically shared how he used to have the security guard, Simon, in splits when swiping his ID card upon entering and exiting the office by making beep sounds from his mouth. When I told him no wonder Surd & Lay fired them both, Viru chuckled.

Simon kept paying brief visits, and Viru shared more anecdotes about Simon and Surd & Lay. I wished I had not agreed to Reva's choice of restaurant and stuck to Viru's instead.

Luckily, their bonhomie was cut short when Simon got busy by the arrival of a large group clad in formal wear, seemingly gathered for a business dinner.

Later, when Simon passed our table, Viru joked, "They must be from Surd & Lay. Put hot chilies and extra spices in their food."

I turned to what Viru often called my favorite game of guessing what our kids must be doing at that moment.

Viru interrupted, "Mandy, our kids are having fun with their grandma. We should talk about ourselves, about *you*, for a change."

"What about me?" I curled my brows, observing Viru's transition from trivial chatter with Simon to assuming a grave pose as if expressing a premeditated thought.

"Yes, you. About your dream."

"My dream? What dream? How do you know?" I asked, wondering when I had spoken about my scary graveyard dream.

"You worked for it. Cleared exams. Attended courses and that shadowing program. That's how I know."

I realized Viru was talking about my dream of becoming a doctor.

"Oh, I see. That chapter is closed, Viru," I returned sadly. "You know my answer. Why do you keep bringing it up? Some dreams remain dreams."

"Mandy, all dreams remain dreams until you act on them. You must never stop chasing your dreams."

"Chasing my dreams! Even if it's at the cost of a tiger chasing my daughter?"

"What does that mean?"

"You don't know what that means? My obsession with that shadowing program, which I failed by the way, almost got Reva killed. Had I been careful, I could have prevented that mishap."

"How could you have prevented it?"

"By stopping Reva from going to that jungle. I could have met Tim's friends or talked to them before permitting Reva. But I did not. My gut feeling warned me then, but I ignored it. My ambition had blinded me."

"Mandy, I told you before, it wasn't your fault. Our daughter is grown up. You can't interview every person before she meets them."

"I can, and I will. How can you say that when you know what we're dealing with? No, Viru; whenever I get selfish, my children suffer the consequences."

"Okay."

"What do you mean, 'okay'? What do you want me to do?"

"Nothing. Leave it. Don't apply for med school."

"Viru, I told you I can't. Ryan and Reva are my priority."

"I understand. That's fine."

"Moreover, I failed that shadowing program."

"You failed because of a rigged evaluation."

"Yes, but in the end, only the result matters. They won't select me. Applying is a waste of time and energy."

"It's okay," Viru replied coldly, slurping his creamy mushroom soup—Simon's recommendation. I made mouth-watering soups at home, but he would not slurp once.

I hated Viru for doing that. He always stirred up the logs to fan the dying fire. He would broach a topic out of nowhere and abruptly drop the conversation in the middle before I could finish my reasoning. I had more to add to my convincing argument, although I was not sure if I was trying to convince him or myself.

Simon brought a cake adorned with a sparkling candle to the elderly couple's table, and the gentleman, young at heart, joined by the strangers in the restaurant, sang happy birthday to his beaming lady.

Contrasting with the dazzling lights on the street marking the advent season, we had a fine dinner under the soft-lit ambient lights. Viru looked overly satiated after devouring Simon's choice of main course, which he claimed was the best in Abbynton, and reciprocated with a generous tip supplemented by his ludicrous jokes.

Back home, two things from the restaurant stayed with me: the flavor of strawberry cream pie in my mouth, and the subject of Viru's unfinished discussion in my head. I didn't mind the former; still, my mint-flavored toothpaste eliminated the last traces of the dessert from my tongue. I just wished bedtime brushing could also wash out the quandary that Viru, now snoring on the bed, had seeded in my mind.

Unable to sleep, I opened my laptop. One webpage led to another, and before I realized it, I had started filling out my application for medical school.

Despite being out of touch for months, writing a profile summary and updating my resume and other documents came naturally to me. Like a chunk of butter melting on a warm pot of my triggered subconscious, the details hitherto buried flowed onto the form.

I would have finished my application in one sitting had I not been distracted by movement in the hallway. I moved to the door, thinking perhaps Mom, seeing the light on, was heading upstairs to check on me.

"Ryan! You're awake?" I exclaimed in surprise. I could expect anyone but Ryan to stand outside my door at midnight. I checked my voice and asked softly, "What happened, honey? Are you alright? Come in."

Ryan's weary eyes, sweating forehead, and glum face scared me.

"What's the matter, Ryan? Did something wake you up?"

Ryan shook his head, enhancing my anxiety. Nothing could terrify me more than watching him suffer silently.

"Then what is it? Look, no matter what happens, I'm here for you. Nobody can hurt you. But you must tell me. I can't help you if you don't."

Fighting back tears, Ryan opened his mouth with an effort, "Mom."

"Yes, tell me, dear."

"I can't sleep."

"You can't sleep? I see. Do you know why that is? Is there anything bothering—"

"I can't sleep, Mom." Ryan began to sob uncontrollably.

"Okay, okay." I embraced Ryan, "So what if you can't sleep? Look at me. I can't sleep most nights. I couldn't sleep tonight either. It's no big deal. You'll be fine, Ryan."

Reva appeared at the door. "What's wrong, Mom? Ryan!"

"Shh, speak softly, Revu."

"What's wrong?" Reva whispered. "Why is he awake? Is he crying?"

"He can't sleep."

"He can't? But he always sleeps!"

"It happens sometimes. You go back to sleep. I'll take care of him. Come, honey. Sleep here, with me and your dad."

As I lay holding Ryan in my arms, Viru slightly opened his eyes and mouth as if to speak, but went back to sleep in the next moment.

I told Reva it happens, but I had never expected it to happen in Ryan's case. In the last eleven years, he'd had trouble waking up, rather than sleeping. Ryan would sleep within no time on anything that supported his back and head, let alone his bed, which was his most precious possession. He loved his sleep so much that, given a chance, he would reside in that world forever. This was the first time he had woken up by himself at nighttime.

What in Loka could keep Ryan away from his fondness for sleep? I wondered.

Could it be his fondness for Britney? She was the only person capable of making Ryan miserable, and knowingly or inadvertently, she was doing that.

I considered that I had been naive in believing the opposites attract theory. My love for my loner son had deluded me into thinking that the talker, Britney, would find a permanent friend in the listener, Ryan. I had thought that another talker—Ted—would not interest her because then who would listen?

We keep justifying the possibility of a desired outcome of the things we can't control. These things, put together, constitute destiny. How can I tell who someone will end up with when I could not have said the same for me twenty years back? Now, I am next to this man in hibernation, who was persuading me this evening to reflect on my ambition, and I fell for it. How can I pursue my dreams when my son cannot pursue sleep?

What does Viru know about Ryan's pain? Reva came to see from the other room, but mister funny man didn't even wake up. I will not let him distract me again.

As much as I dread it, some people do end up alone. But not my son. He is not alone. He has me, his mom.

Lost in thought, I allowed the mother in me to take charge, once again forcing my aspirations into the backseat.

Chapter Three

Sleep is a state of suspended consciousness of the surroundings. In sleep, not only are living things—or minners, in Jack's queer terminology—oblivious to the activity in Loka, but also to their predefined round trip to Shloka.

In this magnificent arrangement, the almighty had awarded the gift of exception to my son. Ryan would make a conscious journey to Shloka, aware of the mystical world, capable of wandering and venturing out at will. Perhaps this rare power captured his fascination for sleep.

But nothing is more powerful than circumstances that can disenchant us even from our everlasting obsessions. He would not share with me, or perhaps did not realize himself, but I knew Britney's indifference was depriving him of his sleep.

Last night, Ryan clung to my arms like a vine wrapped around the boughs of a tree. It took him a long time before he finally slept, to my great relief. Seeing him on our bed in the morning, Viru also found it odd knowing Ryan had trouble sleeping last night.

Relieved by the noticeable peace on his face despite his closed eyes moving randomly, I decided to let him sleep and skip school.

What is the point in waking him? I asked myself. *The only one that could interest him is the cause of his pain.*

I resented this heartless world, Loka.

I wondered if Ryan was better off before, when he lacked these worldly emotions. Or perhaps he never lacked them, only now he could no longer hold them inside.

After Viru went to work, Reva went to school, and

Caesar went to my bed to join his sleeping buddy, Mom and I reminisced on my childhood days over tea. She would be taking her return trip to India in a week after her most extended stay with me post-marriage. Still, we hadn't had a chance to take a trip down memory lane.

We laughed, remembering my obsession with collecting tiny rocks and pebbles when I was little. I would bring rocks from every place we visited and put them in plastic jars. I had four or five of them in my room full of colorful stones.

Upon returning from his work trips, my dad could afford to forget candies, but not pebbles for me. Whenever he did, he stealthily picked up one rock from outside our house, wrapped it in gift paper, and presented it to me by cleverly taking it out of his work briefcase.

Mom recollected how excitedly I would tell her, "Mom, see, that place has rocks just like we have here!"

My older brothers Ajay and Arjun would tease me, declaring Dad did not bring me anything from his trips. He took rocks from my other jars and gave them back to me in gift paper.

We recalled the summer holidays we spent at my maternal grandma's—some of my best childhood memories.

Ajay and Arjun loved to play cricket on Grandma's sprawling lawn. A lot of effort went into making their ball from scratch. My brothers would borrow Grandma's old clothes and cut them into thin laces. They would then roll one lace over the other as tightly as possible and ask Mom to feel the firmness of the round mass in the making.

Mom's approval at the manufacturing stage was vital for them to move to the next step: wrapping it in Grandma's old socks and sewing it. Thus, household production would yield a product with only labor and no capital, thanks to two over-enthused manufacturers, a disinterested quality checker, and a generous supplier.

Being little and almost useless, they would exclude me from their play. Frustrated, I would run away with their precious homemade treasure.

Chased by my angry brothers for stealing the ball made of Grandma's worn-out clothes, I would find refuge in the clothes worn by her. She would cover my head with the loose end of the long waistcoat she wore and wrap her arms around my back. I felt safe holding on to her belly.

"She loved you very much," said Mom. "'This girl is just like me,' she would say. Turns out she was right. You resemble her: same eyes, same nose. Even your fingers are supple like hers. She also had a long thumb," Mom told me, holding my hand.

When the wave of nostalgia had swept over us, Mom went to her room to rest, and I stood by the living room window, smiling as if looking out at my childhood.

I noticed Britney, clad in a warm jacket and fur cap, on the street, walking toward our house. When I didn't hear a knock on the door, I curiously grabbed my stole and opened the front door. Britney had entered her house. A minute later, she came out, now locking her door.

"What's up, Britney?"

"Hey, Mrs. Sharma," Britney returned in a raspy voice.

"Everything okay? Why aren't you at school?"

"Taking a sick day. I caught a cold last night."

"Ah, are you okay?"

"Yes, I took Tylenol. Getting better, but my throat hurts."

"Where are you going?"

"Ted's place."

"Is Ted at home too?"

"No, he's at school. His Mom's there."

"Hmm. You can come here if you like. I can make hot soup for you. Great for colds and sore throats."

"That's okay, Mrs. Sharma. Mom already talked to Ted's Mom. She told me to go to her."

Seeing Britney going to Debra's place hurt my feelings. I knew Elena was acting cold lately, but she had never assigned anyone other than me to watch over Britney in her absence.

Our friendship had had its lows and highs, but had never come to this. It felt like a selfless responsibility I shouldered for years had become a thankless deed. Since she was little, Britney had taken our place as an extension of her house. I could not tell if it was indeed Elena or if Britney was no longer interested in visiting Ryan's house.

An hour later, my fractured ego was bandaged when Britney knocked at my door and said, "Mrs. Sharma? Hot soup will do."

Suddenly, the kitchen became my stage, and taking out my best spices and the ingredients for chicken soup gave me an adrenaline rush. I made two large bowls of soup, childishly believing it would keep Britney from Debra all day.

What does Debra know about babysitting? I thought. *She's never raised a girl.*

The next moment, I checked this spiteful thought with my next one. Debra had known something I would not wish upon an enemy, let alone a mother—the loss of her offspring. I hoped our relationship could normalize one of these days.

I don't eat chicken, but I was confident my soup was better than the mushroom soup that Viru had guzzled last night, to which he had commended Simon for his recommendation and presentation.

Britney's validation seconded my thought. "This is yum, Mrs. Sharma," she said.

"I have more. Take as much as you want. It clears congestion and relieves throat pain."

"Thanks, but this is enough for me. I must go to Ted's Mom. I told her I'd be back soon."

As much as I was offended and wanted to find out the truth, I could not muster the courage to ask the girl if it was her wish or her mom's will to replace me with Debra. Though Britney had kept my respect by sparing a fraction of her time for me, she didn't seem apologetic about awarding a larger share to Debra.

Broaching another topic felt like meddling with a child's personal choice, but thanks to Britney's tight schedule, little room was left to evaluate moral principles.

"Britney, honey, why don't you talk to Ryan anymore?"

"Ryan? I talk to him. Why do you ask?"

"Because I don't see you play anymore."

"We play, Mrs. Sharma."

"Listen, you are a big girl," I said, feeling short of words, "and growing up, we make new friends and sometimes forget our old friends. I know it's not my place to tell you who to make friends with and which friends to keep, it's just that Ryan finds it hard to adapt to change. You two were close, and now I hardly see you around. Ryan is fond of you, but now he feels ignored."

"Did Ryan tell you that?"

"That he feels ignored?"

"No, that he is fond of me. And, yes, that other one, too."

"No, he told me nothing, but I can tell. He doesn't share much. You know him."

"That's it. That was exactly my problem."

"What was your problem?"

"He was not sharing anything with me."

"Yes, well, he can't express himself like you."

"But I kept asking him, and he wouldn't tell me. I told him I would not talk to him if he kept hiding things from me, but he didn't listen. So I became upset and stopped talking."

"Wait, what were you asking him? What was he hiding from you?"

"A secret."

"What secret?"

"A secret about his project."

"What project? Did he receive a project from school? He didn't tell me that."

223

"Not school. Ryan doesn't like school projects. It was a huge project. I call it Project Fix."

"Honey, I think you lost me. What is Project Fix?"

"Okay, it's hard to explain. It's about the virus."

"The virus?"

"The rages virus. Ryan helped to fix it. He worked many nights on the project to calm everything down."

I was stumped, and my mind refused to believe what Britney had just said. Did she know about Ryan? And more bafflingly, did Ryan tell her something?

"Could you elaborate? What do you know? How did Ryan fix the virus?"

"He made animals sleep for a long time. That calmed them and slowed the virus. It's a complex thing with a lot of testing required. Ryan did all this on a high-tech computer."

"High-tech computer? Where's this computer?"

"He changed sleep. So, the computer will be in the sleep," returned Britney, as if the answer was obvious.

"Did Ryan tell you all this?"

"Yes, only after he finished Project Fix. He didn't tell me before, even though I asked. I stopped talking to him because he broke our pact."

"What pact?"

"We made a pact to tell each other our secrets. I used to tell Ryan everything, but he didn't do the same. But one day, he told me how he remembers everything from his sleep. He travels to the prettiest places."

"Did you believe him?"

"Of course, I did. Ryan either speaks the truth or does not speak at all," said Britney, perplexing me with her clarity of mind. "Then he would tell me about his sleep activities every day. It was so cool. Then he stopped talking about sleep, said he was working on a project, and couldn't tell me anything. It was Project Fix."

The realization struck me that though I had first-hand experience of the conscious journey of the sleep world,

Britney managed to access the treasure of Ryan's nightly adventures, something I had not. The idea of Ryan choosing Britney over me for sharing made me envy her and feel displeased with him. But I would still give Britney credit for unquestioningly trusting Ryan.

"Okay, so you were upset with him for not telling. Then, he told you about everything, including Project Fix. What now? Why don't you talk to him like before?"

"Because I made a mistake. I told Mom, and she was not happy. She thinks Ryan makes up stories. She said, 'How can you believe in such fantasies?' Then I made another mistake: I tried to convince her. She told me I couldn't talk to Ryan anymore. So, I have no choice. Now, I only talk to him secretly."

"You do? When?"

"Can't tell you that. It's our secret."

"Oh, so this you can't tell me? Okay, tell me this: Your Mom didn't believe you, but you are still telling me all of this. What made you think I would believe you?"

"Because you know about it. Ryan told me that you know more than him."

Talking to Britney was like sitting on a rollercoaster of revelation, cruising through the twists and turns of emotions. The facets of human behavior have complex dichotomies. I always wanted Britney to get close to Ryan but didn't expect—or perhaps wish—Ryan to reciprocate equally. His reciprocation always felt like an exclusive right reserved for me.

Knowing all was well between Ryan and Britney was a relief, but a fresh question bothered me.

Perhaps she knows the answer, since she already knows so much, I thought.

"If you two are talking and sharing, why does Ryan look depressed? He had a hard time sleeping last night."

"He did?"

"Yes, that's why I let him sleep this morning."

"What do you mean? Did he wake up late?"

"No, he's still sleeping now."

"What? Where?"

"In my room."

"Why is he still sleeping? Did you try waking him?" asked Britney nervously.

"No, but why? What happened? Are you alright?"

"Mrs. Sharma, you need to wake him. Now. He should not be sleeping so late," uttered Britney with panic as she dropped her spoon in the leftover soup and hurriedly rose from her chair.

Chapter Four

Britney was blessed with two remarkable traits: being chatty and carefree. Ted was the only other kid who could compete with her in the talkative department. However, she was the undisputed queen of nonchalance. I barely ever saw any form of anxiety overcome her relaxed demeanor. Therefore, watching her rattle over Ryan's oversleeping—his favorite pastime known to the entire neighborhood—bemused me.

"Mrs. Sharma, you should wake him," she said anxiously.

"Relax, Britney. I will wake him. First, you sit down, honey. Here, drink some water and talk to me."

Sinking back into her chair, Britney gulped the glass of water in one breath.

"Feel better?" I asked, and Britney nodded. "Okay, tell me now. Why do you think Ryan should not be sleeping?"

"Because it's not safe."

"Safe? For who?"

"For him."

"But why? What's the problem?"

"The problem is, we don't know where he is. He can get lost."

"He can get lost," I repeated to absorb the vague reply. "In his sleep?"

"Yes."

"Britney, I believe you know by now that we all take a trip in our sleep. Everyone travels to the same place and comes back. Ryan will be doing the same."

"What if it gets hard for him to find his way back in his sleep?"

"Of all the people, if anyone knows the way well, it's

him. We take a set path without realizing or remembering it afterward, but Ryan consciously knows one hundred ways back and forth. I don't think that's a reason to worry."

"No, Mrs. Sharma, you don't understand. I know Ryan knows the path well, but there's one place he ends up where he gets lost. He doesn't know what to do and where to go. He told me this."

"He told you that? That he gets lost and can't find the way?"

"Yes. You asked me why Ryan is depressed, that's why."

"Okay, Britney. Tell me what Ryan told you. What happens? What's this place like? Where is it?"

"I don't know where it is. Ryan doesn't tell me much. But he's terrified of this place. It's a dark place. He says everything speaks."

"Everything? Do you mean every*one* speaks? Everyone who?"

"Not everyone. Everything speaks: the air, the grass, and the stones."

"What, they talk like people? Air, grass, and stones?"

"Yes, the air cries, the grass whispers, and thousands of stones yell at him."

"Thousands of stones?"

"Yes, there are rows of stones. It's a large place. So many sounds make Ryan nervous."

"The stones are in rows. Are these tombstones? Does this place look like a graveyard?"

"Oh! Yes, probably. I didn't think of that."

"Okay, what else? What does Ryan do?"

"He runs around trying to escape the place and sounds, but he can't. They just become louder. He feels he is being followed. Scary shadows move on the grass."

"Does he see or know anyone trying to cause harm?"

"I don't know. He didn't tell me anything."

"Does he get stranded like this often? When did this all start?"

"Not long ago, I think. Ryan only told me two days ago

after I asked him for the hundredth time. He hates to talk about bad news."

"Did he tell you how he gets out of this place?"

"He didn't. I don't think he knows either. I think he blacks out."

"Did he tell you anything else?"

"That's all I know, Mrs. Sharma," she said. Then suddenly she remembered, "Wait! He sees a lady."

"A lady?"

"Yes, he mentioned there was a woman. He didn't say anything else about her."

Britney's unexpected disclosure helped me connect the misplaced dots of my repeated dream, yet the picture was hazy. The petrified child in my dreams with whom I felt a close affinity was Ryan. And the hands holding him from stumbling perhaps belonged to the woman Britney had mentioned. Something assured me about the hands. I vividly recollected that they meant to care rather than crush.

My heartbeat suddenly began to surge, and so did my urge to rush upstairs. But the presence of Britney kept me seated, effortfully keeping a calm exterior.

"Britney, I'm glad to know how much you care for Ryan. Don't worry about Ryan; he'll be fine."

"But, Mrs. Sharma, we must wake him up to find out if he's fine."

"Yes, I will in some time. He was tired last night, so let him sleep a bit longer. I think you should go. Debra must be looking for you."

"What about Ryan?"

"Honey, Ryan is a strong boy. He knows his way. And I'm here too."

"I want to stay," insisted Britney.

"Your mom will be upset if she finds out you came here. She wants you to stay at Debra's. You should respect her decision. I'll speak to her later, and then maybe you can visit as often as you like. Okay?"

I could sense the hypocrisy in my words, and perhaps

229

Britney did too, but it was for a reason. She reluctantly rose from the chair and walked to the door.

As soon as Britney left, I sprang up the stairs. In my bedroom, Ryan was asleep in a sideways position, unchanged since I saw him early in the morning. Next to him lay Caesar, also motionless.

As usual, I ran my fingers through Ryan's silky hair, calling softly, hoping he would open his eyes like every morning, smile, and wrap his arms around my hand.

But Ryan did not budge.

When stroking his hair and calling louder each time did not help, I moved closer, shaking him forcefully, but to no avail. Caesar, who would otherwise wake up at the drop of a pin, lay listless despite my yelling and jerking him.

I could see now why Ryan was scared to sleep the previous night. He perhaps feared getting stranded in a dark, unknown place. I wished he had confided in me, even with the same fragment of information he shared with Britney.

Concerned, Mom came in and found me panicking. "What happened, Munni?"

"Mom, Ryan won't wake up. I've tried everything. He won't move. And Caesar, too."

"But why?"

"Something is wrong, Ma. I don't know what to do. Wait, can you look out? Your drishti might find him."

"I don't know, Munni. It's only noon," returned Mom, hastening toward the window and looking down the street. "I can't see anything. Drishti only works at night. Nowadays, even at night…"

She didn't finish her sentence, and continued to stare without blinking. When two minutes passed without a word from her, I asked, "Mom, what is it? Do you see something?"

"I did. Several visuals—all hazy, though. First, I saw this street, lonely and deserted, like never before. Then I saw a blank space, white like snow. Some marks appeared on it like strange letters in black ink. It became clear in the next moment that they were not letters but men emerging from the milky white space. They were all in black; black hats and black cloaks."

"Keepers," I mumbled.

"I heard them talking but could not interpret anything."

"Then?"

"Then something strange happened. My vision slipped to another place. Fog all around with a speck far away. Soon, I could see someone coming closer. I saw the face when the mist withered and the person came close enough."

"Who was it?"

"Mom."

"Mom? Your mom, my grandma?"

"Yes. I don't know why I would see her. Makes no sense. That's it; that's all I saw. I didn't see Ryan."

"Hmm, that's not much help. Ryan could be in trouble. I must find out."

"But how, Munni? What will you do?"

"The only way to find out is to go where he is. Wherever he is, I'll bring him back," I resolved. "If I'm late, tell Viru and Reva not to worry. And you too, Ma. And don't wake me under any circumstances."

"Take care, Munni. I'll pray every minute," said Mom, struggling to hide her nervousness.

I lay next to Ryan, slipping my arm underneath his head, supporting it like a pillow, and holding his hand with mine. A few uneasy minutes passed while I lay with my eyes closed. The violent jerk followed by a great fall did not happen. I wondered if I had bungled the transition procedure or if the process had become obsolete.

Why does the mode of execution play hide-and-seek when the necessity of action attains desperate levels?

Irritated, I sat up. "It's not working, Ma. I don't know if I'm missing something or trying too hard."

"Weren't you in Ryan's room last time?" Mom asked thoughtfully.

"I was. Yes, I was!" I jumped off the bed.

It struck me that Mom's stress levels had surpassed mine, yet she still had her ability to think correctly. We were in my bedroom, and all my previous conscious escapades into Shloka had initiated from Ryan's bed.

I carried a listless Ryan in my arms and hastened to his room. To be accurate, I also placed Caesar on Ryan's bed. Repeating the procedure, I prayed to God with closed eyes and bated breath that I got everything right this time.

Ryan's bed shuddered, and I heaved a sigh of relief. I wondered if anyone else would feel a sense of relief at slipping down into the dark abyss. They would if they had braved this before and knew every minner falling asleep unconsciously took a similar plunge. And most importantly, if they were a mom desperate to find her son. The irony was that although my son was lying beside me, I did not know where he was.

If it weren't for Antar, anything falling what seemed like countless miles down at supersonic speed would surely shatter into pieces like a glass pane hitting the solid ground. But I landed with a gentle thud and in one piece.

What I landed on was now waiting to be unveiled by my eyes. The white light hitting my eyes signaled to my brain, revealing I had not landed on solid, but liquid matter. I was amazed to discover I was lying steady on the water's surface, though I was not alien to Jantar's magic.

I sat up in the middle of a vast, deep sea. The same or similar to the one I had crossed with Jack, Ryan, and Caesar on foot on my first visit to Jantar. The sea on which I would neither float or submerge.

The sky was blue and clear, and so was the sea. Sitting on the carpet of the water's surface, I caught sight of the magnificent aquatic life right beneath me, stretched deep and far, embracing the vegetation at the bottom. Jellyfish, starfish, dolphins, crabs, octopuses, turtles, and many other animals I did not know existed all swam in the soothing symphony. I could not say if they were temporary transports from Loka or permanent residents of Jantar.

Curious, colorful fish formed rings around me, poking my legs and back now and then. I stood up, and the adorable rings contracted around my feet.

Looking around, as far as my vision could aid, I could not see anything but water. Then, I noticed a tiny object miles away. Walking toward it and squinting, I realized it was a tree in the middle of the sea. I could not tell whether it was floating, or if its roots grasped the seabed or spread on the surface. Also, it was hard to know if the tree was there before, or had emerged just now.

I walked toward the tree. Surprisingly, it grew in size with every step forward. I remembered Jack telling me once that in Jantar, one covered more distance in a few steps when walking on water than land. In no time, I arrived near the broad trunk of the gigantic tree.

The tree was so high that I could not locate its top from where I stood, as if penetrating the sky. Looking underwater, I could not see the bottom of the tree, but instead its inverted image, so deep that, again, I couldn't spot its crown. In the clear water, it seemed like the tree pierced the sea.

As I wondered what to do, I heard a splash behind me, and I turned around.

"Hello, Mandira! I was expecting you."

"Jack! Where's Ryan?"

"I will tell you soon, but first, come with me."

"No! I will not go anywhere until you tell me. Is he alright?"

"He should be fine."

"What does that mean? Where is my son, Jack?"

"Well, we are looking for him."

"Why? What happened? Why are you looking for him?"

"Monsieur Ryan has not returned. Our search teams are—"

"Not returned? From where?"

"From Shloka."

Chapter Five

A door slid open in the enormous trunk of the infinite tree that was identical but opposite above and below water. I gave in to Jack's appeal to follow him so he could better explain everything he knew about Ryan's disappearance. I could not tell if he had a point or intended to distract me by changing location. Given my mental state, stepping into the tree would not impress me, just like walking on the water had not.

As we walked in, the darkness slowly melted away as if time had fast-forwarded from black night through morning twilight to the luminous noon. The familiar sphere-shaped bubble appeared and sucked us in. I remembered it as one of the detachable compartments of a bubble-shaped metro we took last time.

In the least expected direction, our bubble compartment descended gradually, like a soap bubble pulled by gravity. A few meters down, the bubble halted, giving way to a speeding train that looked like a flexible aluminum duct hose. Moments later, a high-tech, all-glass airplane with keepers inside steered past us.

Moving further down, we encountered colorful balloons floating in the air carrying passengers. I felt like we were parachuting down an enormous waterfall with no clear beginning or end. Infinite skyscrapers, mammoth structures, and monuments of advanced architecture surrounded the waterfall.

Although watching an ultramodern complex unfold inside a tree was not a banal everyday event, the striking observation for me was the foundation on which the whole thing was built. To my ordinary eyes, it was thin air. Trains cruised, riding on invisible tracks. Hundreds of modern vehicles, many without tires, drove on a transparent highway spiraling around us.

There was no floor, yet the keepers in black overalls walked casually. No chairs, yet they sat chatting in groups. No stairs, yet they stepped up and down carelessly. Pools looked like tons of water in giant glass tubs.

"Jack, what is this place?"

"This is the city of Keeperton."

"Keeperton! It's a city? I thought we would go up in the tree."

"No, the tree is underwater. You saw its shadow above water. Keeperton is an underwater city. The legendary Sir Doug Downunder designed it. I told you before, remember?"

"Yes, I think so. But why are we here? Didn't you say you would tell me about Ryan?" I asked. In my present frame of mind, any visual experience, however elevated, could not excite me.

"I did, and that's why we are here. Well, almost. See that building?" Jack pointed to a massive oval-shaped structure resting in the air in the middle of several other skyscrapers.

The structure looked like another bubble similar to ours, only differing in shape and size. Our bubble approached the great bubble and attached itself to its wall. Next thing I knew, we were inside the egg-shaped building, and our ride had disappeared.

It was all white; there were no corners, walls, a roof, or even a floor to ascertain the shape of the place; just a plain white canvas.

Jack stepped forward, and I followed him. I noticed something ahead. A few specks appeared initially, and shortly after, they looked like letters in black marker typing in real-time on a white sheet.

"Just like Mom said," I mumbled softly, but perhaps keepers' ears could catch the words even before they came out of my mouth.

"Your mom saw this place? Her range of drishti is farther than I thought. Not just limited to the keeper zone."

Soon, I found myself in the middle of a commotion. Keepers were walking around, talking to each other in an unintelligible language. Many hastened, though I was unsure where to, as the to and fro looked the same—all white. The hustle and bustle of the place was akin to the New York Stock Exchange trading floor of the eighties. The difference was that there were no papers, furniture, or electronic gadgets, and hundreds of people were dressed alike.

"Jack, when will you tell me what these people are doing?" I asked.

"What do you think, Mandira? They are the members of the Keeper Task Force, the most skilled keepers of Jantar—the experts in completing the top tasks. They never fail to accomplish their assignments, and they have only one right now. Finding Monsieur Ryan."

"Finding Ryan? Is he somewhere around here?"

"No, he's in Shloka, as I told you. This is the planning team. There are many more out in the field. But my purpose in bringing you here was to introduce you to somebody. Look over there."

Jack pointed to my left. An egg-shaped transparent compartment was hanging slightly above the ground with someone in it. Moving closer, I saw a partially bald man from the front, older than Jack, with shiny silver hair and a longer beard. He was sitting on nothing, staring at nothing—or perhaps something my vision could not perceive.

"Who is he?" I asked, and the man raised his caterpillar-like silver brows at me.

The softest-spoken words I had ever heard came from Jack's mouth as he said, "Sir, this is Mandira, Monsieur Ryan's mother. And Mandira, this is Sir Lockman Keyhole."

"Oh, Sir Lockman Keyhole! Nice to finally meet you."

Sir Lockman nodded without any change in expression and said, "We will find him."

"Thank you. But where is Ryan?" I asked.

Sir Keyhole returned to staring into the distance, as if he had not heard me.

"Sir Keyhole? Hello?"

"He will not speak more. A man of few words," said Jack, pulling my arm gently. "Monsieur Ryan is the only reason he came down to Jantar from Parloka."

"Jack, I get why you brought me here; I can see you people are making an effort. But I don't see Ryan. Where exactly is he, and why is it so hard to find him?"

"I see you want details of the effort and can't be content just with the competence of the people making it. So, let's head to the site."

Our bubble ride returned and took us out of the white space into a dimly lit tunnel where it attached itself to the side of a moving metro with similar bubble compartments.

The bubble train exited through a cavity of the enormous tree—aka Keeperton City—and cruised forward on the surface of the calm sea.

*

We arrived at the gigantic gate of Shloka that stood tall and broad like no other structure. Humans and animals in large queues entered and exited the gate steadily.

"Shloka is a vast land with blocks assigned to minner species. Let me show you," said Jack, waving his hand at the gate.

Suddenly, a thick fog surrounded us.

"Do you see these?" Jack pointed toward the rectangular frames. Many door frames without doors were the only visible objects hanging in the air amid the fog. Those frames emitted light flickering continuously, as if somebody had installed faulty light bulbs.

"Jack, what am I looking at? Where are we?"

"You are on the other side of Shloka's gate. And these are the entrances for minner species like cats, dogs, humans, et cetera."

"Oh, small gates inside the big gate! What's with the flickering lights?"

"That's minners going in and coming out. It's happening so quickly that it gives the illusion of flickering light. Inside each block are the houses, each a replica of the other. I cannot show that to you. You can think of those houses as dream boxes; no one can tell the difference from the outside. Every minner occupies a unique box. Monsieur Ryan is inside one of the gazillions of identical-looking boxes. Finding his box is like a needle in a haystack—or rather a strand of hay in a haystack, for that matter. The thing about these boxes is that everyone enters or exits alone. Nobody accompanies them or can tell which box they went to, not even the keepers."

"Are you saying Ryan entered his box alone and now won't come out?"

"Precisely."

"But why? What's the point in going into those boxes?" I asked, irritated. "And why must one go alone? What can you accomplish by being home alone?"

"Why are minners born alone, and why do they die alone? If you look for broad logic, nothing that happens will make sense, and every activity one does will seem like a worthless accomplishment. Alone is the way of life for minners. Being alone in Shloka rejuvenates them and prepares them to face another day. Alone is not lonely; it's healing."

"Okay, even if I believe in your philosophical words of being alone and not lonely, why can't you keepers identify a minner's box? Can't you trace it? Don't you have something similar to CCTV cameras installed in those boxes?"

"CCTV? Mandira, Shloka doesn't work based on lousy minner technology."

"Wow, what arrogance! You keepers claim to be our caretakers and think you're smarter, yet you have an unsupervised place that the entire planet visits."

"Sorry, Mandira. I didn't mean to offend you. The whole idea of Shloka is about no interference, even by the keepers. Being alone means nothing if you're being watched."

"Jack, what could be happening inside Ryan's box? Why hasn't he come out?"

"I can't tell for sure. It looks like Monsieur Ryan is trapped. It's just his box; all the other boxes are fine. Minners are coming and going without problems."

"Do you think his life could be in danger? Ryan was terrified. Britney told me he finds himself in a graveyard. I dreamed of him desperately running from creepy shadows, terrifying noise, and whatnot."

Jack became momentarily thoughtful and said, "Yes, Mandira. You got a peek into Monsieur Ryan's box. I'm surprised you are also blessed with the power of drishti, like your mom. She catches a glimpse of Jantar, and you can glimpse into future events when inside your dream box.

"Unfortunately, Monsieur Ryan didn't speak about it to any of us. He doesn't ask for help. He likes to deal with his problems alone, which is not always a great idea. I won't keep you in the dark. Remember I told you about Dr. Dhingra?"

"Dr. Dhingra! The scientist who supplied poisonous elizer to the daggers and cured them with the anti-elizer?"

"Exactly. The Intelligence Agency of Jantar—IAJ, for short—believes he is behind this. Somehow, he confined Monsieur Ryan in his box."

"But why would he do that? What did Ryan do to him?"

"Revenge, Mandira. The devil desires vengeance more than the blind desire vision. The blind wishes to see, but the devil chooses to be blind. The elizer Dr. Dhingra stole was meant to destroy the minners of Loka. Monsieur Ryan foiled his plot by manipulating Jantar's cycle of wheels and saved Loka."

Jack's language had evolved from the time of scant vocabulary, where words felt like outcasts in his sentences, to the overflowing glossary, where he offered synonyms to my correct word usage. Advancing a step further, this time he was articulating responses in metaphors and similes. But nothing could impress me at that moment.

"Did it not occur to you keepers, with so many enemies, that this place could be dangerous without surveillance?"

"Mandira, the framework of Shloka has worked for ages without issues, and the enemies have surfaced only recently. The keepers have upgraded their security, and daggers have stepped up their evil designs. But you mustn't worry. There isn't anything more important for Kendram than to find Monsieur Ryan."

Jack's emphatic words did not convince me. An important lesson I had learned was that one must rely on a plan rather than mere assurance.

"What now? What's your plan to bring Ryan back?"

"The plan is simple. Find the box and rescue Monsieur Ryan."

"How are you going to do that? What exactly was Sir Lockman Keyhole doing?"

"Sir Keyhole was studying the logic of assigning the dream box to an individual to see if there is any way to identify Monsieur Ryan's box. Not an easy task, as Shloka was designed by Sir Patchman Sinkhole, Keyhole's father when Loka came into being. The foundation was built on the principles of ambiguity and privacy at a time when traitors within keepers didn't exist. Also, an army of keepers inside the human block is randomly searching the area and the boxes," said Jack, pointing at the keeper commandos momentarily appearing and vanishing around us.

"Can we walk into the block and look for Ryan?"

"Yes and no. We can go in but cannot look for him together. I'm a keeper, and you a minner. If we enter the block, I can roam around, but you will be whisked into your box and transported back to Loka. I cannot accompany you beyond this point. Better leave it to the experts. Not much we can contribute here. I wish I knew Monsieur Ryan's box or somebody who could lead us."

"I know somebody who can help."

"Who?"

"My grandma."

"Your grandma? How would she know? She is a minner of Parloka," said Jack with a derisive chuckle.

"So? Didn't you tell me once that she comes to Shloka regularly looking for us?"

"I did, but she randomly enters the boxes and rarely gets lucky. Her finding of any of you can be nothing more than a fluke. A shot in the dark."

"Jack, do you mean it when you tell me I am wise?"

"Of course, I do, Mandira."

"Then you must respect my wisdom."

"I do, Mandira, but what makes you think that your grandma can help?"

"Connecting some dots. My instinct tells me she has an idea, but I can't prove anything."

"Alright, if you insist," said Jack, holding up his fist like he was clenching sand. "But I must tell you this: not only are the boxes alike, but also the paths leading up to them. Forget dead minners like your grandma; even the best of keepers can't tell the difference." Opening his fist, Jack threw the invisible sand up in the air.

"Who will you inform and when?"

"I just did. The IAJ."

Though Jack claimed to have shared with the intelligence agency, given his dismissive attitude and bizarre hand motion, it seemed as if he had tossed the whole idea into the trash, as if it was no better than a crumpled piece of paper.

In the next moment, I saw a familiar figure emerge from the thick mist. Tears rolled down my cheeks like water from a dripping tap.

Chapter Six

It took some time for my eyes to adjust to the dark before I realized I had woken up. My eyes fell on Viru, nodding off on the chair beside the bed. Only when I turned my head and saw Ryan next to me did I fully return to my senses. I removed my arm gently from beneath his head and nudged him.

Ryan did not move or open his eyes. Caesar also lay listless beside him.

Sitting up, I shook him and begged, "Ryan! Wake up. Wake up, honey!"

Viru woke up and turned the light on. "Mandy! Are you awake?"

Reva came running from her adjoining room. "Mom! What is it? Is Ryan okay? Did he wake up, Dad?"

Viru shook his head to Reva and, seeing me deeply concerned, asked, "Did you see Ryan in sleep, Mandy?"

Amid my pondering, everything that Viru and Reva said fell on my ears like garbled speech.

"Mom?"

"Mandy?"

"Hold on! I'm thinking! Please!" I returned brusquely.

I strained my brain hard, trying to invoke the latest shreds of memory at Shloka's gate. Thankfully, my memory did not evade me for long.

I was stood with Jack at the inner side of Shloka's gate, amid the mist, staring at the hanging door frames that he said were the entrances to minner blocks. In the blocks were the zillions of identical, uniformly laid dream boxes meant for individuals, and Ryan was allegedly trapped in his box, impossible to locate easily.

My eyes had welled up with tears when I saw Caesar emerge from the haze. As I embraced him, Jack told me that Caesar had been tirelessly working with the Keeper Task Force in randomly searching the dream boxes.

After his tacit assurance, Caesar disappeared back into the mist, returning to work with enhanced resolve.

I struggled to remember what happened next as several seemingly unconnected flashbacks interfered with the chronological order. I recalled Jack telling me he heard the news about Dr. Dhingra. I didn't bother asking how he could talk to me and simultaneously listen to the news, as I was more curious about the information than its transmission mode.

"Dr. Dhingra was found eliminated," Jack had said.

"Found eliminated? What does that mean? Is he dead?" I'd asked.

"Yes, dead. But not what the minners think it is when they move from Loka to Parloka. Elimination means permanently ceasing to exist in all the worlds. It's *actual* death."

The definition of actual or perceived death was, again, not my prime concern then, so I quickly moved onto the more pressing question.

"Understood. But how did he die?"

"No idea yet. He was found dead."

"Where?"

"In Parloka."

"He was found dead in Parloka? Didn't you say he was behind Ryan's disappearance?"

"Yes, as per IAJ. But now it doesn't add up."

Next, Jack had excused himself on the pretext of looking into Dr. Dhingra's death, but I felt there was more. Usually, his poker face would not give away his inner emotions, but this time, wrinkles of concern had appeared on his forehead. Moreover, not once had he left me alone in this mystical place on previous occasions.

Surrounded by the clouds of uncertainty, I had waited uncomfortably without moving from my spot, as Jack directed before he left. Several keepers appeared and disappeared around me, and my hope flickered like the light coming from the entrance doors of the dream blocks.

Several restless moments later, an orange spec popped up at the entry of the human dream block, turning next into a candlelike flame. As it approached closer, the flame grew in size to a white blaze, erupting right in front of me.

After a hard blinking reflex at the flash of light, my eyes landed on a surreal figure.

Awestruck, I rose from the floor and gazed at the person before me. Like anyone, I had not seen an angel or God, but he closely resembled the ethereal image in my head. The mesmerizing aura he exhibited held me spellbound.

He wore a snow-white cloak instead of the tattered rags sown into a gown. His face looked bright and less wrinkled than tanned and sweaty, and his hair was curly and brushed as opposed to messy.

And his smile lit up the place like it would seeing my freshly cooked and packed meal. The appearance could deceive me, and so could the features, but that smile was ingrained in my mind. My memories from two years ago at the Saint Thomas Metro Station had returned.

"How are you, Mandira?" he'd asked me.

"Sebastian? It's you!" His voice removed my remaining doubt.

"Yes."

"Hi! It's great to see you after so long, Seb. Or should I say, Chief Joseph?"

"Seb will do. The homeless old man that you fed every day."

"Until you disappeared, just when I realized you were the chief."

"What was the point of staying, knowing I would no longer get your delicious food?"

Seeing Sebastian was comforting as he had not appeared

as Chief Joseph before. His calm demeanor was helping, too; still, I couldn't wait to enquire about it. No wonder he read my mind and spoke before I asked.

"Ryan is safe."

If I were to pick from anything I'd ever heard or said, those three magical words from Sebastian would always top the list.

"Really?"

"Yes. He's alright. You need not worry about him. Sorry you had to go through this trouble."

"Where is he? Can I see him?"

"Yes, you will, soon after you're up in Loka. You will reunite at your place."

"What happened to Ryan? How did he get trapped in there? Would you mind sharing something, Seb?"

"I wouldn't, but it will take some time to explain, and I need to take care of a few things. You will find out soon, Mandira. I promise."

"Seb, I trust every word you say. But I need an assurance that Ryan is safe now and in the future. And also we, his family."

"Okay, let me show you something. I don't think you will need any better assurance," the chief told me, snapping his fingers.

A person appeared next to him, sending shivers down my spine. Everything was menacing about him—his rough face with cuts and marks, his fuming red eyes, and his muscular build apparent despite the black cloak he wore. The sight of him brought back nightmarish memories that swam across my eyes. His clenched fists and death stare unsettled me, making my blood boil angrily. He was the one who had tried to obliterate my family and plotted a wipeout of Loka two years back before going missing.

He was the devil. The dagger. The son of Chief Joseph. He was Hogdon.

Two bright rings, horizontal and vertical, surrounded him. He was caged in those rings that sparked at his slightest movement.

"Mandira, here is the cause of your worries; the source of all the troubles. You can be at peace now. This troublemaker will rot in hell."

Seb's hatred for the devil made me speechless. All I could do was stare right into his furious eyes.

"I must go now. Let me leave you with a happy memory. *Au revoir.*"

After a brief appearance, like any VIP, Chief Joseph had vanished with Hogdon in the mist, with several questions unanswered. His parting words of leaving me with a happy memory made me curious, until I saw somebody emerge from the fog.

The expression *blood is thicker than water* not only holds literal, but its density can be felt when seeing long-lost loved ones.

"Munni! Oh, my dearest Munni!" she said, tearing up.

She looked beautiful and younger than when I had last seen her about sixteen years ago, before she left us. She wore a purple headscarf and a gray waistcoat with a belt that brought back my childhood nostalgia of following her everywhere around her big house without letting go of her belt even for a minute.

"Grandma!" I yelped, choking on tears. "I missed you so much."

We embraced affectionately several times, still yearning for more. Her hands looked rough but felt soft as I held and kissed them.

"You're so pretty, my little Munni! How is my Rani doing? And her two monkeys?"

"Mom is doing good. She's with us these days. And the monkeys, well, they are big now." I chuckled at the recollection of my older brothers Ajay and Arjun. To her, my brothers and I were still little children.

I had always regretted not being able to bid my final goodbye to Grandma when she passed away because I was giving birth to Reva. An unexpected wish to meet Grandma and break the barrier between death and life was fulfilled thanks to Chief Joseph.

"What else did she say?"

Mom's words broke me from my reverie. She, Viru, and Reva were sitting with me in Ryan's room, listening attentively.

"She said, 'Tell Rani I miss her. She's her father's favorite; he talks about her all the time.' She also said, 'Tell Rani to take care of herself. She's the emotional one.'"

"She said that? I don't know why she thinks I'm emotional," Mom said, wiping at her tears.

"What else?" asked Viru, as if expecting a word from Grandma for his well being.

"I don't know. It's hard to remember everything. It feels like a long dream. I felt relief in her eyes, as if some burden was released from her shoulders. And yes, she said, 'Munni, you are the strong one. Your child is the future. You protect him; you protect the future.'"

All our eyes were now set on Ryan, still lying on the bed, listless. Then, the miracle happened. Ryan moved for the first time, as if the energy of the first ray of light or if the power of our collective gaze instilled life in him.

Ryan's half-opened eyes met mine first, in his direct line of sight. He then noticed his dad, sister, and grandma surrounding his bed, staring at him with wet eyes and wide smiles.

Feeling awkward with the spotlight on him, as always, Ryan addressed us all, "Come hug me."

Bursting into relieved laughter, Viru, Reva, and I leaned over and hugged Ryan. Despite his reluctant offer, Ryan was uncomfortable with our group hug, as expected. Mom kissed his hands. Caesar was up, too, and eagerly joined in the cuddle session.

An hour later, I heard muffled sounds from the living room. I came downstairs to find Britney knocking on the glass door.

"Hey, Britney!" I said, sliding the door open.

"Hi, Mrs. Sharma!" she said softly. Her voice was still gruff from her cold.

"What are you doing here? Come in! It's freezing outside," I said, seeing her shivering in a T-shirt and shorts. She looked weak.

"I can't. Mom's in the shower; she'll be out any minute. How's Ryan? Did he wake up?"

"Oh, Ryan." Realizing the purpose of her hushed dropping by, I returned with a smile, "Yes, he's awake. He's doing great."

Her eyes turned away from me the next moment, and her face lit up. Looking in the direction of Britney's gaze, I found Ryan standing at the foot of the steps behind me.

"Well, you can look yourself. He came down to see you."

Gazing at Ryan, Britney's green eyes sparked with joy, and she stopped shivering. Moments later, without a word, she darted back into her house with restored vigor.

Chapter Seven

A dull thud woke me, and I saw Viru enter the bedroom.

"Sorry, did I wake you, Mandy?" Viru asked.

I knew his tactic of deliberately hitting the door against the door stopper attached to the side wall and then playing innocent.

"Viru, it's Saturday," I said dryly.

"Door's fault, Mandy. I didn't mean to wake you. And a Saturday for *you*. Laborers like me don't get a break, even on Labor Day."

"A break from who?" I asked, wrapping the duvet around my shoulders.

"Who else?"

"What's he doing now?"

"Making out. On the streets. At freaking minus ten degrees! He's a Casanova of dogs now. Now it's not only Tulip but other bitches going crazy after him. A classic example of when you get the attention of the queen bee, all the other bees start hovering around you."

"What's the problem? Is he making out with all of them?"

"No, he's still faithful to Tulip. But now all dog owners avoid me. Before, it was only Mrs. Walker. They wonder how a dull dog suddenly became desirable to their bitches. The day when Mrs. Bergenza's cats start licking him is not far away."

"What's wrong with that? You should be proud. Didn't you tell me Caesar was a rockstar?"

"Nah. He's just a naughty dog with superpowers."

"Ah, okay. So, he's not a rockstar, and I'm not a superhero anymore?"

"Now you're joking, Mandy. You two are the supporting cast. The main lead is my son, who perhaps doesn't even know or care about it," returned Viru as he walked out of the bedroom, heading downstairs.

Viru's admiration for Caesar and I had lasted only about a month from the day of the big revelation when the hideous bears Duma and Billa stormed into our house. His humorless jokes had returned, and so had our status of being taken for granted, now as the mere sidekicks of the superhero Ryan.

I stayed in the cozy bed for some time, remembering my sweet dream before Viru had interrupted with his usual morning grumble.

I'd dreamt of lush green grasslands sprawling beyond my field of vision. Grandma was walking on the grass barefoot, with Ryan holding her waistcoat belt. Ryan's every step on the meadow gave me the sensation of grass blades teasing my feet. Strangely, I was not participating directly, yet very much part of the dream. Ryan laughed with Grandma like he never had before.

It was New Year's Eve, and I had planned to make my best delicacy for the evening. Usually, Viru would throw a party, but the neighbors were indifferent to us this year, thanks to the misadventures.

I missed Mom, who had taken over the kitchen and made me lazy by relegating me to helping part-time with the chores. Since her return to India before Christmas, I had reclaimed my role in the kitchen and also promoted Reva from doing nothing to cutting and chopping.

After finishing breakfast—my easy-to-make omelet-stuffed croissant sandwich, Ryan's favorite—Reva and I headed back to the kitchen to prepare for the evening special. We decided to make the dessert first.

Viru and Ryan, clad in their winter suits, and Caesar in his natural fur headed out to the driveway. The reason for their enthusiasm was not the activity that Viru would otherwise hate, but testing the new tool to perform it. As

Viru shoveled last night's fresh snow out of the driveway with his brand-new electric snow shovel, Ryan and Caesar found fun walking into the range of the blowing snow and getting sprayed all over.

Not content with the driveway alone, thanks to the joy of operating the new machine, Viru, Ryan, and Caesar then moved to clear the back deck.

Taking a quick break from my kitchen duties, I checked out their backyard amusement and noticed I was not the only one. Britney stood by her window, peering at Ryan's snow shovel game. The longing in her eyes to join the play made me sad.

In the afternoon, Reva got busy reading (her newfound interest), and Ryan and Caesar continued their usual chasing games. Tired from shoveling—the only work he had done since morning, besides walking Caesar—Viru took a nap.

I dropped by Elena's, and her jaw dropped at seeing me at her door after such a long time. Handing her a bowl of my freshly made carrot pudding, her favorite dessert, I invited myself into her house.

Sitting in her living room, I spoke after a long, awkward silence. "Elena, I miss you. I want my old friend back; I don't like the new one. It sucks. Look, I can understand you find me weird. Like the other neighbors, you think I do some twisted magic. Can't you take me as your queer friend? It kills me when you ask Debra to look after Britney, not me. She can't play with Ryan, and I was like her other mom. I miss our gossip. I miss *you*."

Elena's eyes were wet. She sighed and took a long pause before speaking. "Mandy, I saw you that night. You and Caesar stood at the door looking out at countless animals, all looking back at you. It blew my mind. How could so many different species gather peacefully in one place? It seemed they knew you, and you knew them. And then they disappeared, just like that.

"I couldn't sleep for nights. I thought, *Whatever it is, Mandy will tell me. She's my friend.* But then you spoke to me

251

like nothing had happened. You said the bears attacked, and Caesar saved you, that's it. I was disappointed. I felt like I never knew you. I lost the comfort we shared in telling each other things. Knowing even Ryan was sharing with Britney but not you made me more mad. All I wanted from you was an honest conversation, no matter how impossible or inexplicable the things seemed."

I realized my presumption about Elena's indifference strained our friendship. I never addressed the elephant in the room, but judged Elena for forming an opinion about the incident. I assumed that the neighborhood gossip about me had influenced her. All I needed was to talk to her directly.

A candid conversation mends friendship, and a preconceived notion ends it.

I clarified that the trying inquiry by the authorities and the fear of its repercussions prevented me from sharing the extraordinary revelation, and promised to tell her all. We sobbed like sisters and bonded over the carrot pudding.

Another person overjoyed by our patch-up was Britney, who finally got an open visa from her mom to visit our house, and she instantly exercised the privilege. Britney's chatterbox form returned after a long time, and Ryan, as usual, listened quietly and nodded. Ryan continued to be a miser in expression, but his eyes depicted his new year's wish was fulfilled a day early.

I sneaked up on them a few times, hoping Ryan would spill the secrets of his Shloka escapade, but in vain.

Britney played with Ryan for the rest of the day to make up for lost time until her mom called her home for her evening supper.

The dinner table came to life with bowls, servers, plates, dishes, spoons, tumblers, and us. Ryan, the choosey one, satisfied his latest obsession with cheese by relishing my paneer (Indian cottage cheese) dish dipped in a tomato-based curry.

Despite having the luxury of trying all the choices, Viru

and Reva focused on butter chicken. As a vegetarian, I restricted myself to *dal makhani* (black lentils cooked with butter and cream) and paneer items. Caesar started with dessert, simultaneously eating *gulab jamun* soaked in sugar syrup and carrot pudding.

Viru and Reva sang my praises, often bordering on flattery. Viru yet again gave me what was not his to give: another of his frivolous titles, this time, Culinary Queen.

Reva pestered me by repeatedly telling Viru, "Take another bite, Dad. Tastes even better."

"Alright, stop it now. I already said yes. What else do you two want?"

Every year, Reva expressed her desire to watch New Year's Eve fireworks, and I would turn her down due to Ryan's discomfort with crowded places and late-night waking. This time, I agreed to stay home with Ryan and Caesar and let Viru and Reva have fun. So, butter chicken was not the only reason to butter me up.

An hour after Viru and Reva left for the Old Port and as Ryan and Caesar were sleeping, I retired to my bedroom. As I went to draw the curtains, someone on the street drew my attention. To my surprise, Jack stood by the streetlamp, looking at me.

I quietly stepped out of the house and down to the street.

"Jack! What are you doing here? Is everything okay?"

"Everything is perfect, Mandira. I came to give you New Year's wishes."

"It's still New Year's Eve, and I don't believe you visited me just for that. Tell me, what is it?"

"Chief Joseph had promised you to tell everything, remember? I'm here to fulfill his promise."

"Oh, was he serious? I thought he said that to get rid of me."

"The chief doesn't give his word for nothing."

After speaking big words in the chief's honor, Jack got to the business of full disclosure.

After fleeing from the trial in Parloka two years ago, Hogdon secretly engaged with dagger sympathizer Dr. Dhingra through his wicked supporters. Dhingra invented an anti-elizer to treat daggers debilitated by elizer induced as a punishment by keepers.

Dhingra was not a devil, just misled into thinking the daggers would quietly move on after recovering. When he realized Hogdon's plot of misusing elizer to destroy Loka, he broke ties with him and threatened to expose him. In response, Hogdon eliminated Dr. Dhingra. The demon son of Chief Joseph used Dhingra while he was alive and also after his death.

Hogdon didn't commit wrongdoings openly for fear of losing his supporter base in Parloka, which he still enjoyed. To his supporters, Hogdon was a keeper fighting for his rightfully deserved throne as the next chief. So, Hogdon continued to perform all sinful activities in the name of the deceased Dr. Dhingra.

When Ryan adjusted the cycle of wheels at Jantar to alleviate the havoc caused by elizer-infected animals in Loka, Hogdon used the temporary disorder as an opportunity to sneak into Shloka. He rummaged through the dream boxes for days until he finally found Ryan's box and camped there. It was hard to tell if he just got lucky or figured out some method to get to it.

Hogdon began terrorizing Ryan by creating nightmarish sounds and illusions. On the fateful morning when Ryan did not wake up, Hogdon had trapped him in his Shloka dream box, closing all entries and exits. He tormented Ryan with baffling noises and scary visuals, leading to his nervous breakdown.

Jack told me that any minner's mental disintegration in Shloka opened a hidden door leading to Parloka, and that was precisely Hogdon's plan for Ryan. He knew that stepping into Parloka in this manner would permanently cease not only Ryan's chance to return to Loka, but also to become the next chief. By rule, when contesting for the top job, a contender must be in their origin world, not the migrated world.

Chief Joseph had anticipated the evil designs of Hogdon. When Ryan headed for Parloka, the chief received him just before the entrance to Parloka and prevented his permanent migration.

Chief then located Ryan's dream box, and I was delighted to know who helped him. Jack did not take me seriously when I told him Grandma could find Ryan, but the chief did upon receiving Jack's reluctantly broadcasted message. The chief arrived at Ryan's dream box and captured Hogdon, thanks to Grandma.

Hogdon would have long fled before the chief's arrival had Ryan not shown a remarkable presence of mind, even when in distress. When the hidden door toward Parloka opened, Hogdon made the mistake of underestimating the disoriented Ryan. Intoxicated by the sense of victory, he celebrated too early by revealing himself to Ryan.

Upon realizing that Hogdon was terrorizing him all those nights, Ryan did not just walk out of the door, but stood at its threshold instead.

Perhaps from spending hours at Dr. Lockman Keyhole's labs, Ryan had figured out that prolonged standing at the hidden doorstep would permanently shut that and the other regular doors—like a forced computer shutdown upon malfunction—forcing him out of the dream box. As a result, Ryan was ousted from the dream box, but Hogdon was trapped in it.

Jack also explained how Grandma knew about Ryan's dream box. Grandma had visited Shloka from Parloka frequently for years to catch a glimpse of her loved ones, despite knowing the chances were slim. Recently, she had stumbled upon Ryan's dream box and found him suffering, thanks to Hogdon's abuse.

If necessity is the mother of invention, distress is the father of discovery. Grandma discovered a way to visit Ryan regularly and check on him.

When returning from Shloka, the residents of Parloka follow the direction of an infinite illuminated pole stationed in Parloka. When she left Ryan's dream box, she marked the entire return path with arrows and signs she could understand, leading to Parloka. Then, she would trace the same route back and forth to see him daily.

"How did you know your grandma could lead us to Monsieur Ryan's box in Shloka?" Jack asked me.

"Well, like I said before, I connected the dots. After talking to Britney I realized that the child in my dreams was Ryan, and I had been dreaming about his horrible sleeping experience. I would see hands appearing from the dark like mine, only rougher and more wrinkled, holding Ryan in distress, and Mom had mentioned that my hands were like Grandma's. Then Britney confirmed Ryan saw a woman in the ghostly place. And finally, Mom's drishti spotting Grandma removed all my doubts about the mystery woman meeting Ryan. And if Grandma met Ryan, she would surely know about his box. You once told me that seeing dead people in sleep was real."

"Yes, only in Shloka; meeting dead people is a real encounter, and everything else is a hallucination. Shloka is the only place where the minners of Parloka meet those of Loka. Your logic impresses me every time. Why didn't you tell me this before?"

"You say that now in hindsight. Had I told you before, you would have laughed it off. It's easy to ignore logic when you underestimate the minners."

"I never underestimated you."

"I was talking about my grandma. Anyways, what are you doing with Hogdon?"

"He is being tried in the highest court of Kendram. He cannot escape punishment."

"What if he escapes again before punishment?"

"No way. He cannot fool the keepers again."

I smelled overconfidence in Jack's words, but let him continue speaking.

"Another piece of good news: Mon cher Caesar and his D-Force made another breakthrough in Loka. After a fierce fight, they captured the rogue bear, Billa, with the help of the friendly wolf Assar. Ron and Nikki were also caught. Duma is still at large but won't be for long."

In the next moment, stars began exploding abruptly, dazzling the sky with white, red, pink, orange, and green lights. The incessant bursting noises made it clear that the fireworks illuminating the sky bid farewell to the year gone by and welcomed a brand new one.

"Happy New Year, Mandira. Didn't I say I came to wish you as such? See, I'm the first one."

"Thank you, Jack! And to you, too."

"This year is of great significance. Monsieur Ryan will turn twelve later this year and become eligible for Korsi, or The Meet."

Jack pointed at the sky. The mesmerizing fireworks took the shape of a crown. I formed thoughts in my mind, but no words came out.

*

Two weeks later, while casually browsing through my inbox, an email caught my attention. Confused, I hastened to Viru, who was shoveling snow in the driveway.

"Viru! Viru!"

Viru turned off the electric shovel. "What's wrong?"

"I received a strange email from the assistant dean of the Faculty of Medicine."

"What does it say?"

"It says, 'We are pleased to invite you to Victoria University for an interview session.'"

"You're selected for the interview? That's excellent news, Mandy! Wow!" Viru jumped with joy.

"But I don't get it. I never applied. How is this possible? Could it be spam?" I looked at Viru, who was grinning. "Wait! Did you apply for me, Viru?"

"You had filled out most of the application form, Mandy. All I did was click apply," Viru admitted.

"Oh my God! I'm going to interview for medical school in ten days! Damn it, Viru! Why didn't you tell me before?"

"For starters, you would have argued with me. And secondly, I followed Lord Krishna's philosophy: Do your job without bothering about the outcome. You had done the job; you just needed my lucky fingers to hit the submit button. I tell you, Mandy, I am your lucky mascot…"

Viru's words fell into my ears, but could not climb over the wall of my overwhelming thoughts. Jack's assurance that this would be a year of great significance crossed my mind.

****

About the Author

Rohit Dharupta is fond of underdog stories where the protagonist faces overwhelming challenges on the way to accomplishing unexpected feats.

The concept for the *Order* series stemmed from the idea of a child struggling to meet the societal norms of development playing a significant role in a world beyond comprehension. Halfway through writing the first book, *Order of the World*, the realization struck that the principal protagonist was not the underdog son, as initially thought, but his protective mom.

Rohit believes that the writer can conceive the idea and shape the characters to a point where they find their path, and then from there the story writes itself.

Disorder of the World takes Mandira's family on a rollercoaster of innocent love, coping with loss, enduring mayhem, and braving vengeance.

Thanks for reading! If you enjoyed this book, please consider leaving an honest review on Amazon, Goodreads, or your platform of choice.